CHAMPAGNE
FOR BUZZARDS

ALSO BY PHYLLIS SMALLMAN

Sherri Travis Mysteries
Margarita Nights
Sex in a Sidecar
A Brewski for the Old Man

CHAMPAGNE FOR BUZZARDS

PHYLLIS SMALLMAN

McArthur & Company
Toronto

This edition published in Canada in 2011 by
McArthur & Company
322 King Street West, Suite 402
Toronto, Ontario
M5V 1J2
www.mcarthur-co.com

Library and Archives Canada Cataloguing in Publication

Smallman, Phyllis
Champagne for buzzards / Phyllis Smallman.

(A Sherri Travis mystery)
ISBN 978-1-55278-912-4

I. Title. II. Series: Smallman, Phyllis. Sherri Travis mystery.

PS8637.M36C43 2011   C813'.6   C2010-907605-2

Canada Council   Conseil des Arts   ONTARIO ARTS COUNCIL
for the Arts   du Canada   CONSEIL DES ARTS DE L'ONTARIO

The publisher would like to acknowledge the financial support of the
Government of Canada through the Canada Book Fund and the Canada
Council for our publishing activities. The publisher further wishes to
acknowledge the financial support of the Ontario Arts Council and the
OMDC for our publishing program.

Cover and text design by Tania Craan
Printed in Canada by Webcom

10 9 8 7 6 5 4 3 2 1

for
Hazel Elizabeth Havard
my mother ~ my friend

CHAPTER 1

The back door to the bar opened, filling the hot Florida night with foot-stomping loud zydeco music. A man stumbled through the open door and down the single step. Cursing, he grabbed hold of the tailgate of a red pickup to stop his fall. Slumped against the truck, the drunken man gave a loud belch and cursed again.

While he clung to the truck and waited for the world to right, the door to the bar opened behind him. He threw his right arm back along the tailgate, swiveling his body to face the new arrival. With arms splayed along the tailgate for support, the drunk looked up. "What the fuck do you want?" His voice was slurred and thick but showed no fear.

At the door, the second man looked down the empty hallway behind him and then reached back inside. The gooseneck light over the exit went out, leaving the alley lit only by a faint glow from the window of the men's room. The door sighed shut.

"What the hell?" the drunk mumbled.

The shadow leapt off the step to where the drunken man was still splayed against the truck. "Get the fuck away from me," the drunk said. Those were his last words.

A hammer came down on his head.

With a soft exhale of surprise, the victim slowly released the truck and began to slide down to the ground. His attacker stopped his descent, lifting and heaving the unconscious man into the bed of the pickup, grunting with the effort. Then the killer began smashing his victim's head in with the hammer, giving a harsh groan of exertion with each blow, like a tennis player returning a serve. When he was done, the murderer leaned over the side and pulled up a tarp from the bed of the truck, tucking it around the dead man and hiding the body.

The killer looked around to make sure he was unobserved before he ran down the alley to the street, taking the weapon with him.

It was more than an hour before the back door to the bar opened again and a man came out. He stumbled off the step and fell forward into the tailgate of the red pickup. "What happened to the f-ing light? It's darker than a whore's heart out here."

His companion, still on the step, muttered, "Should've parked on the street."

They looked up at the light over the door while a third man, still standing in the doorway, blocked the door open with the toe of his cowboy boot and leaned inside to switch on the light above the door. "Someone forgot to turn it on."

No longer interested, the two men went to their vehicle. But the man on the step made no move to follow them. He stood by the door and watched, his hands smoothing the shirt over his paunch while he waited for the vehicle to exit the alley. Then he went to the red pickup and got in.

It began to rain. A soft rain, it did little to wash away the heat of the day or the smell of garbage and vomit from the alley.

CHAPTER 2

In a strange awkward dance, a large black creature, its wings stretched out for balance, hopped around on the roof of the red pickup. Another perched on the tailgate while a whole convocation of the ugly creatures conferred on the ground around the truck.

"What's with the frigging birds on Big Red?" I asked Tully.

Tully came and stood at my shoulder and looked out the kitchen window. "Buzzards. They're not just birds — they're buzzards looking for a meal."

"Oh yeah? Well, I've got all the freeloaders I can handle."

"Are you referring to me and your Uncle Ziggy?"

I turned and grinned at my father over my coffee mug.

"You've cut me deeply, Sherri," Tully Jenkins said with his hand on his heart and a hurt look on his face. But he couldn't sustain his impression of damaged pride. Tully was about as sensitive as old leather. Actually that pretty much described my old man. His gaunt face looked like it was made of old rawhide. In his early sixties, his dark hair had only a little gray and his black eyes still shone, the sparkle in them saying he wasn't quite dead yet, thank you. Still a little dangerous, he wasn't a man to be messed with. Well, at least not by anyone but me. Lately I found trashing my dad a whole lot of fun.

My father and I were out at Riverwood, an hour and a bit northeast of my normal stomping grounds of Jacaranda, Florida. These three hundred acres of jungle were my partner's new passion in life.

I don't do country. For me Riverwood was only a place to stash my old man and spend an occasional weekend. And yet, to be honest, I seemed to be spending more and more of my free time hanging out at Riverwood with my dad, just sitting on the porch and having long conversations that went nowhere.

Clay Adams, my business partner and lover, seemed to treat Tully's stay at Riverwood as part of the normal course of events. Tully hadn't said he was moving to Clay's ranch, certainly no one had asked him to; he just sort of went out there and hung around for longer and longer periods of time, moving more of his junk into a bunkhouse that had once housed hired men. The day his fish smoker arrived in the back of his rusted-out pickup, I knew Tully was there to stay.

And Tully wasn't my only family at Riverwood. Uncle Ziggy had moved in with Clay and me after a fire wiped out his home and left his face and hands badly scarred. He'd moved out to the ranch when he had stopped needing his dressings changed. The idea had been that he would stay at the ranch while he looked for a new place to live. It had become the longest property search known to man — so long, I no longer asked how it was going.

Now Uncle Ziggy stepped through the door of the kitchen, letting the screen slam closed behind him. The polar opposite of my father, Uncle Ziggy is about six-foot-three and pushing up near three hundred pounds, a huge barrel of love and joy.

"Mornin', sweet pea," he said.

"Where you been, Uncle Zig?"

Uncle Ziggy scratched his head and looked sheepish. The right side of his face flamed to match the fire-chewed color of the left. "Ah, nowhere much."

Well, well, well, this looked like fun. Uncle Ziggy had a secret.

"Zig's in love," Tully drawled.

I spewed coffee.

"Easy, girl," Tully said, patting my back. "Those fine ladies you been hanging out with are going to run you out of town, you act like that."

I checked out the suit I'd just spent the price of a college semester on. The cost of the suit had given me heart palpitations. I brushed down the black material with my hand, checking for stains. The suit was Clay's idea. Somehow he'd convinced me I needed to dress to project my new station in life, to look like a serious businesswoman.

The ensemble wasn't my idea of flattering. Just to make myself feel like I was still alive, I wore a trashy little black bustier underneath. No need to take this self-improvement thing to extremes — a girl could die of boredom.

I grabbed a tea towel and patted at a damp spot on my chest. "Who's the lucky girl, Uncle Zig?"

"Oh, don't you listen to Tully, he just likes to tease me. Ain't nothin', just like goin' into town for my breakfast, better'n that shit he likes to fry up and I need to get out now and then, blow the stink off and get away from Tully's constant chatter." He shuffled to the coffee pot. "'Sides, you's taken, pretty little thing, I has to look elsewhere if I want a little something in my life."

His remark wasn't as weird as it sounded — wasn't some Southern thing that Northerners always suspect us of. Ziggy wasn't my real uncle. He and Tully had met in 'Nam before I was born and stayed tight so we'd long ago forgotten the little matter of DNA.

I made another pass with the tea towel.

Tully took the cloth away from me and said, "You look fine, girl. Where ye' goin' all rigged out?"

The joy went out of the morning. "I'm going into Jacaranda, got to meet with that decorator Clay hired." Clay had called from his building project up in Cedar Key and asked me to go in and have a look at Laura Kemp's plans for the decoration of his ranch house. He sounded worried. The ranch was supposed to have been finished weeks ago, which was why I had planned on having Clay's birthday party out at Riverwood and not at the Sunset.

I saw Ziggy and Tully exchange looks. What did they know that I didn't? For sure, it was something I wasn't going to like.

Wagging a finger back and forth between them, I asked, "Have you two met Laura Kemp?"

"Yup," Tully replied. Uncle Ziggy ignored the question and went to the fridge for milk.

"And?" I asked.

"And what?" Tully answered. "She came out and measured, told a bunch of guys what to do and then went away again."

They were acting way too casual.

I turned back to the window. "I'm going to pick up the champagne for Clay's birthday party. What's with those stupid buzzards anyway?"

"Clay's right," Tully told me. "You should get rid of Jimmy's truck."

"It isn't Jimmy's, it's mine." The truck and the tattoo on my ass that said "Jimmy's" were the last remnants of ten years of marriage. I was stuck with the tat but I couldn't explain even to myself why I clung to Big Red. I was more than happy to have my no good, shithead husband out of my life, but I held onto the truck against all reason, and the more Clay nagged me to get rid of the pickup, the more stubborn I got.

"Who died in your truck?" Uncle Ziggy asked, coming to stand behind me and putting a hand on my shoulder. "Those birds sure as hell are making a mess of it. Want me to go hose it down?"

"Naw, there's no time. I'll do it in town."

"What you been carrying in Big Red anyway?" Tully asked.

"It's seafood. Miguel bought fresh fish and some crab from the dock yesterday. He used my truck. And I picked up those plants in the afternoon, which by the way I expect you two to help me plant when I get back. I want this place to look perfect for Clay's party."

"Don't know nothing 'bout flowers and such," Uncle Ziggy said, scratching his head and looking worried, like I asked him to perform a lobotomy.

"Well, neither do I, but how hard can it be? We just make sure the green end is up when we stick them in the ground. Everything should be fine. Mostly, plants survive without any help from people. At least I hope so." I set my mug in the sink. "I'll be back in three hours — we'll do it then." I quickly kissed them both.

I'd gone my whole life without exchanging embraces with any of my kin, but lately that had changed. I didn't want to think too closely about the why of this. These days there were lots of things beneath the surface I was choosing to ignore.

I went down the hall and picked up my purse and checked myself out in the mirror in the front hall. I didn't look at all like me: no glitter, no long legs under a wickedly short skirt above dangerously high stilettos. But damn I looked good — if good looking was a mortician's assistant. Plain black, severe and matched with faux pearls, the suit was supposed to turn me into a lady who lunched. I should be able to carry it off until I opened my mouth.

Clay might think he'd turned a sow's ear into a silk purse, but I knew better and so would Laura Kemp. Fortyish, at least ten years older than me, and stylish in a way that I could never be, Laura had once had a relationship with Clay and she was looking forward to another.

No one in Jacaranda expected the love affair between Clay and me to last. Truthfully, I think Clay and I were as shocked as those who watched as cultured and refined met smart-mouthed trailer trash. It was a little like George Clooney dating Britney Spears — jaw dropping and impossible. What were the odds of that working? I asked myself that question every day but I was willing to do pretty much anything to keep it going, even putting on this outfit.

There seemed to be even more buzzards around the truck as I stepped out on the back porch. "Holy shit."

"Don't know if it's holy but there will certainly be shit," Tully said as he joined me on the porch. "You better get Jimmy's truck washed right away or the acid in their droppings will strip the paint."

"You haven't been carrying roadkill in my truck, have you?"

"Now why would I be putting roadkill in Jimmy's truck?"

"My truck," I corrected. "Because I know how you can't pass up a free meal."

"You sayin' I eat roadkill?"

"Oh yeah. You made me late for grade eight commencement because you stopped to pick up a deer that the car in front of us hit. We had to deliver it to your friend the butcher before we could go to the school. All dressed up and you take me to a butcher's."

Tully said, "Sometimes you really are your mother's daughter. You both have a long and nasty memory for trivial details."

I approached the truck warily, watching the buzzards hopping in and out of the bed of the truck. With bald heads that looked diseased, feathers that seemed to shine with a pomade of filth, and feet that were scaly and evil, the buzzards gave me the willies.

Tully seemed to be having the same reaction. He moved closer to me and took me by the arm as if to hold me back. "You sure you want to drive it? You can take my truck or Ziggy's."

Tully's truck was a rattling wreck, held together by baling wire and hope, while Uncle Ziggy's was newish but stuffed with junk. We'd have to unload it first if I wanted to get the champagne and other supplies in it. That would make me late for the decorating maven.

"It's the seafood," I told Tully, "That's what they smell. I'll park away from the office. No one will know I arrived in a pickup covered in bird shit and stinking of dead fish. I'll get it washed after I go to the decorator's. Help get them away, will you?"

Tully roared and flapped his arms, charging at the buzzards and looking rather like a caricature of the creatures he was trying to shoo. As they rose into the air, I ran to the truck with my purse over my head. One thing about sensible pumps, you can move a lot faster than you can in fuck-me shoes, something I might need to consider if I was going to spend any time out here in the great nowhere.

I waved to Tully and backed out quickly before the stupid birds could settle back down.

CHAPTER 3

On my way out the quarter-mile to the road, a small black horse named Joey raced the pickup along the white rail fence.

Clay raised horses on Riverwood Ranch. Florida Cracker horses, horses that had carried people through the palmettos since the time of the Spanish conquistadors. When the first Spaniards came to America and loaded their ships with treasures for the return trip, they left behind their horses, cattle and pigs. The wild horses became breeding stock for the early settlers. Over the centuries the isolation of the Florida peninsula kept the stock unique and became the basis of the Cracker horse.

The number of these horses is dwindling; fewer than three thousand are left now that ranchers use three-wheeled off-road vehicles to check on their beef. Clay seemed to have taken their survival as his personal mission in life.

"Why do you love them so much?" I'd asked Clay.

"They built Florida. A man on a Cracker horse can cover seventy miles in a day. They're versatile, tough, durable and uncomplaining."

"Exactly like me."

"Did I mention they have a short but strong back?"

"Also like me."

"You smell better."

"And I'm more fun."

Clay gave a disappointed shake of his head "But they have a 'coon rack.'"

"Do I have one of those racks or just the normal kind?"

"A coon rack is a gait, a fast walk, almost a running walk." His hands were doing interesting things at the time of this conversation so you'll understand my confusion between a coon rack and what was happening.

"You have a lovely gait too," he'd said.

"Now I know why you love me, the good ride, but don't try seventy miles a day."

"You're built for a pleasure ride, not distance."

"Mmm," I'd said.

I stopped at the road, waiting for an old compact to go by. Joey came up against the fence, bucking and jumping about in frustration at the end of our race. "Stupid animal," I told him.

In the rearview I saw the buzzards fly lazily towards me. "It's this damn suit," I told Joey. "I knew black wasn't my color. They think I'm dead."

I turned right, going west to the coast.

Clay's ranch is tucked between two broad creeks, a private and safe place with only one road into it. To hit a major highway and get anywhere you have to go through Independence, a small town three miles from the ranch gate.

The road ran through the Sweet Meadow citrus ranch, the

next farm to Clay's. Well over a thousand acres, the ranch was strung out on either side of the road. The long lines of citrus trees running away from the road were already in blossom. White blocks of beehives sat here and there among the rows of trees. There's nothing better than orange blossom honey.

For this short space of time in my existence I was content, delighted with my life and in no hurry to be anywhere else. I overtook two Mexican farm workers, wobbling along on bikes like accidents looking for a place to get down to business. Judging by their unsteady progress, riding bikes was a new activity for these guys, but they waved and grinned as if they really knew me and I waved back the same way. Small-town Florida is like that, something we seemed to have lost along the coast with all the newcomers brought in by the hyperdevelopment. I'd gone from knowing everyone in Jacaranda to wondering who in hell they all were.

I slowed down to cross a narrow bridge over Saddle Creek. This narrow stream flows through the east side of town, drains into Jobean Lake at the southwest of town, and then rambles off to the Gulf of Mexico. Criss-crossing waterways birthed the town and now they protect it from highways and expansion.

The town of Independence came into being during the Civil War when a group of ranchers pushed through the mangroves, heading inland along the rivers. Hacking the palmettos as they went, they settled among the bugs and gators of South Florida and raised food for the Confederacy. Barges laden with beef were poled down the rivers to Port Charlotte Harbor, near Punta Gorda, where the cattle and produce were loaded onto ships.

After the war, a railroad was built along the western boundary to take produce and beef from the western side of Florida to the North. This railroad also brought tourists south to places like Boca Grande and Fort Myers and inland to towns like Independence. Large houses were built, winter homes for the rich coming down by rail from places like Detroit, Chicago, Cleveland and Buffalo. The men from the North, men who owned foundries and shipping companies, wanted winter homes like the ones they'd left behind. They built tall Victorian houses of brick and clapboard, making little concession to Southern ways and wisdom.

Against all odds, these houses, Victorian Ladies, survived in Independence, although by the First World War tourists no longer came and these glorious relics fell into decline. During the Second World War an airfield was built to the west. Soldiers on leave filled the town. Many of the gracious mansions were turned into boarding houses for the personnel from the airfield. When the airfield closed after the Korean War, Independence fell on hard times.

Now Independence was just a place that time forgot. The town didn't seem to care. On this glorious March day, with the temperature hovering in the mid-seventies, it looked safe and nostalgic. Maybe Clay was right to spend more and more of his time out here.

I stopped for an old black dog that ambled across the street, so tired he was hardly capable of holding his nose an inch off the pavement. Everything seemed to be in sepia tones and slightly dusty in Independence. Even the lawns were brown and dried out. Houses weren't painted, cars had rusted out where they sat, and there wasn't a hanging basket it sight. Here the stores all spoke to necessity, unlike the shops in a tourist town that said life was about consumption. The only color to catch my eye was the one neon sign in town. Made of red rope, it spelled out "Open" and flashed over the new gun store next to a pawnshop. When I was a kid, back in the eighties, every pickup truck had a gun on a rack across the back window. Guns have never gone out of style in small-town Florida.

In front of the truck the dog stopped, lifted his head and sniffed the air. I did the same. Even I could smell something. That was it. Miguel wasn't using my truck to pick up supplies anymore.

The dog bayed.

I used the horn. He gave one more long mournful sound and crossed the road to flop down in the dusty shade of a red-brick church, exhausted by his trip, but his head was up and he still howled.

After the house of worship came five small weathered and beaten-down houses, leaning against each other for support. They protected the church from a bar called the Gator Hole, a rough sort of place that catered to farm workers and ranchers. Tully and Ziggy played pool in there late in the afternoons and brought back stories that made other bars seem like service clubs.

There was a row of Victorian mansions before the town changed abruptly to country and with it the speed limit. I could hurry on out to the main highway, but on this sunny Friday morning I didn't seem to be in any rush and for once there were no worries chasing me.

16

On my left, a handmade sign said "Used Cows." Used for what, and in what way, the sign didn't say. Ranches, orange groves and thousand-acre megafarms growing all manner of things came after the rail line. In the corners of the monster farms, and along their edges, were small acreages of beaten-down holdings with houses that hadn't seen paint in decades. Resting on concrete blocks, the houses overlooked yards filled with bits of machinery and leftover cars. Every house seemed to have an outdoor living room consisting of plastic chairs and tables set out on bare earth under live oaks. Along here every property had a sign like "Wild Boar Hunting" or "Smoked Fish for sale" or even "Bush Hog for rent."

Twenty-five minutes down the road, at the boiled peanut and veggie stand, I made the turn onto the freeway and back into the modern world. It was like crossing a magic line from the past to the present. The thruway running north and south up the western side of Florida separates two realities: the high rise–high rent area along the coast and the farm towns to the east.

I stepped on the gas to join the world again.

CHAPTER 4

I crossed the lift bridge at the north end of Cypress Island. The blue waters of the Gulf of Mexico were spread out in front of me. I bumped down over the iron grating and onto the main street of Jacaranda with a smile on my face. I was home.

The palm-lined main street was filled with ice cream–licking tourists wearing wrinkled shorts and tee-shirts declaring what they loved. Under the banyan trees in the park a barbershop quartet was singing to a crowd of people sitting on folding chairs.

Laura Kemp's office was in an elegant Spanish building from the twenties. At the west end of the commercial district, her office was as removed from the crass bustle of the retail trade as it could be, not a tee-shirt shop in sight.

I pulled into the municipal parking lot around the back and parked as far from the building as possible. No need for the pride of the Junior League to see the white splotches covering Big Red, or catch the decided whiff of something nasty that I smelled. I'd stop at the car wash as soon as I was finished with the decorating queen and then I'd pick up the champagne for the party.

I was late. I started to hurry, and then reminded myself that ladies don't run. "But what if the house is on fire, can they run then?" the silly person who lives in my head asked. I pulled down the jacket on my stupid suit and took tiny little steps, as if there were a giant elastic around my knees.

Down the bricked alley and around to the front on Main Street I minced.

The windows of Laura Kemp's Decorating Shoppe were tastefully done. Inside, it was cool and dim and crowded with furniture, lamps and small pieces to fill up your mantel. An elegant woman glided towards me and said, "May I help you?" This was quickly followed by, "Oh, Ms. Travis, I didn't recognize you." The suit must be working if I was unrecognizable, although in this straitjacket my own mother wouldn't recognize me. Actually, my mother, Ruth Ann Jenkins, would say, "Oh honey, why you all done up like someone's maiden auntie? No use hiding your treasures under a bushel basket, darlin'." Ruth Ann always had her treasures well on display. And just to make sure everyone noticed them she covered them with rhinestones. Maybe rhinestones were just what this black shroud needed.

"Come this way, Laura is waiting for you," the elegant woman said. Was there a rebuke in those words, a slight disapproval? And when had I become so sensitive?

Laura Kemp looked up from an antique desk. Blond and beautiful, she smiled sweetly at me. She stood and stretched out her hand. "Hello, Sherri." Shit, why didn't I leave the price tag on my suit? Oh, I remember now, suits like this didn't have price tags.

Laura was wearing a winter green linen suit, loosely cut and wrinkled, with elegant shell jewelry, big and chunky jewelry. Now that's the look I wanted, but somehow I never could do elegant. Slut in heat, redneck ho and trashy tart were all looks I can manage easily, but understated elegance always escaped me. Naked, and with a really good pedicure, was the only way for me not to screw up being properly dressed.

"May I get you an iced tea?" she asked.

"No thank you. I'm a little pressed for time, got an important meeting." Score one for me. I was learning how this social thing was done — get in first with the lie and insincerity.

"Of course." She waved a hand at a chair and I sat.

Around the elegant, cultured women that Clay dated before me, my self-confidence plummeted. It was easier for me to deal with a crazy drunk or a crackhead than a woman wearing an Armani suit.

"I'll just show you the boards," Laura said. "Clay has been a little undecided about this. I know you aren't interested, since it is Clay's house, but he did want you to see them." Score ten for Laura and nothing I could say that was going to get me back to even.

"These are the materials," she said, bringing me a shallow basket filled with material swatches, all browns and beiges and other muddy colors.

Laura Kemp glided towards the wall covered in pictures of furniture while I stared down at the basket full of shit.

"Isn't there any color?" I fingered the nubby, coarse materials. "You've seen the house, it's Victorian." The house had surprised me. Two stories tall with attics on top of that, it was fronted by a curved front porch enclosing two bay windows separated by tall twin doors. On each rounded end of the porch sat a half-dozen old wicker rocking chairs that came with the house. Gracious and welcoming, the ranch house had not been what I expected.

"Victorians need color," I said. Why was I arguing; what did I care? It wasn't mine. I can never get over the feeling that Clay and I are temporary. A little walk on the wild side for him, a little bit of the good life for me, but transitory, even though I wanted it to be more than that.

She turned to face me, raising one eyebrow in surprise, or was it disgust? "Oh? I didn't know you were an interior design-er." She stretched her mouth. "Oh, that's right, you aren't. You're a bartender." She turned back to look at the pictures up on the wall. "I've gone for a mid-century look, updated Swedish modern, teak and steel, with the addition of leather."

Shocked, stunned and without words, I stared at the wall of pictures while she blathered on about her concept. She pointed to a couch with a straight back and set on aluminum legs. It looked like furniture from a union office.

I rose to my feet and tried to get back into the game. "I can't imagine stretching out on that," I said, pointing to the couch.

"I don't think anyone will need to stretch out on it. This is the main reception area of an exquisite residence and not a homeless shelter."

"Just who are we meant to be receiving?"

She looked at me, doing that trick with the one eyebrow again and said, "In your case I really can't imagine."

Okay, bitch, enough of playing nice. What was the one thing that would twist the Kemp's knickers? I handed her the basket. "This won't do. We are planning on living in this house. It isn't a show house but a family home."

Really I'd never once considered living on the ranch although Clay had suggested it over and over. I'm a city girl. Why did I care how Clay did it up? He could tart it up in pink ribbons for all I cared. "We are going to live there…" I hesitated and then added, in case she didn't quite get the concept, "…together. It has to please both of us." The subtext to this statement was "There ain't no way you is ever going to get your skinny ass back in Clay's bed. So give it up, bitch."

She gave a silent sigh and jutted a hip. "That's not what I hear. I understood from Clay that I was to have free rein. He only told me to show you my design because he thought it might amuse you."

"Amuse me? Lady, you're what's amusing. And I'd tell you where to stick your mid-century-design shit but from the look of you, it might just pass for a good time and about the only action you're likely to get."

This suit, my power suit, was really working for me, but my plan to show more class had gone down the toilet.

CHAPTER 5

I was on fire with indignation. Driving down Main Street, the big oops happened. How annoyed was Clay going to be with me for pissing off his decorator? And what about the seventy to eighty people coming for a party in one week's time? A party in an empty house, which once upon a time would have been my ideal, wasn't really the style I was going for. What was I going to do about a party in a house without furniture?

Laura Kemp had already had the inside of the house painted top to bottom in a soft cream and all the old cypress floors had been redone. I dialed Marley. She was with a patient and wouldn't take my call. Dental hygiene wasn't as important as my problem so I headed on over to the office.

Marley's my best friend, has been since grade school, and she follows every trend going in home decoration, knows everything about it and loves to shop. Except these days she was recovering from the end of her love affair with David, a man she thought she was going to marry. She'd fallen into a huge pit of despair from which we couldn't seem to drag her.

Marley looked up from the open mouth of her patient. Her red curls had turned into a shrub from which her pale freckled face peeked. Her glasses, still new and startling, were as round and full as headlights. She pulled down her mask and said, "Where'd you get the suit?"

"Same place you got the hair." I turned and walked out of the room. She followed, closing the door behind her and snapping off latex gloves. "What's up?" she asked.

I told her. Marley went into a fit of laughter.

"Clay used to date that bitch," I said.

"Was there anyone in the social register he didn't date?"

"I think he did it so none of them could tie him down."

"Well, if that story makes you happy. My bet is he was just horny and rich and could get away with it."

I slapped her on the arm but not hard enough that she was going to retaliate and lay me out in my new suit. "What am I going to do?"

"I suggest you rent or buy some furniture."

"Will you help?"

"Hell, yeah. Spending someone else's money, how great is that? But where's the money coming from?"

"Good question. Buy now, pay later if it's my money. But Clay will cough up the dough. He just might not see the need to rush out and do it in a hurry. But here's what I figure. We can hire a bunch of chairs and tables with long tablecloths and pretend we left the house empty on purpose. We can set some up on the porches too. I already bought lots of Japanese lanterns and fairy lights to twinkle in the trees. We only need to buy geegaws for the bathrooms and a few little things, just enough to tart the place up a bit."

Marley said, "Surprise parties never turn out well."

"If it isn't a surprise there won't be a party. Clay doesn't like birthdays."

"Then why bother?"

I thought about it for a second. "Truthfully, maybe being younger is the only thing I have on my side. I'm thirty-one and he's forty-five in ten days. He hates being fourteen years older, puts him at a disadvantage, but he has money, class and all the good things, so it doesn't hurt to remind him I have one thing he can't ever have again."

"Wow," she said, "you're a bigger bitch than even I knew and I always gave you lots of credit for that."

"Thank you, it's lovely to impress someone. Will you come out this weekend and help me decide what to do?"

"Sure." But Marley wasn't looking at me as she said it. She was looking out the window. I followed her gaze. A turkey vulture sat on the roof of Big Red. Now, a turkey vulture isn't something you see every day in downtown Jacaranda.

"Shit," I said.

"What?" Marley said.

"Something about Big Red, there were buzzards sitting on it this morning."

"Probably the suit, you look like you died and someone forgot to close the lid."

"Go back to torturing the guy in your chair."

"Oh, forgot all about him. I finish early today. I'll pack a few things and come right out."

The turkey vulture had hopped down from the roof and was in the bed of the truck by the time I arrived. He was pulling at something, holding it down with his feet and grasping it in his beak and pulling hard. I waved my tasteful black clutch purse at him. He squawked in annoyance but took off, not far, just to the middle or the street, waiting to see if I abandoned whatever he had fallen in love with in the back of my truck. I looked to see what it was. It was a hand.

CHAPTER 6

I screamed and jumped away as if the vile claw might reach for me. I looked around to see if my scream had brought anyone. I was alone. Just me and the thing.

Had I really seen what I thought I saw? I leaned forward, stretching out my neck to see the gruesome details without moving any closer. Holy shit! It was still there. Really, it wasn't much of a hand. Just bones in the shape of a hand since much of the meat had been stripped away.

Crazy jumbled thoughts tumbled over each other in my brain. Who did the hand belong to? How did it get there? But the biggest question of all was what were you supposed to do when you find such a thing? Of all the dangers Ruth Ann had warned me about, nothing ever came close to this.

Still terrified the thing might reach out and grab me, I edged forward to see what was attached to the hand and saw a leather watchband encircling the wrist bones. Above the watchband a scrap of red plaid stuck out from under the tarp. It wasn't just a stray hand. The lumpiness of the covering told me the owner of the hand was probably under the tarp.

"Holy crap." I started to crumble to the ground in shock but remembered the cost of the suit and leaned against the car behind me instead. I disabused myself of any faint hope that the person was sleeping and it wasn't a dead body in the bed of the truck. If he wasn't dead it sure must hurt like hell when the vultures went to work on him. I stifled my hysterics with the back of my hand and dug in my bag for my cell phone. I definitely needed help here. I punched in a nine and a one but just before I added the last digit the practical part of my brain took over. This wasn't an emergency. The man was already dead. Should I take him to the hospital or to a doctor? Well that was pretty much ditto for the emergency number, not a lot they could do now. What in hell was I supposed to do with a dead body? Drive it to the morgue? And where would that be? What I needed was the police.

Detective Styles, with the Jacaranda police force, was the cop in charge of the investigation when my husband Jimmy was murdered. Tough but honest, I knew I could rely on him. I pushed Styles' number only to be told by his electronic voice that he was away for a week and giving me an alternative number to call if the problem couldn't wait for his return. I didn't make another call.

My brain, over its initial shock, was working again. This body had nothing to do with Jacaranda. The buzzards sitting on the truck before I ever left Riverwood said it was already there when I slid behind the wheel that morning. The Sunset Bar and Grill was slowly getting on its feet and didn't need any bad publicity about people dying of unnatural causes around Sherri Travis. I was already part of too many colorful stories in Jacaranda. I liked the idea of taking my troubles to new territory. Besides, maybe the guy in my truck hadn't died a violent death. Perhaps he had been feeling sick and climbed in there to rest but instead he'd died, died of natural causes. It could happen.

I wasn't buying any part of the story I was telling myself. Only one thing was clear. The guy was quite dead so it didn't matter to him where his death was reported and waiting wasn't a problem; nothing was going to hurt him anymore. I scrambled into the driver's seat and hit the lock button, keeping myself safe from the thing in back.

Freaking out and seriously melting down, I tore out of the parking lot, while saying, "Take it easy, take it easy." The last thing I needed was to be stopped by a cop, with a dead body on board.

And within blocks I realized I'd made another serious mistake. I shouldn't have driven back along Main Street with its stop and go traffic and the sidewalks crowded with people who wove in and out of stalled traffic. At every crosswalk I waited for someone to look into the bed of the truck and start shrieking. If that happened I'd play dumb, my best act.

I should have at least made sure the hand was covered. Yeah right, as though that was going to happen. No way was I getting close to those bones.

I crept through town waiting to be caught, expecting the waking nightmare to get worse.

Once I crossed over the causeway to the mainland my panic subsided and my heartbeat eased its mad tattoo. It was even better when I merged onto the freeway. I thought my troubles were over. Not even close.

That's when the wind caught the tarp, sending a blue corner snapping back and forth outside the back window, the grommet striking the window like a bony knuckle rapping to demand entrance. Why the hell hadn't I tied the tarp down? But then I would have had to get close to the monstrous thing, would have had to reach into the truck bed and pick up the tarp, pull it tight over the body and see the hand again, touch what it had touched. No, no, no…not going there. Let it flap.

Too many Stephen King books gave me a vivid picture of what driving around with a dead body on board meant. At any moment that hand would slither into the cab and grab me, bony fingers wrapping around my neck and choking off my breath with a maniacal chortle. My head sank down closer and closer to my collarbone, going into protection mode, to make death by skeleton as difficult as possible.

CHAPTER 7

Independence was now full of shoppers — pulling out of the hardware store parking lot in front of me, stopping to talk to neighbors or just jaywalking. I drove through town at a snail's pace and watched the sky for the return of the buzzards.

When I turned off the road and onto the long twisting lane to the ranch house, my heart was going triple time. "Thank God," I breathed. My relief was boundless.

Tully was out in front of the house on a riding lawn mower, going around and around in circles, a cloud of dust following him as he cut what was supposed to be lawn but was mostly weeds and bare patches.

Near the house the driveway divided, one fork going left to the barn and the working part of the farm and the other arm going around to the front of the house. I went right and pulled up in front of the house. I slammed into Park and jumped out of the truck while it was still rocking. "Dad," I screamed, running like no lady should or could.

Maybe it was that one word or maybe it was the way I tore

into the yard, but he'd already shut off the tractor and was running across the lawn towards me.

He swept me up into his arms without asking anything, just holding on tight to stop my trembling. "It's okay, it's okay," he said over and over, although he obviously didn't know how untrue that was.

Uncle Ziggy came down off the porch in his awkward limping jog. "What's wrong, what is it?" His hands gripped my shoulders while Tully made meaningless soothing sounds as old as time.

I freed an arm and pointed to the truck. "There, there," I said. They both looked to the truck and Tully asked, "What, honey, what is it?"

"An arm, a man I think, there."

They started towards the truck, holding me between them. "We have to go to the other side," I told them at the tailgate. "It's sticking out over there." I stared at the blue covering, waiting for it to move. We shuffled together around the truck with the two of them still holding onto me. I balked when we got closer to the thing. "I can't," I said.

Tully left me with Uncle Ziggy and went and lifted the covering.

Tully jumped back. "Jesus Christ."

So that answered my question. The hand was still there. I'd been praying it would disappear on the drive out from Jacaranda.

Ziggy pulled me away and shoved my head into his neck so I couldn't look at the thing in the back of the truck. "Who is it, Tully?" Ziggy said.

It took some time for Tully to answer. "Head's pretty battered but it looks like Lucan Percell to me."

"Oh no," I whimpered. Lucan Percell was the man Clay had driven off his land for poaching the turtles along Saddle Creek. Lucan Percell had bagged about sixty soft-shell turtles when Clay caught him. When Clay called the Florida Fish and Wildlife Conservation Commission he was told that the mass hunting of soft-shell turtles was legal; only the gopher tortoise was protected. A long and heated war had begun between Clay and Lucan. Only Clay's threat to have Lucan Percell arrested for trespassing could keep him off Saddle Creek and keep the turtles safe.

It couldn't be a coincidence that Lucan Percell's body was found on Clay's Riverwood Ranch. "Oh no," I said again. Trouble had surely come to visit.

Uncle Ziggy led me away, up onto the porch, shoving me down into one of the wicker chairs. He left without saying anything while I leaned forward, putting my head between my knees and took deep breaths.

"Drink this," Uncle Ziggy ordered, holding out a glass of amber liquid. The whiskey burned all the way down. I handed it back to him and croaked, "More."

"Nope, you got to stay sober." Tully climbed the steps to the veranda.

"Great! Of all the times for you to turn into a tea-totaller on me. Just when I need a friend the most."

"We have to decide what we're going to do."

"I already know what I'm going to do. I'm going to call the sheriff."

"Nope," Tully disagreed. "I'm going to. I'm going to put the truck under the drive shed where it was and call the sheriff. Tell him I just found it there."

I shook my head in denial. "It's my truck and I've been driving around Jacaranda all morning. People saw me. One thing I learned from Styles, no matter what you tell the police, or any other authorities, you're stuck with it. Any inconsistencies will come back to bite you."

"You sure you don't want your dad and I to just take him out and bury him somewhere?" Uncle Ziggy asked. "Clay's got hundreds of acres of wilderness out there with more than one gator hole to drop him into. Even if the gators leave anything of him behind, cops will think he just had an accident. Everyone knows he poaches all 'round here."

"Zig's got a point there."

"Everyone knows he and Clay don't get on. You aren't listening; I'm going to tell them I found his body. Clay will be well out of it. No matter what happens, no one can think I killed him."

"All right, don't get excited, we'll do whatever you want," Tully said, patting my shoulder.

"Sure we will, sweetie," Uncle Zig agreed, but he didn't sound like he thought it was a real good idea, more like he just wanted to keep me from totally losing it.

"Can I have another drink now?"

"Nope," Tully said.

"Well, this is a hell of a time to go AA on me."

"You need to stay clear-headed," Tully said and went to look up the sheriff's number.

CHAPTER 8

I ditched the suit and was back on the porch in time for the first official to arrive, a deputy named Michael Quinn. He introduced himself calmly, like he was making a social call. Tall and slim, his good looks would normally have held my attention but today nothing was going to distract me from the horror in my truck.

Deputy Quinn listened to what I had to say and then went to his car and got out a small canvas carryall. At the pickup, he pulled on disposable gloves before lifting the blue tarp. He spent some time considering what was before him and then he gently lowered the tarp.

A second car arrived in a cloud of dust, a red bar of lights flashing, and a yellow door swinging wide even before the car was fully stopped, as if by rushing the driver could reverse what had been final hours ago. The man who stepped out and surveyed the scene was a man very much in charge.

Beside me, Ziggy said, "Sheriff Red Hozen."

The sheriff headed for my pickup at the double and reached for the tarp. The deputy stretched an arm to stop him, said something quietly and then handed the gloves he held in his hand to the sheriff.

The sheriff struggled into them before he pulled back the tarp and examined the body. "Shit." The sheriff slammed the tarp down.

"What's got him so upset?" I whispered.

"It doesn't seem to be what he was expecting," Tully replied.

"Or who," Ziggy put in. "Looks like he already had it figured out who it was going to be and is disappointed."

"Now why would he think he knew who was dead in the back of Jimmy's truck?" Tully asked and handed me a mug.

I looked at it dubiously. "What is it?"

"Ma always said tea was best for shock," Tully told me.

"In that case Grandma Jenkins must have drunk a barrel of it, given the Jenkins brothers' bad habits."

A newspaper that Ziggy had been reading when I slammed to a stop in front of the house was scattered around my feet. I bent down to pick it up as the sheriff headed our way, the built-in tidiness for guests kicking in.

"I'll do that, baby," Uncle Ziggy said, coming to help me.

At the foot of the stairs the sheriff took off his hat and wiped his forehead with the back of his hand. "I'm Sheriff Hozen," he told us. The red hair that gave Red Hozen his name was fading to white, a transformation that was nearly complete in his crisply trimmed goatee.

Sheriff Hozen was dressed in freshly ironed matching brown

shirt and pants, as if he had dressed for the occasion. As neat and tidy as they were, his shirt was a little tight, his paunch straining the dark buttons. He resettled his hat precisely.

Tully introduced us and said, "Come and sit down, Sheriff."

After he climbed the stairs, the sheriff chose to stand but he did remove his wire-framed Ray-Bans and sink back against the railing. "I need a little more information, Miss Travis. Start at the beginning and tell me everything."

I did as instructed.

He didn't write it down. That surprised me.

"The pickup was there all night?" he asked. "You didn't have it out yesterday after you arrived, is that right?"

"That's right. Tully drove Uncle Ziggy and me into town to the café for dinner. The truck was here when we left. Least I think it was." I looked at Tully and then at Uncle Ziggy. "Wasn't it?"

"Far as I remember," Tully said. "My truck was by the bunkhouse, not under the drive shed, so I had no reason to look and see if Jimmy's pickup was there."

"Who is Jimmy?" the sheriff asked.

"The truck used to belong to my deceased husband, James Travis." I turned away from the sheriff. "Do you remember if it was there, Uncle Zig?"

Uncle Ziggy set his badly folded newspaper on the floor beside him. "Wouldn't likely have noticed it if weren't." He smoothed back his hair. "Course, what am I saying? We'd 'ave noticed it being driven out the lane. Suppose it had to be there as long as we were, sure would have noticed it leaving." Tully and I nodded in agreement at this sensible statement.

Sheriff Hozen wasn't interested in our musings. "What time did you arrive yesterday?"

"About four. The truck was full of plants, not a body in sight. Dad and Zig helped me unload the plants. We put them under the tree and watered them and then we came out here for a cold drink. We were going to plant them today." My voice choked up, our normal life shattered by death.

Uncle Ziggy reached out and patted my arm. "No matter, honey, I watered them for you. Those pretty little pink things will be fine."

The sheriff barked, "Who else had keys to the truck?"

"No one. But I leave spare keys behind the visor so anyone can use it if they need to. It wasn't locked."

"So anyone could have driven the truck away or met Percell here."

"Was he killed here?" I asked.

Sheriff Hozen's lips tightened. He didn't like being questioned. "Too early to say. He could have been murdered elsewhere and placed in the truck. There was no one on the property to see what happened, to see if someone took the truck off the property?"

I shook my head. "Mr. Sweet worked until I arrived and then left for the day." Howie Sweet was Clay's foreman, the man who looked after the ranch day to day and kept it going while Clay was away making money. Howie Sweet was also the man who had owned the ranch before Clay bought it. The Sweet family had been on this land for three or four generations as the family went on a long, slow slide into oblivion. Pearl and Howard Sweet only had one daughter, Lovey, and a granddaughter named Kelly. Lovey owned a small diner called the San Casa on the main street of Independence.

"Did you know Lucan Percell, Miss Travis?"

I shook my head. "Never met the man. Is that who the dead man is?"

"Seems like it. That's what the driver's license says."

"Was there money in the wallet?"

He thought it over before answering, "Some."

"So it wasn't robbery."

The sheriff scowled at me.

I felt it necessary to add, "If he was killed for his money, killed in a robbery, the killer would have taken the wallet. Of course, maybe the body isn't that of Lucan Percell. Maybe someone stole the wallet and then the robber was killed and his body was put in my truck. Maybe that's why the head was battered, so no one could identify him."

Sheriff Hozen was not real pleased to hear any of my ideas.

"If it is Lucan, what was he doing in Jimmy's truck?" Tully asked, getting into the game. "What was he doing in the truck unless he was killed here?"

"Nothing to say he was killed here," Ziggy answered. "Could have been killed somewhere else and dumped at Riverwood, someone wanting to make it look like Clay was involved."

"Look," the sheriff said, his voice loud. "This isn't helping. I just need to know facts and not conjectures. What do you actually know to be a fact, Miss Travis? What do you know happened?"

"Nothing, I know nothing about this. It may seem that it's

just careless to let your pickup be used as dumping ground for murder, but I know nothing about it. I don't know how a body ended up in my truck." I couldn't turn myself off; words just tumbled out of my mouth. "It's just stupid. Why would some-one kill Lucan and put him in my truck, especially if it was done out here. Why load him into Big Red when there's all that land to hide him in?" I gave a broad wave of my hand in case he wasn't sure what land I was talking about. "Doesn't make any sense."

The sheriff had had enough. "Mr. Adams, where can we get in touch with him?"

I turned over this information. I'd talked to Clay after I'd called the sheriff. Laura Kemp had already phoned him earlier and from his frosty tone I was lucky there was only one dead body on Riverwood. I also assured Clay there was no need to come home, not that he'd offered.

"You'll have to come into the station and make a statement about all this."

"Of course, although you now know all I know."

The sheriff frowned at me and then turned to Tully and Ziggy and asked, "Have you seen any strange men around Riverwood?"

They answered in the negative and then the sheriff asked, "How about you, Miss Travis?"

I shook my head. "Only these two very odd guys sitting here, they're pretty strange."

My words pained him. "We're looking for a man seen in this area. Likely our killer, so if you see him call me at once. I'll leave Deputy Quinn in charge here. I'll have to go tell April Donaldson, the woman who lived with Lucan."

The sheriff's words brought back bad memories of
Detective Styles coming into the Sunset and telling me that
Jimmy was dead, not that I had believed Jimmy was dead.
Reality didn't sink in for days, and then the horror of what had
happened to Jimmy, the horror of them only finding bits of
him out in the mangroves, well, that nearly swamped me.

"April's the only one that's going to care that Lucan is dead,"
the sheriff added. "Most everyone else will be relieved. Come to
the office tomorrow and someone will take your statement." He
was done with me. He turned and jogged down the steps.

Tully said, "He sure won't miss Lucan from what I hear at
the Gator Hole."

"Why?" I asked. "What did he have against Lucan?"

"Lovey Sweet, Howie Sweet's girl. She and Lucan had a history and now the sheriff fancies his chances with Lovey."

"Ain't hardly likely," Uncle Ziggy put in. "No way, no how.
A woman like that ain't gonna to have no truck with a man like
Hozen, nearly as old as me and no more honest than he needs
to be from what I hear."

"Ziggy loves Lovey," Tully told me. "Covets her."

"You're just a man that naturally has evil thoughts, Tulsa
Jenkins, always have, always will. You just don't understand
friendship between a man and a woman."

Tully snorted with laughter.

I was too baffled by what was happening to join in this fun.
"Seems to me the sheriff was expecting someone else when he
looked into the bed of the truck — even hoping to see someone else there."

"I thought the same," Tully agreed. "And why's he asking
about some stranger?"

"Maybe he doesn't think anyone in Independence would do such a thing."

I was still trying to wheedle a drink of something stronger than tea out of Tully when Howie Sweet showed up.

CHAPTER 9

We watched Howie Sweet stop to talk to the sheriff. They seemed on very good terms, but then Howie was a long-term resident of the area, part of the old establishment.

Howie shook his head, denying something. The sheriff patted him on the shoulder and hurried off, getting into his car and tearing out of the yard, nearly colliding with an ambulance coming in.

"Little too late for an ambulance, isn't it?" Tully asked.

Various other cars pulled into the yard. We watched as men got out and put on white suits over their clothes before they pulled on blue gloves and went to my pickup, carrying their cases. One man climbed up into the bed of the truck and knelt down. I looked away. I didn't want to know.

Howie turned away from the scene as well and climbed the stairs to join us on the front porch. He looked like a man who had lost someone near and dear to him, which was strange because Uncle Ziggy said Howie and Lucan Percell had a long, hate-filled history with Lovey Sweet as the source of their vendetta.

Howie collapsed down into the wicker chair like a man whose bones had just given out. We all sat staring at him, waiting to hear what he made of the death of a man he hated.

"Lucan Percell?" he asked, as if he couldn't quite believe it and needed it confirmed.

"Seems to be," said Tully.

Leaning forward, with his hands hanging down between his knees, Howie stared straight ahead. Silent and shocked, there was no doubt this had hit him hard. Suddenly his eyes widened and he sat up a little straighter. "I know…" he started to say and then gave a little shake of his head and went silent.

"What do you know?" Tully demanded in a harsh voice more designed to scare than coax.

"Nothing, ain't nothing," Howie answered and slumped back.

"Don't be a fool," Tully told him. "You know anything you better speak up."

Howie shook his head and jutted his jaw.

I caught Uncle Ziggy's eye, nodded at Tully and cocked my head to the side.

Uncle Ziggy pulled himself to his feet. "Tully, let's go see what the deputy is going to do with Jimmy's truck. We'll have to find something for Sherri to drive if they're going to keep it."

"Well, it sure is time to get rid of it now, isn't it, Sherri? You don't want to be driving around in a hearse," Tully said and followed Ziggy off the porch. Howie Sweet was thinking hard on something and hardly noticed they were gone.

"I need a drink," I said to Howie. "Let's go in."

I'd said the magic words. Howie was on his feet and through the door before me.

I poured Jack Daniel's into a glass and added a little water. "Ice?" He shook his head and reached for the glass. Howie's hand trembled as he took it from me, drinking the whiskey down as if it was an antidote for snakebite and he'd just been bitten bad.

He shuddered a little and set the glass down on the counter.

"You seem real upset by this."

"It's a surprise, it surely is," he said. He pushed the glass towards me. "Such a shock to think someone would murder Lucan and put him in that truck."

He watched me pour a second drink, a little stronger this time, while both his palms smoothed out his shirt stretched across his broad girth.

"Why are you surprised that someone killed Lucan?" I asked, holding out the fresh drink and watching him.

"Don't expect a thing like that."

"From what I hear, if ever there was a man who was born to be murdered, it was Lucan."

Howie nodded his bald head, his eyes fixed on the glass in my hand. "A bastard," he agreed. "Everyone in the county hated him."

I remembered what the sheriff had said. "Not April Donaldson."

"No one much bothers with April."

"Including you?"

He didn't answer.

"She's just lost someone she cared about," I told him.

"They wasn't married. It isn't the same."

"That's nice and Christian of you." I handed over the whiskey. His hands still trembled as they settled around the glass but this time he sipped at the liquid.

"Tell me."

His faded blue eyes met mine. "What?"

"As you say, the sheriff's men aren't bagging your best friend out there. Everyone knows you two were enemies so you can't be that devastated by his death. Something else is going on here. Do you know how that body ended up in my truck?"

He drew himself up. "I don't think what I know or don't know is any of your business."

"Wrong answer. I'm in this shit and I don't like it. You were the only one who could easily have taken my truck. I'll make sure the sheriff understands that; maybe I'll even tell him I saw you do it if you don't can the attitude."

"You can't lie."

I laughed. "Lying is one of the few things I excel at."

He frowned.

There was something I was really curious about. "Even without knowing about my lying you already seem to think the worst of me, Howie, why is that?"

"'Cause you and Clay ain't married. You're living in sin and that's just wrong. Pearl says so."

It was hard to believe that living with someone without marriage could still be an issue, which shows exactly how different things were in Independence from Jacaranda. Back in Jacaranda it was close to being the normal way of things.

"It ain't right," Howie declared.

"Well, that's the least of the problems on Riverwood. There's something else going on here. Cough it up or I'm out the door to the deputy. I can be just about as bad as Pearl thinks I am."

He grimaced.

"I mean it, Howie."

"I took your truck," he muttered into his glass with a voice barely loud enough for me to hear the words.

"Say again?"

He looked up. "I took it. I would have asked if you'd been here, but no one was home."

"Where did you take it?"

"To the Gator Hole."

CHAPTER 10

"I thought I'd just go out for one quick drink. See, Pearl was at choir practice with our truck. She don't like me drinking." He fell to studying the glass again.

"Let me get this straight. Pearl went out and you snuck over here and stole my pickup."

"I didn't sneak over."

"Howie, you were sitting outside under the oak, not fifty yards from the end of the lane, when we went into town. You saw us, we all waved, and you knew no one was here. You came over here and drove away in my truck. What do you call that?"

"I always have use of the farm trucks. Clay says."

"It wasn't a farm truck. It was mine."

"Didn't think you'd care." Howie was petulant and sorry for himself at getting caught, trying to make me the one in the wrong.

"I wouldn't care except for the dead body you picked up. That was one hell of a hitchhiker." An idea kicked in. "You didn't pick up anyone, did you?"

"Nope. And no one knew I was driving your truck either. I made sure no one saw me leaving in it and I parked it around back at the Gator Hole, only a few cars there."

"Even though you didn't think there was anything wrong with taking my truck you took all those precautions?"

"Didn't want Pearl to know, did I?"

"Someone for sure saw you. A red pickup with a ton of chrome is pretty visible."

"Maybe not," he said. "And no one needs to know."

"I know, and the sheriff needs to know."

"No need to tell him." His voice was whining and a fine haze of sweat shined on his bald head. "Can we wait and see if the sheriff figures out what happened before we say anything 'bout it?"

"How likely is that to happen? I'd be surprised if that guy can find his dick in the dark with both hands." I saw the shock on his face. "Oh, sorry Howie. When I get upset all my manners go out the window."

His face was beet red, his eyes wide with stunned surprise but he had the good sense not to lecture. The Sweets were upstanding members of the Baptist Church. Not only did Pearl sing in the choir but they went to church twice on Sunday and to Bible study every Wednesday. The word *dick* had never passed Howie's lips and I was guessing Pearl didn't even know the things existed. But if all that was true and they were the next best things to saints, what was Howie doing sneaking out to a bar?

"Someone's going to remember seeing you in the Gator Hole, Howie."

Howie's scowl didn't lighten. "So? Long as no one tells Pearl it doesn't matter. And no one will tell her — they all know how it is."

"The old boys' club at work. Was Percell there last night at the Gator Hole?"

"Yeah."

"And everyone saw Lucan, he wasn't hiding?"

"No."

"Who else was there?" I asked as I refilled his glass. My years as a bartender always win out. I hate an empty glass and besides, secrets don't stay secrets when you keep the glasses full.

"Everyone."

"Well, that clears things up." This conversation with Howie was like picking burrs from an Australian pine out of my feet, one little round bugger at a time. I waited a moment to see if he had anything to add before asking, "Exactly who was everyone?"

A list of people I didn't know followed before he added, "Oh yeah, Harland Breslau was there, don't remember ever seeing him in the Gator Hole before." Something funny happened in his eyes, and a weird little smile lifted his lips. "He normally is too busy looking after his wife, Amanda. Must have come right in from the farm, had his work gloves in his back pocket." He stroked his stomach, considering this oddity before adding, "He came in with Boomer, that's his son. Don't think they really get along. And then I saw them talking with Lucan. They were arguing with him."

"So everyone heard. Now the sheriff will hear about it."

"May not."

"Why?"

"Sheriff and Breslaus are kin. People don't mess in their business."

"Did you talk to Lucan?"

"Nope."

"Why?"

"Lucan and I never had anything to do with each other."

"The sheriff is going to find out where he was last and place him in the bar and then they're going to look at everyone that was there. Are you sure you two didn't have a fight? Didn't exchange words? If you did you better tell the sheriff before someone else does."

He looked as if his boxers were binding and he was too polite to work them loose.

"Did you have words?"

"Not exactly."

"What exactly?"

"I just said to stay off our land."

Howard Sweet had never been man enough to stop Lucan Percell from taking anything he wanted — turtles from the river or Howie's own daughter, Lovey. From what Tully heard around town, Lucan Percell had had the run of Riverwood before Clay bought it. And it was useless to point out that it wasn't his land anymore.

"Well, looks like someone solved the problem of keeping Lucan off Riverwood," I said. I looked out the window to the silver roof of the drive shed where the pickup had sat that morning. Likely Lucan Percell had been lying there in the bed of the truck while Tully and I watched the buzzards picking at his flesh.

"Orlin Breslau came into the Gator Hole too, just before

Lucan left," Howie volunteered. "Strange, isn't it, the one time that the whole Breslau clan was there, that's when Lucan died."

"You trying to tell me something, Howie?"

"Nope, just saying." He was clearly taking pleasure in some secret knowledge.

"I'm sure the sheriff will be interested in hearing what you have to say."

He snorted. "Don't be too sure. Told you, the sheriff and Orlin Breslau are cousins, been real close their whole lives, and if anything bad comes Orlin's way," he gave a shrug, "well, the sheriff will make sure Orlin's protected."

"Even to covering up a murder?"

"Don't know about that, but there are only certain people in Independence that the law applies to. Some it don't apply to at all and out here, well, the sheriff never stopped Orlin from stealing my water or kept Lucan off my land."

Suddenly I didn't want to hear anymore. I dumped my Jack Daniel's in the sink, sorry I'd pushed Howie to tell me what he knew about Percell. My inclination was to get in Big Red and get out of there, but then I didn't have Big Red and this mess wasn't going to go away.

And in one week seventy-five people were arriving for a party, a party I hoped would be my social debut on Clay's arm. I didn't like to admit even to myself how important this party was to me.

How would Lucan's murder impact Clay and Riverwood? Come to that, what did it mean to me? Bottom line, I didn't want a whole lot of hassle myself. The sheriff had to know I was not responsible for Lucan's body being in my truck and he needed to know the murder had nothing to do with Clay or Riverwood. I just wanted all of this gone so I could get on with my life.

But the problem had been delivered to me in the back of my truck. It didn't get more personal than that.

Was there anything in what Howie had said to me that I needed to pass on to the authorities? I've never been big on helping the police do their jobs or landing people in the stinky stuff, and if I repeated our conversation, was Howie going to tell the police just what he'd told me?

Could Howie have killed Lucan at the Gator Hole and stuffed him in Big Red? Not even this sorry-ass loser could be that dumb, could he?

"If you want to tell Deputy Quinn right now where the truck was last night, that's fine with me, but if you want to wait 'til tomorrow, until you tell Pearl, that's fine with me too."

"Don't want to tell Pearl." His agitated hands smoothed his shirt down over his stomach. "I'll tell the sheriff but not Pearl. Why do I have to?"

Why had I never been able to control a man the way Pearl controlled Howie? "I need to get a bigger whip," I muttered. Howie's face wrinkled in confusion. Well that made two of us. Who would want a wimp like Howie?

CHAPTER 11

Marley's arrival was dramatic.

When Deputy Quinn stepped out in front of her blue Neon to stop her from coming any farther, she threw open the car door and took off like a cat exiting a tub of scalding water.

Marley and the deputy exchanged words. He reached out for her and she landed a foot on his shin, then Marley slipped around him and headed for my truck where all the technicians were working. It was my bet she was thinking one of us was dead.

But give the big guy credit, he may have been wearing cowboy boots, but he turned like a high school quarterback heading for the goal line with the ball, catching her before she was five steps away from him. The cop picked her up with one long arm, lifted her right off her feet and swung her around like they'd just invented some new square-dance step. When he set her down she swung to face him, trying to deke around him. He had her again and there they stood, waiting for the other's next move.

He didn't know Marley. It was going to end badly. When

Marley gets an idea into her head, nothing is going to stop her. That deputy was about to get injured so I hustled down off the porch to cut in on their little hoedown.

"She's with me," I told the cop. Nothing happened.

She may be skinny, and since she and David broke up she's lost even more weight, but there must be something on that bag of bones he was liking 'cause he was holding her real close.

"She belongs here," I said, a little louder in case he had a hearing problem.

He frowned but stepped back a little, reluctantly loosening his hands. Like a shot Marley was around him and holding onto me. This girl just was way into grabbing anything she could. She was sobbing and babbling, "Are you okay?"

"Why wouldn't I be?" I asked. I looked at the cop over her shoulder. He stood with his hands on his hips, heaving and puffing and watching us close, maybe hoping for a second round.

"What's the sheriff's guy doing here then?" Her voice was barely above a whisper.

"Somebody died."

Her nails bit into my arm. "Tully?"

She was voicing my worst fears. "No, no one you know."

With a great intake of breath, she looked back over her shoulder at the cop and leaned in real close, so close her breath tickled my ear when she whispered, "Laura Kemp?"

I pulled her towards the porch, out of earshot, and replied, "Unfortunately not, but someone just as deserving."

"Why are they messing about with Jimmy's truck?" she asked as she sank down into a chair.

I hitched my behind up on the railing. "Because there's a dead body in the back."

"Oh Jesus, Sherri, did you hit someone with the truck?"

"Man your brain is really full of interesting ideas, isn't it? What do you think happened?"

"I just wondered if you maybe—" her hands made uncertain circles. "Well, I wondered if you ran over someone and then put him in your truck." She frowned, maybe already seeing how weird it sounded.

"Nope. Besides, he'd have to be sleeping on the road for me to run over his head."

She joined me on the railing. With our eyes on the activity in the yard, I told her about my passenger from hell and how he came to be in Big Red.

"Man," Marley said, "you have crappy luck."

"Don't stand too close," I advised her. "Never know what might drop on me next and you don't want to get splattered."

We watched for the best part of an hour as people wandered around doing things we could only speculate about. We did a lot of that. Some people left but not many. Mostly they just seemed to come and stand around talking in low voices, looking up at us sitting on the porch like they were looking at exhibit "A." A long black hearse from the local undertaker pulled slowly into the circle of vehicles. They got a stretcher out of the back.

And then a flatbed truck broke from the trees along the drive and came towards us. Right behind it the sheriff sped back in.

CHAPTER 12

The "A One" towing truck pulled up towards the bunkhouse and then back into the turnaround.

The sheriff marched towards the porch. "We're taking your truck into the lab to do the forensics, testing for prints and such," the sheriff said from the bottom of the stairs. "And we'll need to get samples of your prints to rule them out. Probably be a while before you get the truck back."

"Not sure if I want it back."

Sheriff Hozen shrugged. "Well, it will take some time," he said and turned to leave.

"Wait," I called.

He swiveled around and frowned at me.

"How is—" I started to say "Lucan's wife" but changed it to, "How is April?"

His frown didn't improve. "A little upset. Didn't believe me." He turned away.

When I heard about Jimmy's death I hadn't believed it

either. Hearing about April brought back that pain. "Is anyone with her?"

"Nope," he said. He didn't even stop walking.

We watched the technicians going about their work. Spreading out from the truck, eyes down, they searched the ground for clues.

"What are they looking for?" Marley wondered.

"Maybe they're looking for blood," I suggested. "Or the weapon. Or even signs of someone dragging Lucan to the shed."

"Shouldn't you tell them how the body got in the truck?"

"They're having fun, and they'd probably do it anyway. Besides, no one listens to me."

The technicians were starting to pack up when something caught Marley's eye. "What are all the flowers for?" Marley pointed down to the bedding plants sitting under the tree.

"I was going to plant them for the party."

"You were really going all out for this party, weren't you?"

"Seems like it."

"You can't have it now, can you?"

"Maybe they'll find the murderer real quick. It would be all right then to have a party, wouldn't it, if they solved it?"

Marley shrugged. "I don't know."

"Not like we knew him real well. I never met him. And none of us were involved, didn't even happen here, so it has nothing to do with us really."

"I just love the way you wiggle, girl."

"'Sides," I said, "everyone is coming from Jacaranda. They won't know a thing about it."

Marley pointed at the plants. "Those flowers are looking a little worse for wear, aren't they? They need to get in the ground or they'll die too." She hopped down from the railing. "Let's do it now."

I said, "I just don't think this is the time to be planting flowers."

She picked up a plant in each hand. "If I don't do something I'm going to jump out of my skin. Besides, the dead guy will be planted soon too."

I followed Marley reluctantly down the steps. For Marley a dead body in my truck was horrible but now it was over and she was back to important matters, like the flowers.

But I was never going to forget a buzzard holding down Lucan's hand with its talons while it pulled off his flesh, never forget the naked bones and death dropping into my life again.

Even though I'd never known Lucan Percell, our lives had intersected hideously, and his death brought back my past, a past haunted by violence. My memories were like a wound that had scabbed over but hadn't quite healed, and this new death peeled away the protective covering from my wound. Maybe I was never going to heal completely; maybe I was always going to have an open sore that life could rub raw at any moment. I felt alone and caught in a dark whirlpool that no one understood or could see but me.

I sat on the bottom step and watched Marley spreading out the flowers in the bed under the tree until she had them in a pattern she liked, making order out of chaos, and then beginning to dig them in while I sat there asking myself questions to which there were no answers, but it never stops me from asking them anyway.

Slowly the searchers were ebbing away, slamming doors and starting engines, going back to their own reality.

Tully opened the screen door and said, "You girls better come in an' have a bite." He looked down at me and smiled. "Food will make you feel better."

"I don't think so." The thought of eating made my stomach do a funny little dance.

"Then come in and at least have a coffee." Tully went back inside, letting the screen slam behind him.

Marley stood up, a plant in each hand and whispered, "Your father cooking is a novel idea and more than a little worrying."

"Yeah," I agreed. "Hopefully, whatever he's serving up has come out of a package or the freezer, not something he's liberated from a stretch of highway."

"Oh, shit," Marley said. "I'd forgotten about that."

But the changes in Tully were nothing to the surprise I awoke to.

CHAPTER 13

It was barely sunrise, and not even Marley was up, so it took a while to realize the ringing wasn't in my head.

I grabbed the phone. "What?"

"Good morning to you too," Clay said.

"You're doing this because I upset your girlfriend, aren't you?"

"I thought you were my girlfriend."

"Oh? I thought I was more than that."

"This conversation isn't getting off to a good start but then no conversation with you that takes place before nine goes well."

I rolled onto my back. "Tell me why you love me then."

"Because I'm a glutton for the perverse…as opposed to the perverted. Now, let's start again," Clay suggested. "Good morning."

"Good morning." I pulled the covers over my head, taking the cell phone with me. I was trying to calculate how many minutes more sleep I could get before Marley barged in.

"Any word on Lucan's murder?"

"At this friggin' hour of the morning? Even murderers are still in bed."

"Right. You don't sound like you're ready for a long conversation so I'll give you my news and let you get back to sleep. There are three storage units of furniture in Sarasota. It belonged to my parents. Plus there's a few things in there I've picked up at auctions. You might want to have a look and see what you think of it before you start buying stuff."

"Wait, you're saying you have a whole load of furniture?"

"Yup."

"Antiques?" I was awake now.

"Depends on your idea of antique — mostly it's just old."

"And some of this you bought...didn't just inherit?"

"Yeah."

"You sound embarrassed."

"Well," he fell silent.

"Why? Why are you embarrassed that you're the owner of antiques or mostly old furniture, or that you held on to your folks' stuff?"

"Why do you care? Just go have a look at it and we'll talk later."

"Did you tell your fancy decorator about this furniture?"

"Not really. Right out of the box she had her own ideas. Wasn't too interested in what I thought."

I figured it was because Ms. Kemp was decorating the house for herself, for when Clay saw the light and went back to her.

"I won't talk about how much you've cost me in Laura's fees if you don't ask a lot of dumb questions, okay?" He gave me the details and told me where to find the keys. "I thought I knew you," I told him, "But you still have a few surprises for me, don't you?"

"As I'm sure you do for me, my little beach-bar Mona Lisa."

"Not much of a compliment, she's fat and plain."

"But she has that mysterious smile."

"Yeah, while mine's just plain dirty, far better than mysterious."

"I've been thinking about you and some dirty things."

"Tell me."

"Nope, I'm going to hang up now before I get all excited. Try not to pick up anymore hitchhikers, bye."

I didn't even get a chance to say goodbye. He knew I was going to start digging into the how and why of this treasure trove. Like why were none of these pieces from his family in his penthouse, which Laura Kemp had also decorated? Clay was uncomfortable with the whole subject while I was delighted. I went to wake Marley, which was also delightful.

"We're going riding first, remember? You promised," Marley said. "Then we'll go look at the furniture."

"Fine, but you ride Joey." Clay had saved Joey from an abusive owner, but I was on the owner's side in this argument. Joey was an animal even more stubborn and vicious than I was. That horse deserved to be abused. A gelding, he should have been much calmer, but someone forgot to tell Joey. Originally I thought if I could learn to handle Joey I could ride anything but he'd already dumped me twice. "I'm riding Wildflower," I said and headed for the door.

"No way," Marley replied, throwing back the covers and swinging her legs out of bed. "You were the show-off who thought she could handle Joey, so handle him, tough girl."

I led Joey into the center alley of the barn. His coat was sleek and black; his intelligent eyes were set wide on either side of a white blaze and his alert expression said, "This looks like fun." He had everything but manners.

As I clamped the crossties on Joey, Tully came into the barn and asked, "How come Howie Sweet didn't turn up this morning? Did he say anything to you?"

"Nope. Maybe he slept in, or maybe he told Pearl he was at the Gator Hole and she put him in the hospital, or maybe he's been arrested for murder." I threw the saddle on Joey's back and reached under his belly for the cinch. "Whatever happened, there was no sign of him this morning. Marley and I turned the horses out."

Tully came to my side and kneed Joey in the gut to get him to empty his belly full of air, a neat trick Joey had. When I snugged up the cinch he'd blow out the air and leave a loose saddle.

"Are you sure you want to ride this guy if he's as bad as you say?"

"I told Clay I'd make sure he got exercised."

"Well, he's a trickster," Tully said, and gave another yank on the belly strap. "This horse has more attitude than brains. You two are a matched set."

Marley was talking a mile a minute as we walked the horses

back the lane. Fresh air is happy gas to Marley but to me it just smells funny. I like my air like I liked my wine, full-bodied. My lungs need a little more ozone, a little cigarette smoke mingled with the smell of stale beer, to work properly.

The joy that had come back into Marley the night before was even more pronounced this morning and her enthusiasm for everything around her knew no bounds. I wanted to strangle her but I was too busy watching Joey's ears. Apparently they were supposed to tell me when he planned on dumping me.

The day was pleasantly warm, unlike the unbearable heat we'd been experiencing, and there weren't even any bugs. Joey was behaving like a prince. That should have warned me things were about to turn to rat shit.

I pointed ahead of me and off to the left of the trail, to a small black sow with five little piglets trotting behind her. "Look."

Joey, who was even less trusting of nature than I was, danced sideways while keeping his eye on the sow. I patted his neck, trying to soothe him and watched his ears.

The sow and her family disappeared into the underbrush and Joey decided to walk on, tossing his head in indignation.

Things went along glowingly for another ten minutes. Joey and I were getting along faultlessly, forming a partnership and bonding when I saw what looked like the branch of a tree across the path. The log moved. "That can't be right," my brain was saying. "Logs don't move."

CHAPTER 14

Seven feet long, or maybe even over eight feet, Joey and I didn't stop to measure it, the snake slithered across the trail in front of us. Joey jumped. Like an Olympic champion, he stretched out and sailed high in the air, clearing the reptile by at least his own height.

At lift-off I grabbed for his mane, the horn, anything that would keep me onboard. When he touched down I was thrown forward, nearly catapulting over his head. I lost my right stirrup.

I'd lost the reins in my grab for the horn and now the stupid horse was off for the next county. Going like spit and cutting in too close on the corners, branches were slapping me. I forgot all those good things I'd been told, like keeping my heels down so my foot wouldn't go through the stirrup and get me dragged behind Joey when I fell off, and I was going to fall off, no doubt about it. It was just a matter of time and finding a spot to land.

I was curling into a smaller and smaller ball, like a little burr, just trying to stay with him. I suppose if he'd been a race-horse this would have encouraged him to go faster but Joey didn't seem to need any encouragement.

And then he suddenly stopped. I listed to the right and, in a losing battle with gravity, slowly slid off. When I hit the ground I started to curse the stupid, brain dead, ugly walking piece of carrion called Joey.

Marley sat there, arms folded on the horn of her saddle, not at all concerned for my wellbeing, and grinned down at me.

"I could be hurt," I screamed at her.

"No pain, no gain."

I got off my ass and climbed back on Joey, too mad to be afraid. Fear would come later. It often does with me.

"What the shit was that?" I asked. "Was it a snake?" Joey was now only interested in cropping grass

"An Eastern Indigo, they're rare," Marley said.

"Thank God for that."

Marley, a nature lover who went on hikes and even raised money to save this and that, went on and on about the snake. "I only caught sight of the last of it disappearing into the bushes after you and Joey took off." Her eyes and cheeks glowed.

"Runaway horses and snakes bigger than me, if I had a gun I would have shot both of them."

"That would have been a mistake, at least shooting the snake. Indigos are really good to have around; they eat lots of mice and things. They live in gopher tortoise burrows. Think we should go have a look for a tortoise burrow? That would be neat to see."

I offered her my view of her mental state.

"Maybe not," Marley said.

"I've had all the nature I can take for one day," I said. "Let's go back."

"Best to walk on a little farther, just so you can show Joey who's boss."

"Oh, I think he knows that already."

I followed Marley down an eight-foot-wide path cut deep into the jungle. The path was the width of two passes with the rotary mower Howie used to keep it from getting overgrown. Each week he drove the tractor out through the brush, around a small lake to where a stream came in from the Breslau property to the east and then back again, leaving a green lane behind him. It was a path Joey knew, but any unusual thing on it would set him doing the sideways cha cha. Now he walked sedately on, past Spanish moss waving and flowing in the breeze, without a hint of anxiety. The rustle of the thick palmettos at the base of the oaks didn't even seem to bother him. He strolled along like a real gentleman — for about ten seconds.

"Watch it," Marley warned. "Not so close."

Before I could pull him back, Joey stretched out his neck and nipped at Wildflower's flank. The little mare screamed in pain and indignation and shot forward while Joey tossed his head, prancing and playing innocent.

Wildflower, being a lady, settled down immediately while Joey sidestepped and shook his head and acted the fool.

"Go ahead of me," Marley said. "Joey likes to lead."

It was too late for her advice. Joey was already trotting forward to take his rightful place at the head of the parade. It would have taken a tank to stop him from being first.

But still, despite his manners I thought we were doing fine. We'd trot a couple of hundred yards farther along the trail, then we could turn around and have a nice quiet walk back to the barn and I'd have exercised Joey just the way I promised Clay.

I just didn't get it. Clay loved the ranch while I thought it would be best to rip up the whole three hundred acres and put in a mall with an enormous parking lot.

Something caught Joey's eye, or maybe tweaked his nose, because he stopped, lifted his head and seemed to be sniffing the air. He gave a soft whinny and sidestepped into the underbrush.

The broken end of a branch jabbed into my thigh. "Stupid, stupid animal."

"What's that noise?" Marley asked. "I thought there was no one out here."

I could hear it now, a mechanical roar, growing louder and more offensive by the second. Clay's land, bordered by a river on the east and a stream on the west, was long and deep, running from one country road to the next one north. Beef cattle had once kept the land clear but Howie had given up ranching years before Clay had arrived. Most of the northern part of the ranch had gone back to nature and could only be accessed from the cleared land around the farmhouse to the south. It was supposed to be a fine and private place.

Three vehicles shot around the bend and nearly ran us down. When they'd halted, Joey and I were boxed in.

Some primeval instinct set the hairs at the nape of my neck tingling…or maybe it was the rifles mounted across the handlebars of their machines that were scaring the shit out of me. The riders were grinning like they'd found treasure. These weren't the kind of men you wanted to be alone in a dark alley with — nor the kind of men you wanted to meet out in the bush.

CHAPTER 15

The noise of the machines was deafening. Joey backed his rear deeper into the brush. Barbs snagged my clothes and raked my body. Branches scratched Joey's sides. He didn't seem to notice.

Forcing his way sideways and back through the underbrush, he worked his way out of the circled machines, then turned and faced his enemies. He blew out a loud snort of disgust and tossed his head.

The guy on the lead three-wheeler was young — late teens or early twenties. I took my eyes off the long gun slung across the handles of his machine and had a good look at the revolver he wore in a holster at his hip. But there was something more in his eyes, something besides guns to worry about. He swung a leg the size of a tree trunk over the seat and dismounted. Hitching up his jeans, he swaggered towards me. Blond and beefy, he would have been handsome except for the sneer and fifty extra pounds that gave him a bloated look.

I recognized the look on his face, a predatory look — like he'd just been handed a brand-new toy. But I'm no one's toy.

I glanced at the two guys behind him. They were staying with their machines, waiting and watching to see how it would play out, maybe waiting to be given orders. No help there. Marley and I were on our own.

The young fool coming towards me smiled.

I have to say it did a lot to improve his looks. Then he licked his lips. I felt like a prime cut set in front of a man who hadn't seen food for days.

"I'm Boomer Breslau," he said, loud and proud like I should know him and be real delighted to be in his presence.

And in a way I did know him. His grandpa's ranch ran alongside Clay's to the east. Clay had lots to say about this family and their use of illegal aliens to farm their land, some twenty-five hundred acres of tomatoes and such.

"I'm Sherri Travis. I'm a friend of Clay Adams. Does Clay know you're here?"

"Friend?" he roared and then laughed, choosing to ignore my question. "I hear you're more than friends. You're the sweet piece that warms his bed."

He moved closer. "He's pretty old for you, ain't he? But when a man has as much money as he does, guess he doesn't have to be real good to keep a woman happy." His laugh warned me. There was no use making nice with this guy. There was only one thing he'd understand and I'd only get one chance.

"Sherri," Marley said from behind me, "let's go back."

"Why you want to do that?" Boomer Breslau said while Boomer's face said, "I can have anything I want. I can have you. And no one can stop me."

"Let's go, Sherri," Marley said again.

Marley was ignoring the fact that there was just this one track, nowhere else to go, and I was pretty sure we couldn't outrun them.

Boomer laughed. "Stick around, girls."

Without turning my head or taking my eyes off him, I said to Marley, "You start back, I'll catch up." Hopefully she'd ride like hell and bring help.

"I'll wait for you," Marley said.

"No. You hurry on back and tell Tully and Ziggy we have company. Make sure they prepare a real warm reception."

"Oh," she said, suddenly understanding.

Boomer Breslau held up a hand to stop her, "No reason to do that."

"Okay, I'm going," Marley said. I heard Wildflower's hooves beating the earth as they galloped away but I kept my eye on the nasty bastard in front of me.

"Now why'd you go and do that?" Boomer asked. "You ain't afraid of me, are you?" He stepped closer, his eyes locked on me. I knew that look, seen it in too many drunk's eyes not to know what it meant. I eased my foot out of the stirrup. He was about to get a taste of my fancy new boot.

Boomer Breslau reached out a hand for me. Joey had him. Took a nice big chunk of his arm and held on, nodding his head and grinding his teeth in delight.

Boomer yelled, a real stupid thing to do around a horse with Joey's nasty and unpredictable personality. The yell set Joey rearing back, pulling Boomer with him. I grabbed the horn, hoping Joey wouldn't topple backwards on top of me, and fought to keep my feet in the stirrups. Joey released Boomer.

Boomer fell back on his ass with Joey's hooves slicing down inches from Boomer's head. Crablike, he scuttled away and scrambled to regain the safety of his ATV.

Joey reared one more time but his heart wasn't in it. I leaned forward and stroked Joey's neck. "Okay, sweetie," I whispered to Joey. "You did just fine."

Then I spoke up to the three men staring at me from their machines. "Now why don't you boys just go on home?" I said. "I'll tell Clay you came by to introduce yourselves."

I turned Joey and cantered back towards the house, trying to decide what I would do if they followed me and ran me off the path into the palmettos. Swear like hell and threaten them with everything under the sun likely. I couldn't think of anything else.

Just when I thought I was well clear of danger, some extra sense, some tingling of the hairs on the back of my head made me look around. Had they come after me?

But it wasn't that. This was a whole new terror. Deep in the palmettos, hidden and fleeting, I looked into the eyes of a man. Dark-skinned, with chiseled features, he had a face from an Aztec carving. I felt the scream bubbling up from my gut. The memory of recent pain and Joey's reaction to surprises quelled the instinct, but my knees must have tightened, must have sent the signal for speed. It was all the stupid piece of dog food needed.

CHAPTER 16

Joey bolted. Any man trying to run us down was going to have his work cut out trying to outrun Joey. We flew along the narrow lane. Palm fronds and other green stuff slapped us, probably adding to Joey's speed. I bent lower in the saddle to keep from being swept away by a branch, glued to his back by panic.

At the edge of the forest I saw Tully and Ziggy careening towards me in Tully's beat-up old wreck. Joey saw it too. He came to a stop and shook his head, spraying me with lather.

"Take it easy," I said, hoping he wouldn't turn around and bolt back into the forest. "Take it easy." I wasn't sure if it was meant for Joey or me. I pulled Joey up close to the board fence of the pasture as the old pickup slid to a stop beside us.

Tully had a rifle across his lap. Ziggy had a shotgun, with the butt planted on the seat, in his left hand. They were looking like this was an everyday occurrence for them, a scary thought.

I panted, "Fun's over, gentleman." I reached down and patted Joey's neck.

"What happened?" Tully asked.

"Met some bad news guys out there, but this fellow finally did something right. He bit the hand that needed it."

Tully said, "We'll just go on out there and have a little talk with those boys."

"Naw, everything's cool."

Tully's mouth was pulled tight into a thin angry line. "Those guys need a lesson in manners, need to be told about trespassing."

"Waste of time," I said, nudging Joey into a walk. "They've already gone."

Tully got his old truck turned around while I walked on with Joey. I was shaking all over with shock. Boomer was nasty but a known threat, at least I was stupid enough to think so. I'd dealt with a hundred guys like Boomer in a dozen different bars. Discouraging dickheads is part of the job for any woman tending bar and most of the grungy places I'd worked in abounded in fools just like Boomer Breslau.

At the moment it was the dark face in the palmettos that was scariest for me. I couldn't quantify it, didn't know what he threatened or why that guy was out there, unless he was a criminal or a crazy person. Any man hiding out in all that wilderness had to be one or the other. It wasn't an easy place to get to. There was only a narrow track, through deep jungle of vines and underbrush, running into the back two hundred acres of Riverwood. There were about a hundred acres of cleared land up near the house but the other two hundred acres had gone back to slash pines and palmettos and was home for gators, wild pigs, panthers and bugs — not a place that most people would find hospitable.

To get there he would have gone in from the lane behind

the barn or have followed one of the waterways into the jungle from the surrounding farms. Those waters teemed with gators.

This much I knew: he definitely didn't want to be seen. He was hiding, and there was a murderer about. Had I just looked into the eyes of the man who killed Lucan Percell? It couldn't be a coincidence that this man had shown up the same time Lucan's body had. What had the sheriff said about looking for a stranger? That guy definitely qualified as a stranger.

I tried to think it through. Had the man in the woods been at the Gator Hole, killed Lucan and hid the body and himself in the truck?

I tried to imagine climbing into the bed of a truck with a dead body, snuggling up real close, and not screaming the place down. Then, while I was hiding there under the tarp, someone gets in the truck and drives me and the body to God knows where. It took a lot of imagination. I couldn't really come up with another scenario that put the murderer at Riverwood. It didn't make sense, but then nothing made sense.

Maybe Howie surprised the murderer when he was bashing in Lucan's head. That's why the man got in the back of the truck, to hide, and that's why he was now out in the underbrush. It was the only situation I could come up with to put both Lucan's body and a man in the truck.

It seemed sensible that when Howie brought Big Red back to Riverwood, the killer had come with him, trapped under the tarp with the body. After Howie parked the truck and went home, the murderer had taken off for the jungle out behind the farmhouse. But why hadn't he headed back to town? It wasn't that far to walk.

I didn't want to get involved with the guy in the woods or

the police and I didn't want any of it to end up in the papers with my name attached. I was hoping it would all just disappear with no help from me. Self-interest is a wonderful motivator and leads to all kinds of sins.

I'd invited seventy-five people to a party, and the number one thing on my dance card was creating a fantastic evening for Clay and his friends on his birthday. Nothing else mattered.

When I got back to the barn Marley was walking Wildflower up and down outside the barn, worrying and waiting.

"Sorry," she said with an embarrassed lift of her left shoulder.

"What for?"

"For running out on you. Those guys scared the shit out of me."

"Me too, thanks for getting help."

She frowned. "Yeah, well…"

I was more concerned about Joey than Marley. I slid to the ground and checked him for damage. There were raised ridges of scratches along both of his sides and when I wiped my hand across his flank it came away with blood on it.

Tully pulled his old truck up in the shade of the barn and creaked his door open.

"He doesn't look too bad," I said when Tully ambled over.

Tully took Joey's bridle and said, "We'll rub the horses down and put them out to pasture. You two look like you could do with a coffee."

"Do you think he's all right? Think maybe I should get a vet?"

"This horse is tougher than he looks." He ran his hand over Joey's side. "Clay says he was bred for country like this — a little scratch won't harm him none."

Marley and I walked in silence back to the house. Now was the time to tell Marley about the man I'd seen. I owed it to her.

And I should phone the sheriff so they could begin the manhunt. But something didn't seem right with this scenario. I was left with one nagging thought. If he was the murderer, why was he hanging about? Why was he staying? And what was Boomer Breslau doing out there? Looking for someone would be my guess.

Marley held the screen door to the kitchen open. "If you're not mad, why are you so quiet?"

"What?" I thought we'd already covered this conversation.

"Do you want me to leave?"

"What? Why?"

"I ran out on you."

"No you didn't; you did just what I wanted you to do."

"You sure?"

"Didn't I tell you to go for help?"

"Yeah, but…"

"You did exactly the right thing."

"I'm not very brave," she said, following me into the kitchen and letting the screen slam shut behind her.

"That makes you smart." Her words were another good reason for not mentioning the face in the woods. "Brave is just another word for stupid." If I told the sheriff what I'd seen, Marley would have to be told, that was for sure. I couldn't keep a search party quiet. And if Marley knew there was someone hiding in the woods, she'd take off for Jacaranda and there would be no one to help me. See how selfish I am?

I headed straight for the shower, distance being the best aid to silence. It would also give me time to think things over.

I wanted to present Clay and myself as a real couple. Nothing too fancy, just down home and settled. I was even going to have family present. Although Tully and Ziggy were a risk, I was trusting them to be at their most charming. I'd even bought them both new shirts to wear.

Having the sheriff's men around would interfere with my plans. And, after all, there was nothing to bring the murderer back to Riverwood, was there? That was the last place he'd want to be.

Whatever was happening way out back of beyond, it had nothing to do with me. Just as in Jacaranda what happened a block away was none of my business, same thing in the country. If it happened way out there, it was none of my business.

After my shower, I'd checked all the doors and windows in the big old house, thinking I could lock it up and make us safe. It was a crazy hopeless chore, with five entrances and double that number of windows on the ground floor, some of which couldn't be locked.

And it didn't stop there. The house had porches, the true living space, all around it. Anyone could climb up on the roof of the porches and get to the second floor that way. Any idea I had of keeping intruders out was quickly evaporating. No way could you secure this house. We were sitting targets for anyone wanting in.

I knew Clay kept a handgun in the closet of our bedroom but if I started carrying it around with me it would take some explaining. Besides, my record with firearms wasn't good — they always ended up in the wrong hands. Best not to go armed.

In the kitchen Marley announced, in a tone of disgust, "She fell off again." Seemed she'd gotten over her worry about deserting me.

Tully shook his head in disappointment. "You used to be so athletic, always winning things in school, what happened?"

I poured a cup of coffee. "Well, you see, back then there was no horse named Joey involved." I took my coffee with me and went to try the bolt on the back door. "That horse is a waste of space." The lock had been painted over multiple times and probably hadn't been used in years.

"What are you doing?" Tully asked.

"There's a murderer around, best to be safe. I figure we should keep the house locked for a bit."

Marley's eyes grew wide. "I hadn't thought of that. Do you think he's still here?"

"Naw." Tully waved the thought aside and clomped over to get a coffee mug off the rack. "Never was here. It happened in Independence, and he's long gone from there." He poured his coffee and took a seat at the old enameled table. "'Sides, you gals got Ziggy and me. Don't worry."

Ziggy and Tully didn't actually look like the dream team when it came to home safety and Marley's face was showing her concern. "I'm glad you're here looking after us, Mr. Jenkins, but it can't hurt to keep the doors and windows locked for security."

"Honey, I keep telling you, call me Tully."

"That's awfully hard to do…" she smiled at him, "…after all these years. But I think Sherri is right, we should lock up until the sheriff gets it sorted out."

"'Cept you'll die of heat, without a breeze going through. And how are we going to get in and out?"

"Right, I forgot." I sipped at my coffee. "You and Uncle Ziggy will expire without access to the kitchen. An interesting side advantage, my two favorite mooches will have to stock their own fridge. You do have a fridge out there, don't you?"

"Got a fine fridge. Trouble is it's full of beer, no room for food. That's why we come here. Tell you what, leave the door unlocked when we're here and we'll make sure we lock it if we go out. How will that be?"

It would have to do. But still that face was shimmering in my worry zone.

When Marley went off for a shower, I asked Tully, "What do you know about Howard Sweet?"

He rubbed his right temple with gnarled arthritic fingers. "His family was rich people who used to winter in Independence. Bought this property for the future but never really lived here. His daddy come down to Florida back in the thirties. Had some kind of big dream, you know how it is with Northerners, always got some get-rich scheme, but it didn't work out. Howie, he was borned here and never knew no other place but he wasn't any better at making things turn out than his old man. He had those two big guys living to the east and west of him, both trying to get his land to fill out their own and get control of his water. He couldn't fend them off. There was some

problem with disease in his stock. Old Howie seems a bit para-
noid on the subject, thinks it came from unnatural causes,
thinks someone was trying to drive him out. If so, it worked.
Howie went into debt to restock. Sweet Meadow Farm bought
about three hundred acres to the west to get control of the water,
but Howie Sweet was still way over his head in debt, that's why
he sold out to Clay."

"Was the debt just from restocking or did Howie have
other needs?"

"Not sure, but I bet there wasn't much left after Clay
bought this place and Old Howie paid off the banks. He let's
on he's doing Clay a favor by working at Riverwood but I
think he needs the money." He rubbed the back of his neck
and added, "And working here gives him a chance to hide from
his wife."

"Why didn't he just sell to one of those other ranchers?"

"'Cause he hates them both. Breslau tried to ruin him
and…well, it goes way back. I don't rightly know the ins and
outs of it, except Lucan worked for Breslau, did his dirty work,
and you know of course that Lucan was the father of Lovey
Sweet's baby?"

"What?"

Tully nodded. "All that didn't make for good relations
between neighbors."

"So Clay coming along and buying Riverwood solved
everyone's problems?"

"Maybe not." He took a sip of his coffee and then said,
"Clay already took Sweet Meadow, the orange grove on the
other side of Riverwood, to court and stopped them from

pumping the creek dry. Sweet Meadow Farm can only take so many gallons a day out of the creek, not nearly what they were taking before Clay arrived. Clay owns on both sides of the creeks up here near the road. Richard Arby, who owns Sweet Meadow, wanted the west side of the creek from Howie so he wouldn't have to pump Sweet Meadow's irrigating water so far. Offered him big money, but Howie wasn't going to let either of them in so when Clay came along, he was the reasonable solution. Clay paid top dollar and Howie and Pearl get to live out their lives on their land, plus Howie has a job. They couldn't have gone on living here if either of those other two neighbors had bought them out, would have had to leave the county. Dying where you were born is something good."

"What do you think is behind Lucan's death?"

Tully shrugged. "Why would you kill someone? Me, I've done a lot of crazy things, wonder I haven't killed someone before now, but never have except in 'Nam. More luck than anything else that one of my fights didn't end with someone dead. But that was always in the heat of the moment, and those days are well behind me." He scratched along his whiskered jaw. "Guess I'd still kill to protect you."

Before this could go to my head he added, "Or Marley, or Ziggy. Only natural to protect the people in your life but I don't get angry or crazy enough to kill for any other reason anymore. What was done to Lucan, well there was emotion behind it. Hate or even fear, there was a kind of madness. The guy that did it wasn't just coldly ending a life; he was smashing a life, different sort of thing."

"Could a woman have done it?"

CHAPTER 17

He thought about it. "If Lucan was already in the bed of the truck, say he was drunk and came out of the Gator Hole and climbed into the back of the truck for a little nap, sort of thing a man can do when he's heavy in the liquor, then a woman could have found him there and beat him to death. A man's skull ain't as strong as you might think. One time, I saw a fella trip and hit his head on an iron gate. This little knob," he made a circle with his fingers, "put there to look pretty, went into his head like a lead ball into water, killed him dead right there and then before anyone could do a thing."

"Maybe Lovey did it," I suggested.

"Hope not. It will break old Zig's heart."

"Why?"

"That's where Zig's been goin' every day; got it bad for Lovey Sweet. He's there every morning for breakfast and every day for lunch. Old Zig just sits there and drools and leaves enormous tips." Tully threw back his head and laughed at this outrageous turn of events. "Myself, I don't go there much 'cause I don't want to step into Zig's territory, being as handsome as I am."

"So where have you been going for some sweet talk, Daddy?"

He gave me an exaggerated wink.

I grinned at him and asked, "You think the sheriff is going to figure out what happened to Lucan?"

Tully shrugged. "He didn't impress me much, didn't seem all that interested in Lucan. Might just pin it on the first person who looks likely. He was asking about someone hanging about and now you meet the Breslau bunch out back. Seems strange to me."

"Are you saying the Breslau clan had something to do with this?"

"Don't know. The sheriff is first cousin to Orlin Breslau. I'm just telling you to remember that blood runs thicker than water out here. Things aren't exactly going to come down here like they would back in Jac. Independence is a small town and there are no disinterested parties."

I started to tell him about the man in the palmettos, but Marley came into the kitchen. She'd put a lime green baseball cap on, pulling her mass of hair up under it. The glasses were gone and she was actually wearing some lipstick and mascara, makeup being one of the many fun things she'd given up while dating David. The Baptist grip on her was starting to loosen.

"You look real pretty, honey," Tully told her. He turned to me. "You better stick real close to this gal today or someone's gonna steal her away from us."

Marley beamed, just lit up like a Christmas tree. Even a compliment from my old man pleased her. Even the fact she knew my old man was a really bad judge of woman didn't stop her delight. Her confidence must have been lower than I realized.

"Can I take your truck?" I asked Tully. "I want to swing by the restaurant and pick up the champagne the buzzards and dead body made me forget."

"Well, sure you can, honey. It might teach you to be more generous with your own vehicle."

"Oh, you can drive Big Red now," I said. "There's something about having a dead body in the bed that has made me go right off it."

"Bet it's only temporary," Marley said and bounced down the hall and out the front door.

I raised a finger to Tully, telling him to wait, and went down the hall after Marley and watched her turn on the tap and start watering the flowers. I went back to Tully and closed the door to the front hall. "I got a little surprise out there in the woods — well, two actually." I told him about the face hidden in the jungle.

"Shit," Tully said. "Why didn't you call the sheriff as soon as you got back?" He thought for a minute and said, "Best you girls go back to town."

"Nope, I'm planning a party, remember?"

"Tell people it's been put off 'cause there's been a tragic accident."

I only had to think about it a second. "Not going to happen. I've asked all of Clay's friends. We're doing this."

"Why didn't you just hold it at the Sunset?"

I didn't want to tell him it was because I wanted Clay and me to look like a real couple, with a real life. "Don't try to get out of cooking at my pig roast."

"Okay, if you won't go back to Jacaranda then Zig and I are moving into the house."

"Thanks, that will make Marley feel much better."

"Tough girl," he laughed. "Nothin' scares you, does it?"

"Only the cost of feeding you two. What do you hunt from the back of an ATV?"

Tully's eyebrows went up. "Me? Nothing."

"Would you hunt for a man on them?"

Tully straightened.

"I see what you mean. Both the sheriff and Boomer are looking for someone. I don't think Boomer wants to arrest him."

From the back porch Marley hollered, "Come on," through the screen door.

I leaned forward and kissed Tully's cheek. "You be careful," I told him.

"Always am," he answered.

I started to leave and then hesitated and turned back, suddenly afraid for him, a black premonition of danger filling me with panic and dread.

"Go on," he said, waving an arm. "Get out of here."

CHAPTER 18

Marley was searching through the glove compartment when I climbed behind the wheel. Not finding what she was looking for she started on the junk on the seat and the garbage on the floor. Tully's truck could substitute for a landfill site and contained stuff from the decade before my birth.

"Did you lose something besides your mind?"

She was now checking down the back of the seats. "Looking for cigarettes."

"Tully quit smoking."

"Oh, really? Just because you've been nagging him?" She pulled down the visor. "These will do," she said, picking up the package of cigarettes that slid onto my lap. She opened the pack and held them out, "Want one?"

"I promised Clay."

"Suit yourself." The smell of the cigarette filled the cab and chipped away at my willpower.

"I thought you quit," I said, sounding as grumpy as I felt.

"Did, but one can't hurt."

She propped her feet up on the dash and opened the envelope with the list of furniture as I backed the truck around and started out the lane. Being a neat, in control, sort of orderly person, Clay not only knew where the keys to the units were, he also knew what was in every container. Very impressive and unusual behavior in my world.

After a failed fishing trip, I once heard my father tell my Uncle Dallas that he couldn't organize an orgy in a whorehouse. That pretty much is a family truth. I come from a long line of people with my uncle's lack of talent in the management department. In my family, not only would the keys never be seen again, no one would have a clue what was in the units, and for sure they would never pay the bill for the storage. And then there would be one more story added to the family legends of how, through no fault of their own, mind you, the Jenkins family had lost out on a great fortune. This epic would probably have some tricky educated person, some person with authority, doing them wrong and making off with their extremely valuable treasures. These stories are a great comfort to people who are their own worst enemies. We polish and embellish them until not a hint of a loser remains, turning them into sagas of evil overcoming decent folk. This ability to rewrite the stories of our own failures is our one true skill.

Marley read the list of furniture to me as I wrestled with Tully's old pickup, which kept heading for the ditch, probably in memory of days past — vehicle repair and home repair being two more things we Jenkins didn't go in for.

"Says here there is a silver tea service in the first unit and, in case you were wondering, it comes complete with sugar bowl, tongs, milk jug and tray, and it is early Georgian. What do you think that means?"

"Money, honey, money…old money and lots of it but I didn't think Clay's folks were all that rich. Maybe it is something he bought later. Can you imagine him going around to auctions and secretly buying things like a Georgian tea service and stashing it away?"

"Not really, but I always figured he had hidden depths. After all, he chose you. It would take a strangely perverted man to pick you from the crop, so buying stuff on the sly is not all that weird."

"A man that chose both me and Georgian silver has very good taste."

"Or a strange sense of humor." She stuck the cigarette in her mouth and mumbled something unintelligible around it. The wind from the open window blew the scarf around her neck into her face as she was taking a huge life-destroying gulp of smoke into her lungs. I waited for the material to go up in flames but she batted it away and squinted at the papers in her lap. She took the cigarette from her mouth and said, "Mahogany dining table, sex chairs, nope, must be six chairs."

"You think?"

"Slide…no, sideboard. That sounds good. I'm getting excited here."

"Lucky you. Must be the thought of sex chairs."

"You have no soul or mahogany would do it for you." She pulled the pages up close to her eyes.

"Hey," I warned. "Be careful you don't set them on fire."

She pushed them away again. "Shit, this print is really small."

"Put your glasses on."

She stuck the cigarette in the corner of her mouth to keep the smoke out of her eyes. Puffing the whole time, she dug through her bag for the glasses. "Better," she said, pushing them up her nose and holding the cigarette to the window for the wind to take the ash. "What do you suppose King Charles spaniels are?"

"My guess is dogs, so you stand in front of me when we open the doors."

It took over an hour to get to Sarasota and the three storage units, but oh, the excitement when we opened them.

It was Christmas and birthdays and Easter and every High Holiday I didn't celebrate rolled into one. We opened the first compartment, pulled aside the blankets and wrappings, screamed and jumped up and down and ran to the next storage unit. We opened it, uncovered stuff and screamed, jumped up and down and clapped our hands, all the time saying, "Look at this, look at this," not really seeing anything but yelling anyway and then we ran to the last container, repeating the action, going crazy with greed and excitement and the beauty of what we saw.

It wasn't just old stuff, but fine antiques packed to the roof. Surely very little of it had come from Clay's family. They'd only become moderately well-to-do when they sold out to developers and moved to a new ranch farther inland. And while Clay's family was Old Florida, they weren't the kind of people who ran things or came out from England with a boatload of furniture. They were just hard-working ranchers who lived at the mercy of nature. This assortment looked like someone had spent a lot of time and energy building a collection.

Marley, the shopping whiz, called out a description of each piece as she found it — an orgasmic adventure for the queen of the garage sales. I started to wonder if she realized she wasn't going to get to take any of it home. Best not to tell her when she was in this state or she could turn vicious.

"Hey," said Marley. "I saw a telephone book in your dad's truck." She looked up from her papers. "Why would anyone carry a telephone book around? Get on the cell and find a mover to take this stuff out to the ranch."

She was now in charge so I did as I was told.

"The best I could do is Monday afternoon," I told Marley when I came back. "Hey, where are you?"

"In here. I think I found an organ."

"Must have something to do with sex chairs, don't touch it, you never know where it's been."

Her head poked up beside a floor lamp with an alabaster shade. "You are a very crude person."

"I know. It happens every time Clay goes away. What do you suppose causes it?"

"You have a mind like a septic tank."

"That's a shitty thing to say."

"Humpf," she grunted and disappeared.

"Hey, come out of there. You're going to bring the whole thing down on your head." There was no response. I didn't want to be there when the accident happened so I went back and checked out the other two storage spaces. Even in a sixteen-room house, this furniture was going to make a statement and impress the hell out of everyone.

"Wow," I heard from deep in the pile when I returned.

"What did you find?" I asked, although to tell the truth I wasn't that interested. The joy of antiques was brief for me. I had something else on my mind and I wanted to get back out to Independence.

"I found a beautiful carved headboard. Must be nearly eight feet tall."

"Gross, come on, let's go."

Her head appeared again. "What's the hurry?"

"I want to get the champagne and get back and make plans. You know, figure out where it's all going to go."

"Oh, good idea." She hurried out now. "Maybe I should take pictures before we go."

"I'm sure Clay said there were some back at the house. Use those." She was going to give me grief when she found out there was no such thing but by then I'd have thought of something else.

"Oh, great, I'm really excited." And she was, at least excited enough to run to the pickup while I locked up.

"I'm planning on measuring the rooms and making floor plans just like they show you in the magazines," she told me. "Aren't you thrilled?"

"Just so long as the guests don't have to sit on the floor, I'm cool." This wasn't exactly the truth. I cared a whole lot more than that. I should have known better. I had never fit into the Travis world, no matter how hard I'd tried. Jimmy's father was a plastic surgeon and Jimmy'a mother was the social queen of Jacaranda. Their world was a million miles from the trailer park on the edge of a swamp where I grew up, even though it was only a twenty-minute drive apart. I should have known it wouldn't work any better trying to fit into Clay's. But I'm a girl who never learns from her mistakes. I tend to stick to the old tried and true errors and make the same screw up again and again. That way I can avoid learning new things.

So here I was, taking a week off, the first in two years, to make everything perfect. In my head I could see the idyllic evening, the soft glow of ferry lights in the oaks, the Japanese lanterns strung along the porch, the house glowing and alive with lights. Along the porch and under the trees would be bistro tables with long white tablecloths and candles. Elegant and refined. I'd daydreamed about this for months. I was trying desperately to keep from Marley how important this party was to me. If she knew, she'd laugh herself silly.

She put down the list she was reading for the tenth time and announced, "I'm calling Jane. She works part-time at the office. I'm going to get her to work for me this week and I'll just cancel the rest of the appointments she can't cover. I'm taking a holiday."

I didn't try too hard to talk her out of it.

We swung by the Sunset to load up the champagne. Marley wasn't going any farther until she was fed a huge lunch on the house. Before the food arrived she started in to tell me that I shouldn't get involved with Lucan's murder. "After all," she reasoned, "if someone killed him in the parking lot and wanted to hide him and your truck was there, if it was just a random thing that he was put in Big Red, it hasn't anything to do with you, has it?"

"You're right, it isn't my problem," I agreed. "I'm not involved and I have no intention of ever getting mixed up in it. Besides I have a new philosophy of life."

"I wasn't aware you had an old one."

"Shut up and listen, this is how it is...I no longer feel responsible for anyone but myself. Whatever happens I just let it flow by." My right hand described the undulation of a stream over rocks as I told her this profound truth. "I'm not in control of anything and I don't want to be in control anymore."

"You never were in control," Marley pointed out.

"Yes, but now I realize it, that's the difference. It's all kinda Zen, this letting the world drift by. My own twelve steps for going through life serenely."

"Weird," she said and helped herself to my chips as the waitress set the plate in front of me. "But not any weirder than some of the stuff I've heard come out of your mouth."

"I'm glad you appreciate it. Now tell me what's happening. Have you heard from David?"

The sunshine went out of her face and she dropped the chips onto her plate. "No. It's over. He wants to work full-time with the homeless, which will just about make him homeless as well when he gives up his own church. He won't have his own ministry anymore, no permanent congregation and no income. He will be subsisting on donations, living the same life as those he serves. His sacrifice means he's also sacrificing his future family." Her food was forgotten as she leaned forward on both elbows and said, "I want kids, want to send them to good schools, have holidays, healthcare, all those things. I don't want my children to grow up in a homeless shelter."

"Sounds perfectly reasonable to me. Surely David sees that and agrees?"

She shook her head. "All he can see is the people who need him. Maybe if I loved him more I'd have been willing to make sacrifices as well."

"Or maybe he doesn't love you enough if he chooses strangers over you. Marley, if he had chosen you, you would have clung to him no matter what. He made this decision without thinking about you. He's asking way too much."

She sighed and said, "He wants me to be a better person than I am; he thinks I can be like him."

"Yeah, well I've promised myself that in my next life I'll be a better person too, no shooters, no nights I can't quite recall, fewer parties and a whole lot less fun. But right now I'm dealing with the here and now and I think you should too. Don't try to turn yourself into some kind of a saint for someone else. You'll end up resenting him."

"And yet I love him. I want to be as giving as David but I still want a home." She leaned forward in her intensity. "That's why I'm going to enjoy this week. It might be the only time I get to decorate a house. I may never have a house of my own."

"Of course you will."

"Not like this one and not if I marry David." Again the big sigh. "I'm selfish."

"You haven't a selfish bone in your body."

She wasn't convinced. "I go back and forth, wanting to be with David and wanting a different life than the one I'll have with him. What do you think I should do?"

"Get a haircut and lose the glasses."

"No, I meant about David."

"So did I."

After we stopped at a paint store for a color chart, I dropped Marley off at Riverwood. Memory is a tricky thing, at least my memory. Lucan's murder and the sheriff's comments about April Donaldson brought back the ache of losing Jimmy, and I was flooded with a sense of pain as fresh and as new as if it had just happened that day, not nearly two years ago.

I wondered how April was handling the fact that Lucan would never walk through the door again. Was she adjusting to this new reality? She'd never hear him laugh again, never even get angry with him or be able to make love to him again.

I went to visit Lucan's common-law wife, the lady the county didn't think much of. I figured April Donaldson and I shared a whole lot. Turned out, so did she.

CHAPTER 19

She looked like an unmade bed in a cheap motel — faded, grubby and sagging. Not a place to stretch out unless you were really desperate.

"What you staring at, Miss Uptown Gal?" she said.

"I'm sorry if I was staring."

She was all elongated bones and hard angles. Her face, long and narrow, was a road map to unhappiness and was dominated by sunken, red-rimmed eyes. She took a deep drag on her cigarette and said, "You and I ain't so different."

And that was what was so frightening. She recognized me right off. Some instinct told her we were sisters.

It wasn't just the loss to violence of the men in our lives that we shared. We both lived on the edge of financial disaster. The Sunset looked like it was rolling in dough, but the truth was it was only a real good thing if breaking even excites you. There were still months I took no salary, months when the busboys took home more money than me. The pitiful monthly check I sent to Ruth Ann said how close survival lived to failure.

It would take only a few small calamities to have me on the same track as April Donaldson, but good God, couldn't this woman at least comb her hair? It hung in long strings around her face, except for one side where it appeared a nest of rodents had set up home.

"My name is Sherri Travis."

"Sheriff told me about you and I recognized you from town. What do you want?"

"I wanted to tell you I'm sorry for your loss."

She snorted. "Oh yeah? Knew Luc real well, did you? Liked him even?"

"No, I didn't know him but I can see you loved him and that you'll miss him. I'm sorry for that. I know what it is to lose people."

Her face crumbled. She put up the hand with the cigarette to hide her grief and cover her mouth to stop its sounds. The knobby shoulders shook under the thin cotton blouse. I stepped closer and put my hand to the shoulder blade sticking out under the faded pattern, wanting to offer human comfort. She gave an animal wail of pain and turned to me, moving into me and grabbing hold of me as if I might be her only salvation from drowning in a sea of hurt.

When she pulled away from the damp spot on my shoulder, she was angry again. "I know what people think of Luc. Probably saying it's the best thing that could have happened. Well, not for me it isn't." She swiped at her nose with the back of her hand.

I stepped on the burning cigarette that dropped from her fingers. The scorch mark wouldn't be visible on the battle-ground of the lino.

"He was good to me," she said with an anguished wail. She dropped onto the couch, knees together and her elbows dug deep into her gut. Her tears started again.

I went to the sink and picked up the least dirty glass I could see. The pipes clanged as I turned on the water. I let the water run over the glass, rinsing it out before filling it and taking it to her.

She looked up at me, holding in the hurt. I offered her the glass and she took it silently.

I went to the living room window and pushed aside the thin bed sheet draped over the window. A thin brown dog, at the end of a heavy chain, was going around and around a stake in the middle of the yard, retracing over and over again the perfect circle he had worn into the earth. The chain itself had dragged over the soil within the circle and torn out every living thing. The merciless sun beat down on the thin spiked grass that spotted the sandy soil outside of the circle. Only about four feet of the dog's journey went through any shade at all. He'd exhaust himself in his endless circuit, fall down in the shade until he recovered, then get up and begin his restless journey again. I'm a pack animal myself, need human company the way I need air, so the sight of the dog staked out like a sacrifice did things to me.

I watched him through two full cycles before April said, "Damn Breslaus. They're the ones that killed Lucan or had someone do it for them."

I let the sheet drop back over the window. "He worked for them, didn't he?"

"Off and on. Used to be their foreman; these days he did their dirty work. That's all they thought he was good for."

"Lots of dirty work on a farm. Just what kind did Lucan do?"

"The kind they pay cash for."

"Orlin Breslau, he's the owner of the Oxbow Ranch, isn't he?"

She gave a quick nod. "Nasty piece of shit, him and that grandson he calls Boomer, meanest bastards you ever going to find. Luc was pretty scared of them when he was sober. Drunk, nothing scared him."

"Did he say what he was doing for them?"

For the first time there was an emotion beside anger on her face — fear maybe, caution certainly. "Why you askin' all this?"

"Born nosey."

"Yeah, that can be a real disability." Her mouth stretched in a smile, making the sadness of her eyes more unbearable.

"Look, can I bring that dog inside?"

"What for?"

"It's hot as Hades out there, must be ninety, ninety-five, and who knows he might just be a comfort to you."

She looked confused but I didn't wait for her to agree.

Only when I jumped over the broken bottom step did she holler, "Careful, he bites."

Shit. But there were no signs of food and the metal water bowl had been turned upside down by the chain. He probably hadn't had water since Lucan left. He couldn't be left there to die. The dog, straining at the end of the chain and stretching his body out towards me, teeth bared and jaw up, started barking. He was a pretty impressive sight. I edged towards him, talking nonsense and walking slow. My good intentions were fading fast with each attempt at a lunge he made for me before the collar, thick and tough, called him up short.

"Good dog," I crooned. My knees creaked and cracked as I sat on my heels and slowly put out my hand. The barking turned to a low growl. He sat and watched the hand ease forward. White flecks of foam sprayed on my hand as he yelped and jerked towards it.

"You're slow," I told him, holding my hand into my chest protectively. "Maybe you don't really want to bite me." I moved my hand out towards him again, talking to him and watching him closely. This time he growled but didn't snap. Under the mottled browns of his stretched skin, his ribs showed. I rubbed his ear. He sank down to his haunches and then eased to the ground.

Slowly, slowly I crept forward and unsnapped the chain from his collar, laying it on the ground and sliding back from him without touching him, moving slow.

"Well, you can run away now if you want. I would. Just keep going, miles of nothing for you to live in, but watch for gators, won't you?" I said and backed away. He stayed there, hunched down, waiting for the blow and watching me. I covered ten feet before I turned my back on him.

I heard him move behind me and braced for the attack. It didn't come. At the steps, I climbed gingerly, staying away from the cracked and rotting boards in the middle, easing up the outside where the steps were firmly attached at the edge.

I heard the click of his nails on the broken concrete behind me. I stopped. He stopped.

I stepped onto the porch. The paint was peeling back off several layers of color, white over sage green over bare gray boards. I looked back and he lowered himself, not quite lying down but certainly not upright. I opened the door, nudging a stray shoe in front of it to block it open. I went in.

His nails went click, click, as he climbed the stairs.

April Donaldson was where I'd left her, the empty glass on the floor beside her. I went to the sink and washed out a bowl and filled it with water. The dog retreated down the steps as I came through the door. "You look like you can use this," I said to him as I set the bowl on the stoop. I went back inside to the click click of his nails climbing up the steps and then the frantic lapping of the water. I went to the fridge and opened it.

"You make yourself at home, don't you?" April said, but she didn't seem unduly disturbed by my rudeness. In the fridge there was a package of gray hamburger still covered in the plastic wrapper from the store. I checked the date and sniffed the package. It wasn't the freshest but the dog would starve before he died of bad meat. Animals seemed to be immune to things that would kill us. I stuck my nail in the end to open the wrap and plopped a good fist-sized glob onto a plate from the sink. Best to start easy. He'd eat whatever I put out and then throw it back up if I was overgenerous.

The dog growled again as I approached him but drool was running over his snarling lips. "Good dog," I started to say as I reached out to place the plate on the bare wood. He lunged and gulped the meat down before the plate made it to the floor. "All righty," I told him. "Looks like that takes care of dinner. You all come in when you feel up to it." I took the plate back inside.

April watched all this without comment and I was starting to think she might have a wheel or two missing from her wagon so I asked, "Will you be all right here alone?"

"Say, what are you, a bloody social worker or something?"

"More like a concerned neighbor."

She snorted. "So that explains why you let me cry on your shoulder."

I ran water over the plate and then put the plug in the sink and searched for dish soap. I twisted around to look at her as the sink filled. "Tell me about Lucan."

She shrugged and stayed silent. Minutes passed and the sink filled. At last she said, "We grew up together, me and Lovey and Lucan."

I turned off the water and looked at her. She considered her hands, saying, "Lovey Sweet was the girl all the boys loved, specially Lucan. Her father didn't think Lucan was good enough for Lovey, caught them together once, and threatened to kill Luc if he didn't stay away from her."

She got out of the chair as if every motion pained her and went for her Winstons. "Lovey is beautiful. You seen her?" She looked at me now with gray eyes that might never shine again.

"Can't remember."

"Oh, you'd remember. She's like one of those old time paintings, lush, you know? Round and sensual, not like those skinny women you see in magazines today, not like me. Luc is Kelly's daddy only he didn't know it for the longest time 'cause Lovey told him he wasn't, said some other man had sired Kelly, but you only have to see Kelly to know she's a Percell, and besides, Lovey was never that sort of girl, you know, the sort that would go with more than one man at a time. No, there was never anyone but Luc for her in those days."

I set a dripping plate in the dish rack and asked, "Why didn't Lovey marry him?"

"I think she was afraid her daddy really would shoot Luc. Mr. Sweet's a good man but when that wife of his gets talking and doing his thinking for him, there's no telling what's going to happen. Besides, back then, seventeen, eighteen years ago, well we were more inclined to do what we was told."

"Wasn't having a child out of wedlock a huge deal?"

"Yup, but then Mrs. High and Mighty Sweet Pants could heave a sigh and say it was her cross to bear but no way was she going to have Luc for a son-in-law. Lovey wasn't but fifteen or sixteen. Not easy to stand up for yourself then."

"But she kept the baby."

"Baptist you know, no abortion and you didn't give away kin. She stayed at home for a few years then she got out of there. From what I hear, she hasn't been back since and old Pearl won't hear her name mentioned."

"Do you think it was Mr. Sweet who killed Lucan?"

But April wasn't listening. "Well look at that there, will ya."

I turned to see what had put the animation in her voice.

CHAPTER 20

The dog crept into the house on bent legs, nose almost to the floor, waiting inside the door to see what would happen before he melted down, head on his paws and his eyes watching us.

"Luc said that was one mean animal but he don't look so bad now, does he?"

"He looks quite normal there," I agreed. "He'll be good company for you. You won't be all alone now."

"Dog doesn't make up for a man."

"Well," I said, stirring the water in the sink with my hand, considering it, "there've been one or two men in my life that a dog would have been a whole lot better than."

She gave a hic and then a rusty laugh, as if she was using vocal cords that hadn't performed in a long time. "That's sure enough true. Some men in my life, well, living with a dog would be a whole lot better." She came to the counter and took up the dish towel, hanging on a drawer knob, and began to dry the dishes in the rack, hip against the counter and one bare foot resting on the other.

I asked, "What do you think, is Howard Sweet capable of murdering Luc?"

She gave a shrug, watching the towel go round and round the plate. "He always seemed like his name. Don't think he'd have made a fuss if Lovey and Luc had married, but not that wife of his." Her hands stopped and her eyes met mine over the towel. "Pearl, Mrs. Sweet, she could do it." She nodded her head in agreement with her words. "She could kill someone, especially Luc. Cruel woman, always hurtful, I remember once coming out of class at the end of the day, I must have been about eleven or so, Mrs. Sweet was at the door giving out invitations to Lovey's birthday party. She gave one to the girl in front of me, was smiling and everything, and when I put out my hand to get my invite she just snatched it up to her chest, gave one to the girl behind me though. She just thought me and my family were no good and never would be. She's real good at passing judgment like that." She opened the cupboard door and put the plate inside. "Lovey saved me some cake. Brought it to school the next day and told me how sorry she was her mother hadn't let me be at her party. Lovey's a nice person."

I rinsed a glass and asked, "What about now, how did the Sweets get along with Luc?"

"Mrs. Sweet still believes he'd ruined their family, and the mister pretty much follows her lead. Mrs. Sweet once told me at the grocery store that she thought Lucan and I were going straight to hell for living together without being married, but then everyone 'round here pretty much agrees with that. They don't hold with living in sin."

"Yeah, I got the same reception. How does Lovey feel about Lucan now?"

"Lovey just didn't want Lucan around, didn't have feelings for him anymore, although his never changed for her, nor mine for Luc." She picked the glass out of the rack. "Funny, seems the person whose life was most ruined by Kelly's birth was Luc's. Never was no saint but he dropped out of school and started drinkin' after Lovey got pregnant and told him it was someone else's child. He done some bad things, sure, but he never stopped loving her. And when he knew Kelly was his child he loved her too. He used to go and watch her play baseball, kind of hide behind the stands where no one could see him, and watch her play. Sit outside her school and that sort of thing. And he gave Lovey money for her." She looked around the room. "Think we just like livin' this way? Every spare cent went for that girl or into a college fund for her."

"He wouldn't even spend a cent on a gallon of paint for the house, never mind anything for me. I work cleaning up at the Blue Haven retirement home, cleaning up pee and worse so we could stay alive and he could give it all away. He'd do anything for that child, and when Boomer Breslau started bothering her, I thought Luc was going to kill that boy. See, Luc never got over spying on Kelly, and he seen Boomer trying to kiss Kelly and Kelly trying to get away. Luc stopped his truck in the middle of the street, got out and slugged Boomer. Fortunately some men broke it up, but Luc was sure mad."

"Did he get fired?"

"Nope." Her forehead wrinkled in thought. "Luc said they couldn't fire him because he knew too much."

"About what?"

"Don't know but something's going on over there. Luc never said what, but it's happening and it's bad. Once, when he was drunk, which was just about every night, and we were watching TV he said that what we was watching on television was nothing. Said that worse things were happening right here in Independence."

I handed her the mug I'd just rinsed out. "But you have no idea what?"

"Nope. Don't want to know either and neither do you."

When I left April's the dog started to follow me out the door. April's face fell but she said, "You can take him if you want. I'm not much for animals."

Clay had talked about getting a dog and a mutt like this seemed to be part of every ranch yard I passed. Lord knows, I needed the early warning system. I looked from the dog, gazing expectantly up at me, to April. She crossed her arms over her flat chest and hunched her shoulders. "All the same to me," she said.

"Naw," I replied. "He's your dog; just remember to feed him, won't you?" I wasn't at all sure she would even remember to feed herself.

Her face lit up and she nodded vigorously. "Sure, Luc always fed him, but I can do it."

"I'll drop back in a day or two but you know where I am if you need me."

There was no answer but I got a slight smile with the nod.

CHAPTER 21

The Breslau place was called Oxbow, at least that's what the old weathered sign out at the road said. I slowed down to look as I went past and then came to a stop.

There was this thing biting me. Instead of my anger fading with the passing hours it seemed to be growing.

The look of unrestrained desire in Boomer Breslau's eyes had pretty well convinced me that if Joey hadn't decided on eating meat instead of hay, I'd be shedding tears. I didn't like being treated like a piece of meat, didn't like being frightened, and I was damned sure it wasn't going to happen again if I had anything to say about it. I wanted to tell Boomer's parents to keep their son away from me or he was going to be real sorry. I backed up and pulled into the driveway.

Heavy steel gates, attached to an eight-foot chain-link fence with barbed wire on top, stood open. It looked like the Breslau family was real worried about someone stealing their tomatoes. Well, they had something else to worry about now. I'd been terrified and it had made me cranky. And if I was going to spend time out here with Clay, live part of my life at Riverwood, the neighbors surely had to know I expected a little respect. And one way or another I was going to get it.

Even with the gates swung wide back from the lane, the place wasn't real welcoming. Instead of, "Welcome," the entrance seemed to say, "Go away and forget about it, fool." I had a brief flash of caution that was quickly overcome by simmering rage.

The house was well back in the trees, not even a peek of it showing from the road. I started up the lane. Just driving through the dark overgrowth, greenery reaching for me on all sides, gave me the creeps. Except for the well-used sand drive, the place had an abandoned feeling as if no one cared enough to cut back the vines and undergrowth encroaching all around.

The remains of a white board fence, now peeling and rotting, ran parallel to the driveway. It seemed that things had once been far different here, maybe a little more welcoming and gracious.

The underbrush thinned and I could see through to the field beyond. I couldn't see anything that looked like a tomato plant in the weed-filled ground next to the lane. Truthfully, I wouldn't know a tomato plant if it bit me. I'm only interested in those round red things when they have bacon and mayo on them, but it didn't seem that this fallen-down sort of place with no sunlight was the spot to grow anything but brush.

A covey of six Bobwhite quails darted out in front of me, hesitated and then fluttered into the scrub on the other side of the drive.

I went around a bend into a place where the brush had been pushed back by a bush hog. The weedy clearing in the trees was cluttered with broken machinery, old cars, a flatbed truck and even a mesh-sided orange hauler, all sitting in various states of disrepair while they decayed in dying grasses. The equipment looked as if the machinery had been left to rot where it stopped when someone was done using it, all abandoned in a casual uncaring way.

Beyond this dumping area the house stood sheltering under huge oaks. Even around the house there was more abandoned machinery. Out of this tumble of broken stuff came three brown pit bulls, jaws stretched and barking to wake the dead. Not one tail among the lot was wagging.

These guys meant their snarls; their bare teeth were just waiting to strip the meat from my bones. The scars on their muzzles and along their flanks proved they'd survived more than one battle, their attitude saying they were ready for another. Every country place comes with a dog, often more than one, but not like these — these dogs were meant for something else, something I recognized.

In the trailer park I grew up in there was an old man, a seriously dangerous man who not even my mother tried to reform. He raised fighting dogs. His dogs were locked in cages on the edge of the swamp behind his trailer. His dogs had overlapping scars just like these. We used to sneak out to see those dogs when Old Man Butler took his prize animals off to fight. To prove your mettle, our gang demanded you sneak close enough to a cage to hand feed a dog. They'd gulp down whatever we stuck in between the wires and then lunge at the fragile metal trying to get at you. They were not pets. Neither were these dogs. At least there'd been some sort of cage between me and Old Man Butler's dogs.

I eased around the circular drive searching the old tumbled-down ruin for signs of human life, looking for someone to come outside and call off the dogs. The house had once been white like the fence, but it was now mostly gray where the paint had crept back to expose the weathered boards beneath. And at one time the house had worn black shutters. Now half of them were missing and the remaining ones looked like they'd packed their bags to go.

Except for the dogs and the three rusting air conditioners falling out of the front windows on the ground floor, it looked like the dwelling had been abandoned years ago. As I considered the building, a large brown mastiff came out from the dark of the porch. A thick chain was connected to a leather strap around its neck. The dog's face was an open mouth, a trap of teeth and white drool. His deep-throated growl overpowered the din of the other dogs.

I reached over and pressed down the lock on the passenger door and then on my own side. I wasn't sure I really wanted anyone to come out of the house. If the family was anything like their dogs, this was no place to take a stand on my need for respect. Maybe I should write them a strongly worded letter. Neighbors like this I didn't want to know.

I looked around. The only bright spot on the landscape was a little cottage tucked off to one side. It was painted in soft lavender with purple trim and had bright yellow sunflowers growing in big pots on either side of the door. It was fresh and welcoming but it was also surrounded by chain-link fence with a fenced chute sticking out to the drive. A battered white sedan sat by the fence, the only sign of an automobile I could see. Always one to take the easiest option, I headed for the cottage.

The dogs followed.

I parked in front of the house and tooted the horn to see if I could get anyone's attention. The dogs, except for the mastiff chained to the porch, were now all throwing themselves at the driver's door of Tully's pickup and waiting for lunch to step out. The purple door opened a crack, just enough for a pale face to peek around the edge. I slid over and rolled down the window a few inches and waved a hand out the opening in what I hoped was a friendly gesture. At least they could see the hand didn't hold a weapon. I was thinking that might be important. If I lived in a place like this, guarded by a pack of slavering dogs, I'd expect all my guests to come armed. A dog jumped up onto the door of the truck, its nails clattering on the window and scratching down the paint. I quickly brought my hand back inside and closed the window.

A tall thin man slipped around the edge of the door and swiftly closed it behind him. He walked to the gate of the chute. The pack ran to him. He opened the gate and edged out without letting the animals into the enclosed yard. He closed the gate firmly behind him and hesitated, which I thought was a big mistake. The dogs surrounded him, baring their teeth. Cursing, the man landed a couple of kicks, driving them back. Still snarling and slinking around, they waited for an opening or any sign of weakness. Focused on me, the guy ignored the dogs.

Forty-five to fifty, blond hair faded to mostly gray, he had a face that sadness had moved into a long time ago and had no intention of leaving. Suspicion, and more than a little trepidation, worried his forehead. He didn't smile, although I was wearing my brightest one.

I slid across the bench seat and rolled down the window six inches. "Hi," I said, sticking out my hand for a shake. "I'm Sherri Travis. I live with Clay Adams over at Riverwood. I just came by to invite you to a party."

He thought about taking my hand but remained undecided. Behind him the door of the little house swung in. I couldn't see who was at the door because they were well back from the opening.

"It's Clay's birthday and I thought it would be great for us to get to know the neighbors." My hand was growing tired of hanging there but I wasn't going to pull it back inside unless he spat on it.

"Harland Breslau," he confessed, as if it were a crime. He leaned forward just far enough so he could make contact and in the most fleeting of touches pressed his fingers to mine and then quickly withdrew them. "Thank you, ma'am, but we don't really go to parties. My wife isn't well."

I leaned sideways to see around him. "Hello," I called and risked my arm to wave towards the house where I could see movement at the door.

"I'd like to meet your wife," I told Harland.

He frowned and looked back to the house. Only a black maw yawned into the dark interior. "My wife isn't up to visitors."

His words were immediately turned into a lie as a wheelchair rolled through the open door and the woman sitting in it called out, "Harland, bring our guest inside, don't keep her out there talking in the hot sun."

His voice was uncertain and tentative when he said, "Guess it would be all right for you to step in."

"Are the dogs going to bite me?"

He frowned again. "They're just crazy beasts, never know what they'll do. Pull your truck right up to the gate. That would be best." He went and stood at the chute protruding from the fenced yard, kicking the dogs that rushed at him. They moved away as I backed the pickup to the gate; evidently they were accustomed to being herded with vehicles.

My heart was beating double time. I took a deep breath and pushed open the door on the passenger side. Once my feet hit the ground I was moving. He held the gate ajar for me and clanged it shut before the first dog could slide under the truck and reach me.

I followed him up the crumbling sidewalk to the wooden ramp accessing the cottage.

The woman in the wheelchair was beautiful. She could be used in an ad that needed the perfect grandmother. She had pure white skin, with just a hint of pink on the cheeks and eyes the color of periwinkle. Her perfect blond hair was pulled back and tied with a black velvet ribbon at the nape of her neck.

She backed her wheelchair away from the door and rolled into the living room where she spun the chair around to face us expectantly. She folded her hands in her lap and waited, totally composed and the queen of her surroundings.

The front door led directly into the living room. It was like walking into a little doll's house, the kind of place a real grandmother would live, with roses and ivy climbing over a big overstuffed couch and the chairs all wearing white slipcovers and rose-covered pillows. The sun poured through crystal-clean windows, flooding the living room with light and glinting off a tiny glass chandelier hanging over a round cherry table. Matching glass lamps, with crystal drops, sat on white wrought-iron tables. Light bounced and twinkled around the room. The bleached cypress floors, very like the ones at Riverwood, were free of carpets. Lace curtains at all the windows were pulled back and tied up to let in the maximum amount of sunlight.

"This is Sherri Travis, a friend of Clay Adams," Harland said. He smiled at his wife, a look tender with love. "This is my wife, Amanda."

She nodded like the monarch she was. "Welcome to our home, Ms. Travis." Her voice, dignified and educated, had a hint of Georgia peach in it.

"Please call me Sherri."

"Of course, Sherri."

Regal and handsome, she smiled at me and stretched a palm out towards the chair beside her. I felt honored to be invited to sit next to her. "We'll have some iced tea, please, Harland."

"Your house is lovely," I told her.

"Not so grand as the main house where our son Justin and his grandfather live but here I can maneuver my chair, and everything is on one floor."

My eyes dropped to the white plastic braces showing beneath her flowing chiffon skirt. I looked quickly back to her face.

"I have Multiple Sclerosis." Her words were matter of fact

and meant for information only, not meant in any way to garner sympathy. "It's very advanced."

"I'm sorry to hear that."

She gave a slight nod in acknowledgment of my words then added, "The good news is that I have Harland. He spoils me terribly, waits on me hand and foot, don't you dear?" She smiled up at her husband who came towards us with a tray and three glasses of tea. She raised her right hand, also in a brace. It hovered there by her ear as she added, "He even does my hair."

"It looks lovely. You're lucky to have such a talented husband."

Harland pulled up a small side table and swung it in front of her. "Harland made this table himself," she said proudly. "It works like a hospital table but it surely doesn't look like one, does it? In fact he's made much of our furniture."

"It's beautiful and I noticed the floors right away. The floors in Clay's ranch house are made of cypress just like these. These two houses must have gone up about the same time. I know it's been a long time since they built with cypress in Florida."

Harland said, "This was the foreman's house, built in the 1890s. Oxbow no longer needs a foreman, so we moved in. It's a well-built house and just needed to be modernized."

"Harland did it all himself."

"I enjoyed doing it." He slipped her glass of tea into an insulated foam holder. "I'm good with my hands."

"And he's incredibly strong and fit." She smiled up at him. "He keeps in shape lifting me about." Harland helped his wife lift her trembling left hand onto the tabletop. He placed her hands around the insulated cup and positioned the straw while she leaned forward and sipped her drink.

Iced tea is just not my thing but I found myself wanting to please her so I followed her lead. "What do you grow here?" I asked when Harland had pulled up a straight-back chair and was seated beside her.

A brief look of fear and maybe even panic passed between them. Harland cleared his throat and said, "These days we've cut way back on our production. We rent out about a thousand acres to another farm." Another look passed between them.

What had I missed? What was happening out here that frightened them both so much? Or was it me? Was I somehow threatening them? I tried out a smile. "Oh, so do you work somewhere else now that you don't farm?"

He shook his head in denial. "Oh no, never worked anywhere else but here." He rubbed the palms of his hands together between his knees. "Don't think anyone else would hire me, I've only got a high school education."

I'd only been trying to make friendly conversation but somehow I'd got it all wrong.

"Nonsense, dear," Amanda said. "You could do anything you put your mind to." He smiled gratefully at Amanda. "Besides," she added, "Harland has to look after me." Amanda Breslau reached out awkwardly and placed her hand on her husband's arm, comforting and calming him. "He's needed here. Justin, our son, is a little young to manage a farm as large as this, and my father-in-law, well he's getting on in years."

I'd swear the look on her face when she mentioned her father-in-law, a look like a poisonous snake had just slithered into the room, made me think she felt about Orlin like I felt about my mother-in-law, Bernice Travis. I'd run a mile through broken glass and crawl through nettles to avoid that woman.

I said, "I met your son today."

CHAPTER 22

Harland shrank into himself, like a turtle pulling into his shell, and took Amanda's hand in both of his.

"I thought he said his name was Boomer. Boomer is an unusual name." I smiled at them to tell them I wasn't any threat. "How did he get it?"

"His grandpa calls him that. His name is Justin," Amanda said firmly. "His grandpa gave him that name because Justin was always loud, even as a little boy. He made so much noise, always banging on things."

"Yes," Harland nodded in agreement. "He was always shouting and destroying things." He looked mystified as if he couldn't understand where this child of theirs had come from. Looking at them I couldn't understand it either. They were gentle, refined people who cared for one another and their son was a pig. Go figure.

"I was ill so much, Justin spent a lot of time with his grandfather," Amanda explained. "At first it was cute the way he followed his grandpa around and tried to be just like him, and then it was worrisome. Boys can grow up too fast, Ms. Travis. Do you have any children?"

"No, ma'am."

"Well," she paused, searching for words, "Sometimes they can be a mixed blessing."

"Does Justin live here with you?" I was picking my way around what I'd come for, trying for a nice way to say, "Keep your brute of a son away from me."

Amanda frowned at my question and replied, "No, he lives up at the big house with his grandpa." Her pleasant face grew hard. Unlike when she was telling the unhappy facts of her illness in a straightforward unemotional manner, her face now showed disappointment and grief. Clearly, Boomer was not the son she had hoped for.

"Still, you are all together and your father-in-law was here to help raise Justin."

"My father-in-law has been a bad influence on Justin, given him too much. It's hard for us to set limits when his grandpa pushes him on."

She was basically saying what I already knew. Boomer was out of their control. "Well," she said, "I guess it's too late to worry about it now. He's a man." Regret etched her words.

No use making any demands on them they couldn't fulfill. Boomer wasn't going to be stopped by Amanda and Harland Breslau, and my request that they do something about their monster child would only hurt them more when they already had a bucketful of pain.

"Now, I've come to invite you to my party for Clay's birthday. It's next Saturday night. Nothing fancy, my daddy's going to roast a pig over hardwood and we're going to have lots of salads and dishes we serve at the Sunset. Come and sit on the porch or under a tree and catch up with the neighbors and meet some of Clay's friends from Jacaranda."

Her sweet smile was tinged with regret. "My chair makes it difficult."

"We'll have lots of big old strong men there to lift your chair up onto the porch or take you anywhere you want to go. Can't pass up a chance like that now, can you, being carried around like Cleopatra? And I surely would like it if you came."

"May we think about it for a day or two, see if it's a good day or a bad day on Saturday?"

"Of course. You do just whatever suits you."

I rose to my feet.

Harland spoke up. "I'm sorry you had to be the one to find Lucan's body." He really did sound like he deeply regretted this bad thing that had happened to me.

"It was hardly your fault, was it?

He looked startled by my words. I tried to take them back, to soften them. "It was upsetting for me to find his body but much harder for April to lose him. Do you know her?"

"Amanda doesn't but I do. In small towns you pretty much know everyone."

"And of course Lucan worked for you, didn't he?"

He looked as if I'd accused him of something immoral.

I was confused. "He did work for you, didn't he?"

"Some." He let go of Amanda's hand and got to his feet, sliding behind her chair and grasping the handles. "We'll see how Amanda is feeling on Saturday."

He was inviting me to leave but his reaction awoke my curiosity so I chose to ignore the unspoken suggestion. "It just seems so terrible. Why would anyone kill Lucan?"

The silence stretched out. Harland's fingers restlessly picked at the rubber grips on the handles of his wife's wheelchair.

"Thank you for being concerned about me, about my being upset when I found Lucan."

He nodded. "I hope your truck wasn't damaged." He pushed the chair towards the door.

Funny thing is I got the impression that he was truly sorry, not just apologizing in a general sort of way.

"You were there that night, weren't you?"

He swung the wheelchair round to face me. The chair and his wife were his defense. "What?" The very suggestion had him panicking. "No I wasn't."

Amanda caught his panic and came to his defense. "Harland never leaves my side," she protested.

"Oh? I must have misunderstood. I thought Howie said you came into the Gator Hole that night, Harland."

"Only for a bit." He swiveled the chair back towards the door, leaving me behind again. Did he want to get away from me or just the talk of murder? But I never have been able to take a hint. "Yes," I told his back. "Howie said you must have rushed right in from working on something, said you still had work gloves in your hip pocket."

The worried face he turned to me said he was waiting to see what came next.

I smiled. "I know these questions sound rude but I'm just so shocked, I need to understand what part my truck played in all this. I don't think I'll ever be able to drive it again." I gave a dramatic shiver. "Did you see my truck parked behind the Gator Hole?"

"No, I was parked out front."

"Oh, that's good." I didn't ask how he knew where Big Red was parked. But maybe that was just part of the general gossip about Luc's death. Independence might know all there was to know about Luc's death.

I nodded my head to show how pleased I was about this. "Can you imagine going out to your car and walking right by a dead body, or even worse, going out there and seeing Lucan being beaten?"

No response. I joined them by the door.

"Did you talk to Lucan?" I asked. "In the Gator Hole I mean."

"No. I only stayed a minute or two. Lucan was still there when I left."

"Someone you knew your whole life, it must be painful for you to talk about his murder."

Eyes downcast, he pecked at the rubber grips.

"Still," I said, "not as painful as it was for Lucan."

Harland didn't look up but muttered, "Lucan was so drunk he probably never felt a thing."

"It was a strange place to hide a body, in the back of a pick-up. I suppose it was to remove the body from the scene of the crime and to delay its discovery."

They made no comment so I tried again, "Do you think that's why the body was put in my truck?"

Amanda jumped into the silence, "We've really no idea. Let's leave it to the sheriff, shall we? It's too distressing to talk about." The subject was officially closed and I had outstayed my welcome.

It was really none of my business and these people had enough problems without being burdened with the evil outside their pretty little house.

I followed them through the door where I took Amanda's hand and asked, "May I come back to visit when I'm next out at Riverwood?"

"Oh, please do," Amanda said, smiling up at me. Behind her Harland was not smiling. He'd be glad to see the back of me and not happy to see my return. "We'd like that," Amanda added. "Wouldn't we, Harland?"

Right on cue he said, "Yes, ma'am, we surely would." He pushed the chair farther out onto the deck.

The crows in the pines surrounding the house set up a raucous clamor so loud we all stopped and looked up at the trees. We were still staring at them when a Chevy Silverado with a crew cab pulled into the yard. "Oh," said Harland.

The truck circled around in front of the house, stopped and then came on to park in front of Tully's beat-up old pickup. It backed up tight to the front bumper. I'd have to backup and pull around it before I could get out the lane.

"Amanda?" Harland asked.

"I'll wait here, Harland," Amanda said. "You go on down with Sherri."

He looked down at her, hesitated and then said, "All right, if you think so."

"We're still polite to our visitors; we haven't fallen that far yet." Rolling her chair backwards a few feet, Amanda distanced herself from us, or maybe from what was waiting for us.

CHAPTER 23

The crows cawed loudly from the pines towering over the deep underbrush behind the little house. We stood frozen at the edge of the porch, waiting and watching. I didn't know what there was to fear but I caught their apprehension.

"Go," Amanda Breslau ordered, starting us down the ramp.

The man that got out of the truck was about seventy, powerfully built and with a Florida rancher's tan, the kind of color that comes from decades in the sun with no protection. It was broiled so deep into the pigment that it was permanent, the kind of tan Tully had.

The man wore the battered straw hat of a working cowman rather than the faux kind sported by an evening cowboy. His boots were heeled but I was betting it was a long time since he'd climbed aboard anything that didn't come with an engine. His smile was all charm and honey but didn't warm his cold eyes. Everything about him said this was the man in charge. Even the dogs stayed well back.

Hands on hips, his faded gray eyes assessed me and took my measure. He said, "Well, who's this pretty little thing?"

Little thing? I stand nearly five eight in my bare feet and normally I wear three-inch heels. I'm not really accustomed to thinking of myself as little, but in flip-flops and next to this bull of a man towering over me the description fit. He was at least six-four and heavy with it.

Harland, nervous as a cat and stuttering, introduced me to his father. Orlin Breslau held out a gnarled hand with a copper bracelet around the wrist.

I smiled as his hand crushed mine and returned his greeting but only for politeness' sake. This man didn't have me feeling warm and friendly. "I'm a friend of Clay Adams," I told him, despite the fact we were both aware that he already knew all about me and my living arrangements.

"He's a lucky man to have a beautiful woman like you."

"She's just leaving, sir," Harland said. "Just stopped by to be neighborly."

But I wasn't going quite yet, no matter how eager Harland was to get rid of me. Here was the man who held the power in the family, the one who could control Boomer. "I met your grandson today," I said.

"Oh?" He was waiting to see how bad the news was, which told me he'd heard lots of awful news about his grandson. I probably wasn't the only one showing up to demand he get the monster under control, but on second thought, given the attitude of Boomer, only an idiot like me would come here to complain about Boomer Breslau.

"Boomer was on Clay's land and startled my horse with his ATV."

"Well, I'm real sorry 'bout that." He didn't say which part he was sorry about. "I'm sure he had no intention to cause you distress."

The roar of an approaching vehicle cut off my reply. The gigantic truck, kicking up dust, was speeding too fast into the clearing.

The black pickup, raised up high on big-ass tires and throbbing with rap music through closed windows, started around the circle to the house but slammed to a stop. It backed up and swung around a broken-down wagon and roared towards us, pulling up at an angle across the back bumper of Tully's truck and boxing it in. With the Silverado in front and the black pickup across the back bumper I was locked up tight against the fence and wouldn't be going anywhere until they decided to let me.

The pickup's door shot open. The noise of gangster rap slammed into us. The word "bitch" cleaved the air. Boomer had arrived.

He jumped to the ground. Grinning, he kicked out at a yapping dog and said, "Get off." When I'd seen him that morning he'd been wearing a long-sleeved plaid shirt, hiding what decorated his body. Now his muscle shirt showed off tattoos, from wrist to shoulder, on both arms. On the right side a tiger stalked down towards the hand while on the left a cobra opened its jaw on the ugly bruise made by Joey's teeth. Across his chest and up his neck tats in red and green ink covered his body like a garment.

"You already met this young man," Orlin said proudly. "My grandson, my only grandchild, we don't do well in the reproducing line. I only whelped one and so did Harland. But this fine specimen here is going to do better, aren't you, son?"

"Don't worry, Grandpa, I'm taking care of that."

Orlin clapped his hand on the back of Boomer's neck and shook him roughly. "Good boy, spread it around, boy, spread it around." Their laughter was an ugly, offensive thing.

Beside me I could feel Harland ease away, distancing himself from the words or maybe from what was to follow.

Boomer pointed a forefinger at me and said to his grandpa, "She's hunting me down." Then he said to me, "I knew you weren't going to be able to stay away from me the minute I laid eyes on you." There was something besides pride in Boomer's eyes. Boomer wasn't quite sane. "Old Man Adams sure won't be enough for a woman like you."

"Justin..." Harland started.

"Be quiet," Boomer said, without looking at him. "Me and this pretty lady are friends, aren't we?"

"Not even close. I came here to tell you to keep off our land and to keep your hands to yourself or next time it won't be just my horse that bites you."

A trill of laughter came from Amanda.

Boomer swung around to his mother.

"Get in the house," Boomer ordered.

"I'm just fine here," Amanda replied. Her chin was up, rebellious and proud.

Beside me Harland shuffled restlessly. He started to return to the house and then halted in indecision.

I spoke to Orlin Breslau. "I hope you can make your grandson understand that when I say I'm not interested, I am not interested." I looked at Boomer. "Stay away from me and stay away from Riverwood." I didn't wait for his response but started moving while waving to Amanda. "It was nice to meet you.

I hope I see you again real soon. Come to Riverwood anytime you can and we'll have tea."

I went to Tully's truck, started it up and jabbed it into reverse, jerking back, nearly into Boomer's pride and joy. I slammed on the brake inches from his bumper. I sat there with my foot on the brake, revving the engine, and shaking with anger, wanting to ram the massive truck. But it would only create more problems with Boomer than I already had.

Boomer got the message. The little prick wasn't smiling as he hustled to his truck and cleared it away for me to leave.

Going out the lane I knew it wasn't over. I'd been around this block too many times not to know the signs of what was coming. No doubt about it. What Boomer wanted, he was going to try and take.

I could see in Boomer's flat and empty eyes that self-control, if it had ever existed, was long gone. Empathy and compassion had been eaten away, and all that remained was a destructive and malignant egotism. If Orlin Breslau couldn't control this bad seed, no one could, and Orlin hadn't even tried. Perhaps he knew it was useless or maybe he was as crazy as his grandson.

Sometime in the not too distant future that brute and I were really going to get into it and there was going to be a shit-load of pain for someone.

CHAPTER 24

I closed the day-old paper I was pretending to read and said to Tully, "Looks like Howie Sweet isn't coming."

"Maybe they arrested him for killing Lucan."

"I hate to say it, but it wouldn't hurt my feelings if it was over that easily. But it would leave Clay with a problem."

Tully snorted and got to his feet. "You think I'm too old to look after a few horses? Come on; let's put them in the barn. Then let's all go into town for dinner. Marley wants to go in before that antique place closes for the night."

A white sedan pulled into the yard. The man who got out of the car and went to help his passenger out was dressed in black and wearing a white collar. Now, when a minister comes to call, right away I know he's bringing trouble with him.

"Pearl Sweet," Tully said, naming the trouble.

The woman who got out of the car and glared up at the house wasn't sweet. Going on looks, her name should be Sour. Heavy and lumpy, with a vinegar face that could turn cream, she looked like she'd never passed a happy moment in her life.

Her mouth turned down, the corners of her deep-sunk eyes turned down and so did all the lines on her face.

As she walked towards us, with the minister following her like a puppy dog, she kept her eyes fixed on me. "Where's my husband?" she demanded, standing at the bottom of the stairs with her feet spread wide. Her fine gray hair flew away from her head in all directions, alive with static, the only animated thing on her.

"Evening, Pearl," Tully said.

Her eyes didn't shift from my face.

"Hello, Mrs. Sweet, I'm Sherri Travis."

She glowered. "You tell Howard to come out here right now."

"I haven't seen Howie since he came over last night when the sheriff was here. This morning, when he didn't show up, we let the horses out and we were just about to bring them in. Are you saying Howie is missing?"

"He came here after breakfast, and never got home again, so don't you bother lying to me."

I bounded to the edge of the stairs. "I'm not lying and I've had enough of the sanctimonious people of Independence thinking the worst of me."

I started down the steps but Tully grabbed my arm. "Easy, girl," he said, slowing me down and coming with me. At the bottom he stepped in front of me. "Now, Pearl," he began, "you're barking up a tree that ain't got no coon in it. There's no one here but the four of us. Come up and have a cool drink and we'll talk."

The door banged and Ziggy stepped out on the veranda.

"Hello, Pearl," he said cheerfully. She didn't acknowledge Ziggy, never took her eyes off Tully and me.

"I smelt whiskey on his breath when he came home last night. If that's the sort of thing that goes on here now, I want no part of it. You know I don't hold with drinking, Tully."

"I surely do, Pearl. I wasn't suggesting you drink no alcohol, just have a cold soda is all and we can talk about where Howie might be. He may be hurt or something, had an accident even."

She straightened, shocked at this novel idea. "Accident, what accident?" She swung to the preacher. It had never occurred to her that her husband hadn't fallen into a pit of deprivation but had been the victim of some calamity. Why would she immediately think he was with another woman? There was an interesting story to be told about Howie Sweet.

"Come and set down for a minute, Pearl," Tully said. "We can talk it over."

She started forward, turned back, hesitated, started towards us again and then stopped. She'd probably sworn she'd never set foot in this house while Clay Adams' Jezebel was in residence. Tully went to her and took her arm, guiding her to the stairs. Pearl turned and looked when she reached me, undecided and conflicted. For a minute I thought she was going to spit on me.

Some folks like to hold onto outdated ideas of sin down here in Florida and things haven't changed all that much in the South from when I was a kid. Every time I think our Baptist past is...well, past, back it comes, ranting and roaring about damnation.

"Have you called your daughter?" I asked. "Maybe she knows where he is."

She frowned. "Lovey and I don't talk. Howard talks to her but I don't."

I made a rude sound and ran back up the stairs to where Uncle Ziggy cleared away the newspapers from the chair closest to the front door.

The door slammed behind me as I went into the house to look up the number for the diner.

Lovey answered. Like me she worked long hours, about the only way to make it in the restaurant business. After I told her the situation she said, "I haven't seen Dad all day. I wondered why he wasn't in, but with Lucan…" her voice caught and she fell silent. Then she said, "Oh, God."

"Do you think your dad is running away?" Bad as that question was I didn't have the good sense to stop there but added, "Do you think he killed Lucan?"

"I don't know. I don't know anything anymore."

"Where else should we look for your dad?"

"I don't know. Here, church, home and the ranch, those are the only places he goes. I've called the minister and he was going over to see Mom, see if she knew where Dad is."

"Does your father have a cell?"

"No."

"Okay, I'm going to call the sheriff."

"I'll do it, might be better coming from me."

"All right, I'll go tell your mother that your father is really missing."

"Tell her…" but that was as far as she got. She sighed and said, "Never mind, she knows already. I'll call you back."

Tully came into the kitchen and got two glasses from the

cupboard. While he put ice and water in them I told him about what Lovey had said. "Doesn't look good," Tully said. "I would have thought Howie was a man who never strays too far from what he knows. Something must have sent him off."

We went back out and told Pearl and the minister that Lovey was getting in touch with the sheriff.

"I'm the Reverend Bates from the Independence Pentecostal Gospel Chapel," the man in black said to me. "We surely do thank you for your kindness."

"Why would you think Howie was here?" I asked.

Behind me Tully said, "Leave it, Sherri."

"No, I won't leave it. Has Howie done this sort of thing before?"

Pearl's jaw worked like she was chewing spit.

"So where did you find him last time he disappeared?" I asked.

Reverend Bates cleared his throat. "Perhaps he's had an accident. We'd best check the hospitals."

Pearl looked at him. "You're right; he could have been in an accident." She was relieved by this thought. She'd rather Howie was dead in a ditch than in the arms of another woman. She set the glass down and struggled to get out of the chair. Getting out of those old wicker chairs with the sagging bottoms wasn't easy at the best of times, but even worse for someone of Pearl's bulk. After thrashing about for a bit she finally managed to break free and get to her feet.

As she went by me she said, "I'll pray for you."

"Could you send money instead?"

"Sherri," Tully admonished.

Her progress down the stairs, on knees that didn't seem to bend, was painful to watch.

"Y'all come again real soon," I called as the minister opened the car door for her.

"You just can't resist, can you?" Tully asked as the door slammed shut behind Pearl.

"Hey, why should I behave better than they do? They were quite willing to think the worst of me. As if I'd have anything to do with Howie Sweet."

He shook his head in disgust, "Let's go do the horses. Joey will appreciate you better than Pearl. You and that horse got a lot in common."

CHAPTER 25

The antique store was called Play It Again. It had once been the opera house in the glory days of Independence. An over-the-top structure with plaster gargoyles and other things stuck onto the stucco façade, bargains overflowed out onto the sidewalk. While Marley and I went inside to check out the deals, Tully and Zig went to the Gator Hole to pick up the gossip.

As we climbed the stairs I said, "You have to give them points for honesty and a sense of humor." I pointed to a sign in the window that said, "We buy junk and sell antiques." Inside, every inch of space from floor to ceiling was covered with stuff, some of it trash and some of it valuable and some just strange, like the pile of projection equipment from the old movie theater that had been in this building back in the fifties. Furniture, household goods and estate jewelry, Play It Again had it all.

Marley was in the throes of a shopping orgasm. "The great thing about Florida," Marley told me, "is people move down here with all their favorite pieces and when they die their kids don't want to pay to have them shipped north again. There are always wonderful antiques to be had cheap."

"If you say so," I said, looking at a table lamp from the fifties with an orange shade and lots of silk fringe. "Maybe I should send this to Laura Kemp."

"Maybe you should check out the price tag before you decide."

I had a look. "Seventy-five dollars?" The price tag killed my shopping urge. "Maybe I'll just slip over to the Gator Hole and see if anyone knows where Howie is. I can buy a lot of beer for seventy-five bucks."

Marley turned a wire rug beater over in her hands in a way that made me pay attention. "I want you right here with the credit card in case I find something we need."

"Don't you think you should wait until tomorrow when we've seen what we've got?"

Something caught her eye. "Oh, look a gramophone."

"I don't think we need one of those."

She tapped me on the behind with the rug beater. "What we need is drapes for those front windows, or lace curtains."

"I'm so not a lace curtain kind of person."

"Great, then don't wear them, but the bay windows would like them just fine."

A handsome man in his late forties came down the aisle towards us. Simon Ghent and Marley had an instant understanding, a true meeting of minds. They quickly forgot I was there.

"I've got the perfect thing," he informed Marley after she told him what she was looking for. "Take them home and try them. If they don't work you can bring them back."

He went to a huge old trunk full of dusty velvet where Marley started making sounds of pleasure like Prince Charming was making all the right moves.

"How much?" I asked. Marley held them up and asked, "How many?"

They stretched some red velvet out between them. The drape must have been over twelve feet long.

"They'll be way too long," I said in relief.

"They're supposed to be. They puddle on the floor," Marley told me. "Excess, it's all about excess, baby, no restraint here."

"Yeah? How much are they?"

"You can have them all for a hundred and fifty."

"What?" I yelped.

Marley said, "We'll take them."

It was another half-hour before I could drag Marley out of there and over to the Gator Hole.

At the door of the bar, the noise from inside was enough to drive you back outside. Tully and Zig hadn't lied about the place, an old-fashioned, nasty, dark-brown hole that time had missed. It was like coming home and I was grinning like a fool.

Inside it smelt of every beer that had ever been spilled on the floor and every bucket of grease that had been eaten there. The floor was made of some kind of wood that was beaten down and turned black from thousands of stomping boots grinding in the dirt. A long bar stretched along the wall opposite the doors. The room was so packed, people had to stand sideways to get a place to plant their elbows and their beers.

A low whistle welcomed us as we stepped inside. At first glance there weren't but half a dozen women in the room and not one of them was under the age of fifty so the hearty welcome was explained. The men cleared a path for us but the noise didn't diminish.

This was the kind of bar I'd come of age in, the kind of bar where fights broke out as easily as laughter. It made my heart beat faster and my lips stretch into a crazy smile of joy.

"Wow, I'd like to have half this crowd in the Sunset," I told Marley over my shoulder as I made my way through the horde of bodies.

Marley leaned forward so I could hear her. "No you wouldn't. They wouldn't pay your prices."

"But there wouldn't be the overheads. It's all relative."

"Looking for someone?" A grinning ranch hand blocked my way.

Tully clapped a hand on the guy's shoulder. "Yup, and she just found him." Tully handed the ranch hand his pool cue.

CHAPTER 26

"Come on." Tully bellowed to be heard over the loud drinking voices. "Let's go somewhere we can think."

"You're getting old, Tully," I shouted back at him. "You come to a place like this so you can't think."

"Yeah, that's the trouble with a place like this. Half the people that walk through the door leave their brains behind."

"Well, I like it."

"You like it so well, why don't you buy it. Dole Legger wants to sell and I wouldn't mind being able to drink for free."

"You already do."

He laughed and looked around for Ziggy, who was still leaning over a shot at the pool table.

Zig looked up at Tully, nodded and took his shot, and then he stood and held out his hand to collect the money from the other guys at the table.

"The big guy hasn't lost his eye," Tully said as Ziggy shouldered his way towards us.

"I think it's all about gaining, not losing for Uncle Ziggy. He's going to hit three hundred soon."

"Already has," Tully replied.

Zig and Tully bulldozed their way through the crush, with Marley and me following in their wake.

"Is it always like that?" I asked when we were on the sidewalk.

"Naw," Tully said. "Only Saturdays, all the hired hands hit town on Saturdays. You don't want to be in the Gator Hole a couple of hours from now."

"Oh, but I do." It would be a walk down memory lane for me, a flashback to a misspent youth I was starting to miss and romanticize.

Tully and Zig walked ahead of us, disagreeing where we should go to eat. Seemed Zig thought we should go to Lovey's café but Tully wanted a place he could get a beer with his meal. Lovey didn't serve booze. Maybe she hadn't strayed as far from her mother's teachings as it seemed.

Their argument was ended by Marley saying, "I want a glass of wine."

We headed past a tattoo parlor to a restaurant called The Veranda. It was a two-story white clapboard house with a broad veranda across the front. The tables on the front porch were all filled, so we opted for a table out back on worn decking under trees strung with lights. The air was full of the scent of orange blossoms from the field behind the restaurant. Soft music floated from speakers in the trees.

We'd barely given our drink orders when I asked, "Okay, has anyone seen Howie?"

"We just kinda asked if anyone had seen him today because he hadn't shown up for work," Tully said. "Some guys thought he was out celebrating 'cause Lucan was dead, figured he was drinking himself silly. Those two had a real bad history. Lucan punched Howie out once."

"Wasn't that all old history?"

"Seems Howie had a long memory for grievances."

"Was there anything else?"

Tully grinned. "Howie has gone missing before. Not quite the upright citizen Pearl would like him to be. Other than that, no one seems to have any idea where Howie is."

"Maybe he's been murdered like Lucan," I offered. The three of them lowered their menus and looked at me. "Well, surely I'm not the only one wondering about that." Their shocked expressions said I was.

Behind Tully a determined man was striding towards us. Tully read my face and turned to see who it was before climbing to his feet and offering his hand.

"Evening, Richard," Tully said, shaking the man's hand. Turning to Marley and me, he said, "This here is Richard Arby. He owns Sweet Meadow Farm, the citrus farm next to Riverwood."

Pleasantries were exchanged and Mr. Arby joined us, leaning on the table and getting down to business. "Your father and I play the odd game of pool over at the Gator Hole late in the afternoon," he told me. "How do you like Independence?"

"Well, I'm more of a beach person, I guess. Not real interested in country things."

He beamed at me as if I'd just complimented his favorite child. "This isn't the place for you; you have to be born here to take to it. If you can talk Clay into selling his farm, I'd be very pleased and pay him top dollar. He'll make money on the deal."

"Have you asked Clay if he wants to sell?"

He frowned and said, "We got off on the wrong foot."

"You'll have to take your offer up with Clay."

"I have. He's being stubborn. He's just playing over there, raising a few horses. I need his water, can't run my outfit without it."

"Maybe Clay has plans for Riverwood," Marley put in.

"What plans?"

Marley shrugged. "I don't know but I'm sure there are lots of things he might do with it. What about making it an orange grove?"

He snorted. "You don't know anything about growing citrus, do you? First of all, he doesn't have enough land. Back in the forties a man could make a pretty good living off as little as forty acres of trees. Not now. Growing citrus isn't a hobby like them horses he has. Over the years I've lost thousands of trees to canker disease, hurricanes, pests and freezing. It took years to build up my spread and even with all I've survived it may be the cheap juice coming in from Brazil that kills me. They have lots of land and cheap labor down there." He raised a forefinger. "That's what makes them the number one producer of orange juice in the world and what makes Florida second. No one here wants to work in an orange grove. They all want to work indoors at something like stocking shelves."

Marley wasn't giving up. "There must be other things Clay can do with the land."

"Like harvesting the turtles?" He laughed. "Adams already tried to stop Lucan from doing that." He leaned forward on the table, counting his arguments off on the fingers of his left hand. "A turtle brings a dollar to a dollar and a half a pound sold into the Asian market. On good days you could take fifteen to twenty turtles, nearly three hundred pounds' worth. Fresh water turtles have been a source of food for locals forever in Florida, and hunting for soft-shell turtles has always been a source of income for many people around Independence. It's called 'cooter' on local menus. You see that listed, you know you're getting fresh turtle."

"But turtles aren't just being hunted for the local area, now," I put in. "They're being hunted to extinction to sell into the Asian market. At the rate Percell was mining this turtle resource it would soon be wiped out — one man's greed overcoming nature and common sense."

"You sound like one of those artists," Richard Arby said. There was no mistaking his disgust.

The artists, glass blowers, painters and potters that had moved to Independence for cheap housing, were very big on the environment, and had supported Clay in his efforts to stop the massive killing of turtles in Jobean Lake and the creeks emptying into it. The argument over turtles had divided the town, with the artists and newcomers on one side and the ranchers and long-term residents on the other. The separation had always been there, but now it was out in the open and bitter.

"Thanks to Clay Adams, you're screwed round here if you was planning to make money off turtle hunting." He stretched back in his chair. "The only thing valuable about Adams' property is the water and that's only valuable to the Breslaus and me." He smiled. Clay's unfortunate position was the first happy thought he'd had since I met him.

I had enough of the joys of farming. "Howie Sweet didn't show up this morning. Have you seen him?"

"Nope, but then Howie and I aren't on the best of terms. He'd hardly stop by."

"His disappearance is a little worrying, given what happened to Lucan."

"Lucan was already halfway drunk when he came into the Gator Hole Thursday night; didn't take much more to have him staggering. His killer should have let him drive home, probably would have climbed a tree with that old truck of his and saved all the bother."

Marley said, "You don't seem too upset at his death."

He shrugged. "So who is?"

"April Donaldson," I answered.

"Well, she'll get over it. It ain't like he's a big loss."

He read our faces, scratched his nose and said, "Excuse me, shouldn't make light of it, a man is dead." His apology faded when he added, "But not much of a man."

We were back at Riverwood by nine o'clock and we all straggled off to our beds shortly after.

City habits die hard. Even though there were no other houses around, no other people, I went to pull the drapes across the window. I hate the bare empty eye of a dark window. I always feel something is out there watching. This time I was right.

I jumped away from the window. There was something out there. Then I saw it again. Now I leaned on the sill to see what had caught my eye.

In the woods lights danced. Not small lights, mind you,

but more like search lights, the kind that hunters mounted on their vehicles to hunt down prey in the dark.

I started to call Tully but what could he do? I sure didn't want him going out there to check out the lights. Whatever was happening out there, well, I didn't want to know.

It was going to be a long night. In a house that wouldn't lock, out in the middle of nowhere, and the only people to hear me scream were two guys in their sixties who could sleep over the sound of each other's snoring. How important was this party? Maybe I should just go back to Jac.

The dead haunt my dreams. Unwelcome and uninvited, they accuse and threaten. That night I dreamt of Jimmy. Suddenly awake and in a sweat, the damp sheet tangled around me, I searched for what had jolted me from my dreams. I kicked off the binding shroud and listened to the dark.

Every sense was alive. Blood pumped madly through my veins. Against the screen a dying insect rattled his death throes. Was it that? Was that why I had awakened? Or was it just the old nightmare of a purple beach cottage, of being chased through a hurricane, trying to find a safe place to hide. In my nightmares I'm always trying to hide. My body was rigid with listening. Feeling hunted — like someone's quarry — was an old, terrifying nightmare, drenching me like my sweat. I'd gone months without nightmares but now they were back.

Somewhere outside in the dark a small animal screamed and went silent.

I strained to hear the sounds of someone coming for me. The same terrifying thought, the cruel possibility night always brought, "Is this the night Lester returns for me?" The monster from my past, my dark obsession, seemed real and true. Certainly the panic and fear were real.

Tonight there was an added dread. Lester wasn't the only one who might come after me. There was a face in the woods. Or it could be Boomer Breslau, loud and sure of himself, breaking down doors to get at me. Tonight there were too many reasons for panic to talk myself out of it. I laid back down, waiting…too afraid to get out of bed, too afraid to turn on the light, too afraid to act.

The old wood on the stairs creaked and then went silent.

CHAPTER 27

I told myself it was just my imagination but that didn't stop the fear.

"I hate this," I whispered to the night. "I won't have this." Anger washed over me, a brief reprieve from fear. "Not again."

Self-doubt kicked in. Had I really heard something?

Easy to say but I didn't reach out and turn on the light to banish the threatening shadows. There was no safety in the light but there was no security in the dark. The sweat drying along my body brought chills.

There it was again. Now I knew what it was, the sound of a footfall on bare wood. It wasn't my imagination. Someone was out there in the hall.

Shivering in icy panic I slid to the edge of the bed and watched the doorknob turn.

"Dad?" My quivering voice begged to be reassured.

In the open door I could only make out a man's shadow, backlit by a light from the hall.

"Yeah," Tully acknowledged. "Just checking, go to sleep, sweet pea," the old familiar endearment. "Goodnight."

"You too, Dad," I forced myself to say. "Sleep well."

A soft laugh, "Old men don't sleep. We only nap." The door closed and I heard him move on.

Hungry for the security I can never find, vulnerable and shaking with fear, I drew the damp sheet around me and huddled down. There was no refuge in the dark, even with my father standing watch. There would be no more sleep for me, no way to turn off the adrenaline and turn on happy thoughts, just as there is no way to ever make myself feel truly safe again.

In the morning I was tired and cranky from too little sleep and angry at the whole world because my nightmares had returned. I was in the barn with Marley, leading the horses out to the paddock, when Sheriff Hozen arrived.

"Is this the horse that bites?" he asked, staying well away from Joey.

Boomer had told the sheriff about our meeting. What did that mean? My trouble antennae went up, seeking out bad news.

"Joey only bites people who deserve it."

Sheriff Hozen laughed and reached out to rub Joey's nose. Joey peeled back his lips and snapped. Sheriff Hozen jerked his hand away.

"What can I do for you, Sheriff?" Joey danced sideways in a semicircle and pulled away from me. I took hold of his halter.

"Lovey called. Howie hasn't showed up anywhere since he left to come here yesterday. We don't usually get involved until an adult has been gone forty-eight hours. He hasn't been out of touch that long. A man has a right to a little fun without the sheriff looking for him."

"The man's been gone for twenty-four hours, which sounds pretty serious to me, and you're laughing. I think his daughter has a right to be worried."

He kept on grinning, "A man wouldn't necessarily tell his daughter all his little secrets."

"One man has already been murdered on your watch and now another man is missing. Maybe it's time you did something besides make jokes. Goodbye, Sheriff." I turned away from him before I did something crazy, like bite him myself.

"Hey, wait a minute," the sheriff shouted. "I need some information here."

When I stopped to reply, Joey danced around to face me, trying to toss his head. I held on tightly and talked to the sheriff over my shoulder. "I have no idea where Howard Sweet is, but I can only hope he is alive and well and not in the need of help because if he's waiting on you…well, let's just hope he's all right." My annoyance at the sheriff communicated itself to Joey and he settled down. It would only be temporary.

Marley walked out of the barn leading a little mare who was about to drop her first foal in two weeks. The sheriff swung his arm wide and shouted, "Now you wait here…" His arm struck the little mare. She squealed and danced while Marley cursed at the sheriff. The Baptists hadn't been as successful at reforming Marley as I'd thought.

"Sheriff Hozen, if you have anything further to say to me, please go wait on the porch until we're finished here." If I'd been cranky before the sheriff arrived I was nearly homicidal now.

"Knock it off," I snarled at Joey, who'd decided to see if I was paying attention. Joey recognized a creature nastier than himself and walked along beside me like a show horse.

The sheriff didn't choose to wait. He tore out of the yard with tires churning out gravel.

I was surprised by an idea. Howie had said that everyone was in the Gater Hole on Friday night. Did that include Sheriff Red Hozen? Maybe the reason Red Hozen didn't seem to be hunting Lucan's murderer was because he already knew who it was. Maybe he was the killer.

And what about Howie's disappearance? Did he know where Howie was? Did the man in charge of the investigation already know everything there was to know about Lucan's death, either because he killed Lucan or he knew who did? Was that what was happening here?

Something was going on. There was no sense of urgency. Red Hozen had a different agenda. In truth, it was some unknown man out in the brush who seemed to worry him. Why?

Someone knew what had happened. But who? Perhaps the man in the woods knew the answer to all my questions.

CHAPTER 28

At breakfast I told Ziggy and Tully about the plans for the day. "Marley and I are going to measure up the living room, God knows why, but Martha Stewart here thinks it's important."

"I'll help you do that measuring if you want," Uncle Ziggy told Marley. "Sherri," he rocked uneasily in his chair, giving me an apologetic look before he stumbled on. "Well, I just think it would go better with you and me, Marley."

"That's putting it nicely," Marley added.

"You afraid of the sight of blood, Uncle Ziggy?" I asked.

He gave a huff of laughter. "Just no need to find out, is there?"

I was so happy to be off the hook for that chore, I was already leaving the kitchen. Marley yelled after me. "What he's saying in a nice way is you're useless."

"I'm getting groceries," I said and beat it out of the house before they could come up with another job.

As I backed Marley's blue Neon out of the drive shed Tully

came around the side of the house and waved. "Marley needs more paint," he explained as he opened the door.

Tully edged by the rack of *National Enquirers*. "I'm going to the Good Spirits and get myself a little good spirit," he told me.

"You don't want to help pay for these groceries first, seeing how you're going to be eating most of them?"

"Nope. It's just great to have a daughter who's as successful as you, bringing in the big money in her fancy restaurant." He pulled a couple of candy bars from the display and threw them in the cart. "Does my heart proud."

"Not to mention your wallet." Tully was walking. "Freeloader," I called after him. Didn't even slow him down.

I was pushing the cart out the door of the grocery store when a black pickup, raised high on oversized tires, pulled into the parking lot. It was coming fast with no concern for pedestrians. I held back, waiting for it to flash by but instead it stopped in front of me. The whole truck throbbed with rap music. The dark tinted window slid down and there was Boomer Breslau. He started to say something but I spun the cart to the right, in the direction he came from, and where he couldn't follow. Whatever trash he was disgorging was lost in the noise of the music.

He roared off behind me. I didn't look around.

Leaning over to put a twelve pack into the Neon's trunk, I felt a hand clamp onto my ass. I straightened fast and shot away from the hand, swinging around to face Boomer Breslau.

He laughed and reached inside the trunk of the Neon,

pulled a can of beer out of its plastic circle and popped the ring. Leaning on the trunk opening with his right hand, he tipped up the can, drinking deeply. Then he wiped the back of his mouth with the hand holding the beer can and said, "Here we are again." He was smiling like he'd just won double jeopardy, maybe thinking I should be real glad to see him.

"You sure are pretty and feisty. I like feisty women. Makes it all the sweeter when they give it up." Another swig of beer. "And you will give it up. I can do some mighty interesting things." He wagged his tongue at me.

The problem with men like Boomer is they suffer from selective deafness. You have to get their attention if you want to talk to them.

I slammed the trunk lid shut on his hand, leaning hard on the lid. His eyes widened in shock and pain and he bellowed like a bull. I had his attention now.

I leaned a little harder. "Listen up, little boy. I don't care if you can stick your head up your ass and whistle Dixie — you touch me again and I'll show you a few things that will teach you to keep your hands and the rest of your anatomy to yourself...those pieces you have left."

He was melting to his knees in pain, his eyes tearing up, so he wasn't really up to adding anything to the conversation.

"Now, why don't you run along home before you really start to piss me off?" I stepped back, putting the car between us to be out of range of a flying fist, while he scrambled to lift the trunk and pull out his hand.

There was blood, lots of it. He held his right hand with his left, staring at it as if he wasn't sure all the fingers were still there. His disbelief turned to rage and it was touch and go if he was going to come after me or give into the pain and run for help. "You stupid bitch," he howled.

I wasn't too worried about him beating the crap out of me. Over his shoulder I saw Tully pulling the neck of a whiskey bottle out of a plastic bag. If Boomer moved towards me he was going to have a real bad headache to go with his very sore hand.

"You no good bitch."

Tully waited. I waited. It was up to Boomer how it ended.

Boomer snarled "bitch" once more and sloped off at a jog with his hand clasped tenderly to his chest.

While we watched him go Tully asked, "He goin' be a problem?"

"Him? Naw."

I went back to loading the groceries into the Neon. My hands were shaking and my insides were crumbling. It wasn't fear of Boomer that was giving me the shakes as much as the shock of my own violence, the hate and anger and rage roiling up inside of me.

Tending bar, there's lots of flirting, innuendo and give and take…only natural, and I always enjoy the banter, but these days I turn real ugly at the least sign of a man stepping over the line. In my head that line is pretty clear, but I was becoming more and more quick off the mark to point it out to anyone who wasn't as aware of it as I was.

I'd been sexually assaulted as a young girl, and survived being stalked and kidnapped by a psychopath as an adult, so now sexually aggressive men surely brought out the worst in me. I was turning into a raving maniac, responding with more violence than the original transgression.

One day I was going to go too far. Or one day I was going to push back at the wrong guy. I knew it as sure as I knew night followed day. It was a great big black dog slinking towards me. The question yet to be answered was, was Boomer Breslau the one? Was he the mad dog who would go for my throat?

Even though I'd told Tully that Boomer wasn't going to be a problem, we both knew I was lying. Sooner or later Boomer was coming after me, coming to put me in my place. He wasn't going to back off and he wasn't going to let it lie.

I needed to start taking precautions right that moment and not wait until it happened.

I looked around real good before pulling out of the lot, kept an eye on the rearview as I turned left and drove along Main Street. Tully was watching the side mirror, but trying not to show it.

"You want to tell me what happened?" he asked.

"I was leaning over putting the groceries in the trunk when he grabbed my ass."

"Thata do it."

"I swear to God if I'd had a gun, I would have used it."

"Time we got you a new one."

I tried to laugh. "Best not. We both know how that's worked out in the past and Boomer's probably in too much pain to come for his revenge."

"That won't last. He'll come another day."

"By then I'll be gone."

But Tully was right. There was only one way back to the ranch, one way in and one way out, a road that I was going to travel every time I left Riverwood, a road that Boomer would be traveling too. He'd be watching.

Boomer and I were going to meet up sooner or later, and more likely sooner. When we did, when we met again, it would just depend how crazy he was, or maybe it would depend on how crazy I was, how it came out.

Either way it wasn't over yet — not nearly.

CHAPTER 29

Marley didn't give me any time to fret about Boomer. She had a plan. By four o'clock all the painting was done and the red velvet drapes were up. We were all as pleased as punch with ourselves.

The phone rang. Marley was closest to it so she picked it up but I reached for it when I saw her eyes grow round and her mouth open in shock.

When I put the receiver to my ear, filth spewed out at me. I hit End and set the phone down.

"What?" Tully asked.

"Boomer," I replied.

"He was saying—" Marley began. "Well…" she couldn't finish. She looked at me in alarm, her freckles standing out like a rash on her pale face.

"He was describing in lurid detail what he was going to do to me," I finished for Marley. "That boy has quite an imagination."

Marley covered her mouth with her hand and whispered, "Oh Sherri, what are we going to do?"

"He's all mouth," I told her. "Forget him." But we both

knew we weren't going to forget that call anytime soon. "Come on, let's get rid of all the paint junk and then I'll make us a great dinner."

While Marley and I cleared up, Tully and Uncle Ziggy held down the porch...at least I thought they were, but when I went out to water the flowers, the two of them had disappeared on me.

I was sitting on the railing and still thinking about watering the flowers, when my mobile rang. Was Boomer going to become a real pain in the ass? I was unlikely to get any help from the sheriff, and getting a new number was going to be another hassle. How bad was it going to be? "Shit," I said and picked the phone up off the wicker table. But it was Clay.

"So what exciting thing are you doing?" he asked.

I walked down the steps and sank down onto the last one. "Well, at the moment I'm watching a whole mob of ants devour a palmetto bug."

"Now that's exciting," Clay said.

"Damn right. The action never stops out here. I can see why you love it."

"Did you ride Joey today?"

I had no intention of going out in the back of beyond and letting Joey dump me in Boomer's or the swampman's lap. The thought made me shiver. The guys in the woods could stay in the woods and I'd stay in the house.

"Nope and it's all Marley's fault. She's had us all getting ready for the furniture coming tomorrow."

"What's to do? I thought Laura had redecorated, thought

everything was done except for bringing in the furniture. She charged me enough. What's left?"

"Measuring and stuff." I turned the conversation to Howard Sweet. "Do you have any idea where he is?"

"Not a clue," Clay said and then added, "maybe Howie knows something about Lucan's death."

"Perhaps no one will ever be held accountable for Lucan's death. Years from now it will be one of those pieces about unsolved crimes they put in the Sunday supplement on a slow weekend. In the Gator Hole the locals will talk about the murder of one man and the disappearance of another to entertain newcomers and give that tired town an aura of mystery."

"Well, you're downright depressing, aren't you?"

"Yeah. I don't think much is happening. Sheriff Hozen has his own agenda and he doesn't think Howie's disappearance has anything to do with the murder."

"Maybe you should go back into Jacaranda until this is settled, until they arrest someone for Lucan's murder."

"What? And miss all the action what with the bugs and things, which is, by the way, the only action I'm seeing these days."

This led to a more interesting conversation. We were just getting to the best bits when Tully and Ziggy drove in.

"I have to go, Clay. Looks like Tully's been in a little accident. The driver's side fender of Tully's truck is crumpled. I'm surprised the front wheels are still working. I'll call you back."

The passenger door screeched open on the rusted truck and Uncle Ziggy lumbered out. He was looking real worried and holding onto the door of the truck while keeping an eye on me as if he might want to bolt right back in. Tully followed Uncle Ziggy out the passenger door. Tully pulled the door out of Ziggy's hand and slammed it shut. He headed for the porch, not a care in the world. There was a large red welt on his forehead with a small cut at the center.

While he was sauntering past me I asked, "Little problem?"

"Not hardly," Tully said, patting my shoulder. He climbed the steps and went on into the house.

Uncle Ziggy came warily forward, staring at me like I was a rabid dog.

"You might as well tell me now and save yourself some bother," I advised him. "What's he done?"

"Ask him."

"I'd rather ask you."

"Oh, it ain't fair," he wailed. "You always pick on me, it just ain't fair, you should ask Tully, he's your pa, don't always be asking me things, and then Tully, he get's all upset with me, then no one's happy with me, why you always picking on me?"

I had to smile. "Just tell me and get it over with."

"Well," he took off his peaked cap and scrubbed his forehead with it.

"Just tell me."

"Don't suppose you'll give me any peace 'til I do."

"That's a given."

"Well, Tully wanted to speak to that young man you had a little problem with, so's we just waited for him at the end of their lane, didn't have to wait too long either, and when he came out, well, old Tully, he just puts the young bastard in the ditch and then he tells him, he says, 'You have trouble with one of us, boy, you have trouble with all of us. You may be able to take my daughter, wouldn't bet on it though, and you may even be able to take me, but that leaves this big bugger here, he's gonna finish you. He's gonna wipe you out.'" Uncle Ziggy settled the cap back on his head. "Then Tully just kind of slammed the little bastard's head back, the way you do, you know, and said, 'So just remember, what you do to one of us, you do to all of us and if one of us is left standing, that's the one that's going to kill you. You got to take us all out or leave us all alone,' that's all Old Tully had to say, only told the sorry piece of shit the truth, maybe he could take you two, but not me, no way, not ever, now I suppose you goin' to be mad with both Tully and me." He gave the cap another tug, waiting for the ax to fall.

"So how did Boomer's hand look?"

"Like he broke some fingers, all wrapped up and everything, won't be writing no bad checks anytime soon."

"You think there's any chance of getting Tully to go to the hospital with me?"

"T'ain't hardly likely."

And it wasn't.

CHAPTER 30

Monday morning Marley was going to meet the movers at the storage sheds. I offered to do it but she insisted on going herself. Claimed it was her car and she would drive it, wasn't going to trust me because I picked up dead bodies and wouldn't let Tully because he ran into trees, his explanation for the fender. I hopped in with Tully to go into town for breakfast at Lovey's café. Tully was going to leave his truck in town to get it fixed so Zig drove behind us. Our convoy didn't get far coming out the drive.

A sheriff's vehicle was parked at the end of the lane. A deputy, someone new to us, held up his hand to stop Tully and came back to speak to us.

"Morning, sir."

"Morning, son. What's the problem?" Tully asked.

"We're looking for a fella that's been seen hanging about out here. You seen any strangers?"

"Son, I'm new to these parts. You're all strangers to me — some are just more strange than others."

The deputy smiled and leaned sideways to check out the bed of the pickup. "Well you just call the sheriff's office if you see anyone you figure shouldn't be here."

"Okay," Tully said. The deputy started back to Marley's car but Tully called out, "Say, what does this man look like?"

"I understand he's Guatemalan, dark and not very big."

"What's he wanted for?"

The deputy frowned. "Sheriff didn't say."

"Think he murdered Lucan Percell?"

"Sheriff didn't say, but maybe." He made his way to Marley's car, checking inside and then to Zig's four by four.

"Does he think we're smuggling someone out of here?" I asked Tully.

"Maybe."

"If the sheriff wants this guy for Lucan's murder, wouldn't he be saying so? And why would we be taking a murderer anywhere?"

Tully watched the cop in the side mirror. "Well, the sheriff wants this guy for something, that's clear. He's willing to sacrifice a man from other duties just to check out who leaves Riverwood."

I turned in the seat to see if the deputy was within earshot. "I bet Boomer was looking for this Guatemalan too when we met him out back. Why would the sheriff and Boomer both be looking for someone and why on Riverwood?"

Tully kept his eyes locked on the side mirror and said, "Boomer must have found something in the woods that told him the guy was out there. Or maybe he saw him, like you did, and that's why they think he's on Riverwood."

Tully raised his hand off the side mirror to wave at the deputy as he went by the truck and said softly to me, "You so sure Boomer was looking for a man out there in the woods?"

"Well, either that or he was hunting, but why hunt on Clay's land when he's got a couple of thousand acres of his own? It doesn't make sense."

"Guys like that just go where they want. They don't care about private property and they just shoot at anything that moves."

"Well, I think they were after human quarry."

"You may be right." Tully turned to me. "Think you and Marley should head home?"

"No. As long as they stay well away from the house, I'm cool." We watched the deputy drive out the lane. I asked, "How is Boomer getting onto Clay's property? I thought there was no way onto it but the lane from the house."

"We're in the height of the dry season; water is low this time of year and especially this year." We followed the deputy onto the highway. "They're probably coming in by going along the stream bed or running up the side where it's dried up. They could go right up to the lake and onto the trail."

The police car pulled to the side of the road and then reversed into the lane when we'd gone by.

Tully said, "I got a bad feeling about this."

Every seat in the café was filled, most of them by men. The reason wasn't haute cuisine but Lovey Sweet, a sensuous lush piece of walking art, a Rubens with a coffee carafe in her hand. Alabaster skin and clear dark violet blue eyes, innocent of pride, and perfect features were all worth looking at. And though her figure might be a little fuller than was popular in *Vogue*, no one here was complaining. Heads and eyes swiveled as she walked by and a sigh, a trembling reverberation of lust, followed in her wake.

I'm not really used to being invisible but with Lovey in the room there wasn't another woman who was going to get a second look. With eyes that smiled and laughed, she called each customer by name and made him feel special, almost blessed, as she leaned over and refilled his coffee cup and patted his back or arm, almost always touching them. All of this was as natural as breathing for Lovey. She wasn't coming on to anyone.

When she reached our table, I asked, "Have you heard from your father?"

She set the coffee carafe down on our table as her smile faded. She folded her arms over her chest and said, "Not yet. He's gone off for a few days here and there, just taken some downtime without telling Ma where he was going, but in the past he's always got in touch with me. Not this time. This is different. I'm scared. I've been calling the sheriff morning, noon and night. Can't figure out why the sheriff isn't taking it seriously. He keeps telling me that Dad has to be gone forty-eight hours before the sheriff's department is supposed to get involved." She worried her lip with her teeth while both Tully and Uncle Ziggy gasped for breath, making fish-out-of-water strangling sounds.

Lovey wrinkled her forehead and said, "The sheriff just makes soothing sounds but I don't think he's doing anything."

"Do you think your dad's disappearance has anything to do with Lucan's murder?"

She looked away, considering her answer, and then said, "I don't want to, but Dad wouldn't go away right now. He knows...well, he knows it's a bad time. I don't know what I'll do if anything happens to him."

Someone called Lovey's name. She picked up the coffee carafe and touched my shoulder. "Thank you for caring about Dad."

"Let us know when you hear from him," I said.

"Sure. I'm real sorry you've been let down. Do you need any help out at Riverwood? Maybe I can find someone for you."

"Don't worry about it. We can cope 'til Howie gets back."

Lovey gave us a small smile and went off to refill more mugs and cause another couple of coronaries.

"Do you think Howie is dead?" I asked.

Neither Tully nor Uncle Ziggy looked at me but at least Tully answered. "Lovey's got a point; it's a strange time for Howie to go off." Tully's eyes never left Lovey's undulating backside. "He loves his daughter and knows she needs him. Why'd he go off on a toot now?"

I had the answer to that. "Because Pearl was about to find out he'd snuck off to the Gator Hole. I can see him going away to avoid that party, but won't it just be worse when he gets back?"

"Lord knows," said Tully. "If I was married to Pearl I'd run long and fast."

"Uncle Ziggy?" I asked just to see if he was on the same planet as us but was not really expecting an answer. None came. Uncle Ziggy could only deal with one thought at a time and the one thought that had him in its grip was Lovey. A million dead bodies stretched out end to end wouldn't have caught his attention. He was definitely in love.

Uncle Ziggy wasn't ready to leave when breakfast was over, claimed he needed more coffee, even though he'd already had Lovey fill his cup four or five times. When the debris of our breakfast had been cleared away, and with it all reason to stay, Ziggy moved over to the counter for one more refill, one more chat, one more small contact with Lovey to see him through his day.

"Can't you get him to take it easy on the coffee?" I asked Tully when we left the diner to go check on Tully's truck. "All that coffee, it's just not good for him."

"Never mind the coffee. When a man falls in love at Zig's age it can be dangerous for his health, period. Last night he was cutting the hairs in his nose to look pretty for breakfast and he damn near took his schnoz right off."

"Think he's going to remember us?"

"The fog will clear when he gets out in the fresh air. He'll be along to pick us up as soon as he gets over mooning over Lovey Sweet, or sweet Lovey as he likes to call her. It may take some time though."

The news on Tully's truck wasn't good. Seems it wasn't worth fixing. In fact, the mechanic refused to let Tully drive it off the lot, which got Tully pretty excited. I could have told Tully it was a piece of junk and dangerous to everyone on the road but he wouldn't have listened.

We sat outside the garage on plastic chairs with three elderly men who seemed to be permanent residents of the garage and waited for Uncle Ziggy. Apparently these three spent their mornings sitting there in the sun and considering the world. Their daily routine was recognized as one of the things that made Independence interesting, and everyone driving by acknowledged them with a wave or a honk of the horn.

We introduced ourselves, although they knew exactly who we were. They seemed quite interested in getting a close-up look at the woman who drove around with a dead body in the back of her pickup. When I'd told them all about the buzzards they were more than eager to talk about Lucan Percell and the town of Independence.

The leader of the pack was a skinny, gnarled man who had said goodbye to his teeth some years back. "That Lucan Percell never did get over Lovey; course neither do most of the men who clap eyes on her. Hardly a man in this town that doesn't get weak in the knees at the sight of Lovey. Any that doesn't, well let's just say maybe they oughta get themselves checked." The man turned his head to the side and spat a line of brown juice into the weeds at the edge of the sand parking lot. The side of the garage was speckled with brown spots from years of poor aim and juice caught by the wind.

"You think Lucan's death has anything to do with Lovey?" I asked.

A corpulent man, the only one not tilting backwards on his plastic chair, cut in with, "Naw, why'd she kill him after all this time?"

I hadn't actually been thinking of Lovey as the killer but I didn't point this out to the big fella. Knees splayed, one going east and one going west, and hands the size of dinner plates planted on his knees, he leaned towards me waiting for me to disagree with his assessment. He looked pugnacious enough to put me down on the ground and sit on me if I disagreed with him so I smiled and nodded in agreement.

"Besides," he continued, "Lucan gave lots of folks reason to kill him. Your man took him to court and that guy over at the tattoo parlor, that artist, told everyone in town he was glad Lucan was dead. Said better Lucan died than the turtles. Course," he paused to pull on his ear, "doesn't mean he wanted to kill Lucan, just that there were lots of things about Lucan that made people hate him. That April, she's the only one that ever cared about him. Don't know what will become of her."

"She's leaving," the tobacco chewer stated. "Going to her sister's north of here somewhere." They worried that around a little, surprised that she'd leave before the funeral and speculating if she ever meant to come back. "Don't think she'll be back," Mr. Tobacco said. "She told Sue Clausen at the nursing home she'd wasted more than enough of her life in Independence."

The bald man smoothed back the hair that wasn't there and tried to puzzle this out. "Don't seem right not to stay until Lucan is buried."

It was Tully who brought up the Breslaus and created the silence you could hear all the way to Tallahassee. Seemed no one wanted to discuss the Breslau family.

"The Breslaus have been hunting on Clay's land," I told them.

The big fat fella frowned, "Just stay indoors and let them get on with it. Don't go near them."

"Just best stay away from that family, specially that Boomer," Mr. Tobacco advised.

Boomer cast a pall over them even when he wasn't physically there and fear settled around the old men like cloaks.

Tully tipped back his chair and said, "Sheriff seems to be looking for someone out our way."

"That a fact?" the fat one said. He didn't seem surprised and I was sure it didn't come as news to him. None of them asked for details.

"Who's he looking for?" Tully asked. His question was answered with silent shrugs. Tully tried again. "Have you any idea why the sheriff thinks this stranger might be out our way?"

"Ain't got no idea," their leader said, turning his head to spit one more time. "Best not to get ideas."

I tried another question. "Know what the guy's done?"

They just shook their heads. Strange they were interested in every other bit of gossip but not this. Maybe they had no idea what was going on or maybe they just didn't want to know. When I tried to ask about Harland Breslau and what they grew on their farm, my questions were met with more uneasy silence, another subject not up for discussion. Nor were any of the other questions I tried. They weren't going to speculate on any of the Breslau clan's activities, even the sheriff's, no matter how innocuous the questions.

Their eyes slid away and their bodies eased off from us. They were growing restless and ready to bolt at the next mention of the Breslau name. The bald one confirmed this when he got to his feet preparing to leave and said, "Always best not to know too much about what the sheriff and his kin are up to, if you take my meaning. Safest just to stay clear of them." The others nodded their heads in agreement and followed the bald guy out of the parking lot.

"Well, we're as popular as a fart at Sunday morning service, aren't we?" Tully said, watching them amble away.

"Yeah and when their wives see them coming home this early in the day we'll win even fewer popularity contests. Whatever's up with the Breslaus, this town wants no part of it." How deep did the Breslau family have their talons into this community? It was pretty clear if I came up against Boomer I couldn't expect any help from the town of Independence.

I didn't share this thought with Tully, although I was pretty sure he had figured it out as well.

CHAPTER 31

The moving trucks delivered even more furniture than I expected. Somehow having it all packed so tightly, piled right up to ceiling, had diminished the amount of stuff. I watched in wonder as piece after piece of furniture was carried across the ramp stretched from the rear of the truck to the front veranda. As Clay had said, some of the pieces were genuine antiques and some were just old. The just old and comfortable went into the family room off the kitchen. Clay already had a television and a couple of chairs in there. Now it was pleasantly overstuffed with lots of places to stretch out and nod off.

It took two hours to unload the truck and place the furniture. Paying the movers by the hour made them more than happy to help us arrange it, change our minds and move it around again. It was starting to look like a real home, a place where a family lived.

By one o'clock the trucks drove out the lane, leaving us in a stack of boxes. Marley climbed right into the nearest one, shredding paper and singing out in glee with every new treasure she uncovered. Pieces of glass and silver began to pile up around her. My job was to take each item where she directed. The cut crystal went to the dining room while the silver went to the kitchen for polishing.

"Look at this," Marley said, holding up a faux Louis XIV lamp with a shepherdess in iridescent pinks and blues on the base. She pulled a ball-fringed shade out of the box and plopped it on top. Another matching lamp was pulled out of the box like a rabbit from a top hat.

"Way cool. Let's put them in the living room for a touch of class," I said.

"You better be joking."

"They're retro. I bet Clay's grandma bought them back in the fifties."

"They are truly gross and ugly. Take them upstairs to the back bedroom."

"Gee, there's even a junk room. Just like a real home."

Marley looked up at me. Her face kind of dissolved before she bit down on her lip and she ducked her head. I turned quickly away and headed upstairs.

I was setting the lamps on a rickety little table that Marley had also delegated to the little back bedroom, when I caught a glimpse of movement through the window. I moved closer for a better look. Back beyond the open fields three ATVs drove along a path at the edge of the woods. At the lane to the farmhouse they swung apart and two went east while the third went left along the paddock. I ran for the binoculars that I'd seen in Clay's office.

When I returned, the ATVs had almost reached the farthest

edge of the pasture. I put the glasses to my eyes, adjusted them and had Boomer Breslau in my sights. I followed him until he came up against a fence and couldn't go any farther. He backed around into the fence, turned and started towards the lane and then hesitated, backing off the gas and turning to look at the house, some feral animal instinct telling him he was being watched. He was looking directly at the house, maybe even looking at the very window where I stood. He wore dark glasses and reason told me he couldn't see me, but reason had nothing to do with the fear creeping up my spine. I jerked sideways to hide. The anger that had made me lash out at him was long gone and cool reason told me I'd made a terrible mistake, one I'd have to pay for and the amount due would surely exceed the pleasure his pain had given me.

Slowly I eased forward, peeking around the edge of the window. Boomer still stared at the house. What was he considering? What was he planning?

He turned away and his eyes went back to searching the underbrush. Something in the woods was more important than coming after me but sooner or later it would be my turn.

The searchers on the east side had reached the end of the corridor between pasture and underbrush and were blocked from going any farther. They turned and slowly made their way back to join up again with Boomer, concentrating hard on searching the underbrush.

Boomer tired of the hunt. He revved his machine and shot ahead fifty feet and then turned quickly and raced back along the edge of the wood, his frantic and mad behavior more designed to frighten his quarry than to find it. Was Boomer trying to scare his prey into making a break for it? As long as the guy Boomer was hunting hid deep in the woods he'd be safe.

Boomer's machine stopped. I used the glasses to check out Boomer's bandaged hand. Only the tips of his fingers protruded from the casing.

He leaned forward and stared into the underbrush. Across the handlebars of his ATV was a rifle. Even as the weapon registered in my field glasses, Boomer fumbled to unhook his weapon and swing it to his shoulder. He laid it across his right forearm and stood up on his machine. Gunfire erupted. The other two machines charged towards Boomer from the east.

Harland Breslau's face came into focus. Harland carried a rifle in his right hand. Kind, caring Harland, the man who looked after his wife with such tenderness, was taking part in this manhunt. And it had to be a man they were hunting. Harland wouldn't have left Amanda to go hunting anything else with his son.

My guess was it would take a whole lot of trouble for the Breslau clan to get Harland out here with Boomer.

They searched along the length of the field but the undergrowth was too dense for them to enter. The three vehicles roared off and I watched them disappear back into the woods. I put the field glasses down on the table and wiped my sweating palms on my shorts. Bad things were happening out there and I didn't know what to do. Telling the sheriff wasn't an option. He knew exactly what was happening. He was the third man who had rushed up to join Boomer at the sounds of the shots.

CHAPTER 32

Downstairs, Ziggy and Tully were both still napping, undisturbed by the sounds of gunfire. "Did you hear anything?" I asked Marley.

"Like what?"

"I don't know what, just some loud bangs out back."

"Old men farting," she answered, grinning up at me.

"Yeah, guess so. These old houses are so well built you can't hear things inside."

Her hands stopped unwrapping newspaper. "You're really worried, aren't you?"

"It's this party."

She waved a hand. "Don't give me that, it's this Breslau guy."

"On sober reflection," I told her, "I didn't handle it as well as I could. Sometimes I act before I think."

She laughed. "Yeah, I've noticed that. I also noticed that your easygoing charm is pretty easily gone these days." Her forehead wrinkled with concern. "You think Boomer is going to become a real big problem?"

I shrugged. "Hard to say with guys like that. Hopefully

someone else will piss him off and distract him from me. I'll be out of here in a few days and in the meantime I'm sticking close to the house. After the party I'm going to scoot right back to Jacaranda and the normal kind of crazies."

"Jac isn't that far away. What if he follows you? What if he starts stalking you? If he's a psychopath like you say, it's a likely scenario."

"Then I know a guy with a big bat that does collections…"

She clapped her hands over her ears. "Stop right there. I don't want to know."

"Why?"

"There's a whole lot of people you know that I don't want to know, and a whole lot of things you know about that I don't want to be involved in." She lowered her hands. "Let's just concentrate on getting the house ready."

"I'm trying to be honest here."

"In this situation honesty hasn't got a lot to recommend it."

"You were asking, so I thought I'd tell you, see what you think."

"These days I believe that thinking should be done sparingly…enough to keep me from walking out in traffic but not enough for me to worry about traffic congestion."

"So I'm on my own here?"

"Pretty much."

The conversation was over and I went back to transporting curios.

Later, maybe a half-hour later, we heard the plane. It was small and flying low like it would if it was crop dusting — only there were no crops out in Clay's nearly two hundred acres of swamp and woods. I stood on the back porch and watched the small aircraft fly north and then south, covering the whole property, and then watched it turn and fly across the whole area from east to west in a grid pattern. Whoever they were looking for, they weren't sparing any expense.

"Wow, look at this," Marley yelled.

I leaned over her and peered into the box. It was something electrical, that much I could tell, but it didn't seem nearly as exciting as Marley thought it was. "What is it?"

"It's a chandelier," Marley replied. She ripped open a cardboard packet and held up a long glass bobble. "And these are the crystal drops."

She set the drop aside and I helped her lift the base of the fixture out of the box. "It's the biggest chandelier I've ever seen in my life," I said. "Is it going to fit in the dining room?"

"Oh, yeah," replied Marley. "I'll make it fit." We set it down and Marley pulled out a second box, flat and rectangular, that was nestled below the fixture. It contained strings of glass, yards and yards of it. Our hoots of joy brought Uncle Ziggy from the back room, rubbing his sleep-tousled hair.

"Why, that's real pretty," he said. "Is it all there?"

"Let's see." Marley started pulling off the cardboard protection from the different pieces, spreading bobbles and bits all over the floor. Then Uncle Zig and Marley set to work reassembling it.

"We'll have to get an electrician to wire it for us," Marley said.

Uncle Zig snorted. "Why you want to do that when I'm right here?"

"Can you do electricity?" Marley asked, her voice full of uncertainty, showing she knew my family only too well.

"Know everything about it," Zig said. "Well, I would, wouldn't I, with all the things I've taken apart, even got some of them back together again." He grinned at her.

By four o'clock those household members who were still sane had rebelled and were sitting out on the front porch with long neck beers in their hands when the sheriff flew in with his normal amount of drama. He was looking a little ragged around the edges, like he hadn't shaved quite so closely and as if his clothes weren't quite so freshly laundered and pressed.

"Have you found Howie yet?" I asked after a cold refreshment had been offered and turned down.

"Nope, Howie will show up sooner or later." A small smile confirmed his lack of concern. "He's gone AWOL before. He'll be somewhere comfortable."

"Got a little bundle of joy hidden away somewhere, has he?" Tully asked. All of the men were grinning. Howard's secret was probably shared by every bit of testosterone in the county, a male conspiracy.

Why do men hide and condone each other's affairs while women in the same situation would rat each other out in a second? Or maybe that was just my own bias from watching Jimmy's friends cheer him on in his wanderings. And then they'd always been shocked when Jimmy made a pass at their wives, which Jimmy would do eventually. Even friendship didn't stop him from poaching on another man's territory. More than one guy had come whining to me and demanding I keep Jimmy from straying — as if I could.

"Have you told Pearl you figure he's safe?" I asked the sheriff.

"Oh, Pearl's got it figured, why else you think she came running 'round here with the pastor in tow? She had the right church but the wrong pew, if you know what I mean."

Uncle Ziggy and Tully broke into gales of laughter at this bit of wit.

"Men are all disgusting," I told them. "World would be better off without the lot of you."

"The world would end without us," Tully pointed out. I was in no mood for this slice of truth.

"Howard Sweet may well be as dead as Lucan. You do remember that murder don't you, Sheriff?"

His face turned scarlet. "City people don't need to come out here and teach us how to do things. My men are working on it, searching for a suspect. Have any of you seen a man hanging about?"

"You mean besides the dead one I found in my truck?" I asked.

Sheriff Hozen went rigid. He growled, "Have you seen anyone about, in the fields or in the woods?" He looked to Tully and Ziggy, "Either of you seen anyone about? There's been stories of a man hiding out on Clay's property." They both shook their heads in denial.

I said, "I don't suppose he'll be wearing a baseball cap that says 'Killer' on it, will he?"

"I just asked a simple question, Mrs. Travis. We don't want anyone else to die, do we?"

"You mean like Howie Sweet?"

"I'd think finding Lucan's body would convince you this was no time for jokes and no time to be at Riverwood. If I were you, I'd go back where I belonged. Where it's safe." The sheriff was trying hard to scare me out of my tutu and doing a pretty good job of it.

"Oh, I surely will think on that," I said. "You do frighten me, Sheriff. I'm just so glad you are here to look after us all."

Tully and Uncle Zig looked at me like I'd lost the last of my good sense. All that orange blossoms and honey was unbelievable to Tully and Ziggy, but there's nothing like it to convince a man you're not related to that he's a hero and you trust him absolutely.

"I know I can trust you to keep me safe, Sheriff," I added for good measure, along with a bit of wide-eyed wonder. Now Tully and Zig were truly incredulous but then they knew me better than the sheriff, although the sheriff wasn't looking too impressed either.

"Good. In the meantime, before you go back to the city, you best keep your doors locked and if you see anybody around here you call me right away."

"But I still don't understand. What does this person look like?" I asked. "So I'll know if the man I saw is the one you're looking for."

His eyes lit up. "So you have seen someone?"

"No," I told the sheriff. Lying to authority is a congenital failing in the Jenkins family, like some fatal illness that runs rampant through the genes. I could be standing beside a three-car pile up, covered in blood, and if a cop asked if I'd been in an accident, I'd say, "Why whatever gave you that idea?

Everything's fine officer, nothing happening here." It came in my mother's milk and now the denial just popped out before I thought about it.

But my reaction was caused by more than coming from a family of liars. Sheriff Hozen wasn't looking too honest himself. He was more interested in capturing this stranger than finding out what had happened to Howie or identifying a murderer. What could this stranger have done that was worse than the killing of Lucan Percell? What was worse than murder?

I said, "But just in case I do see him, I just wondered what this stranger would look like."

The sheriff frowned. He wasn't happy to be giving out information. "Hispanic — we're looking for a guy from Guatemala. If you see him don't go near him, just get away and call for help. He's armed and dangerous."

Armed and dangerous described Boomer and the sheriff.

It started to rain — just like that, while the sun was still shining, as if someone had turned on a shower. We all looked up at the sky, transfixed for a moment by something other than death. The rain fell straight down out of a clear sky, the first moisture we'd seen in a month.

"Won't last," the sheriff said. We nodded in agreement, still watching the rain fall.

"When can I get my truck back?" I asked. "I can't go home without it."

The sheriff said, "I'll check and see if all the forensics are done. I'll have it washed and brought back to you right away so you can get back to Jacaranda."

The sound of the rain pounding on the tin roof of the

porch grew louder and made more conversation impossible, but the sheriff was done with us anyway. He waved a hand at us and raced to his car, peeling away and sending mud flying out in a rooster tail behind him.

The three of us trailed inside.

"You want Jimmy's truck back?" Tully asked, closing the door and shutting out some of the noise of the downpour.

"We're short two vehicles. You and I can share it until you get another."

"But you're really going to drive around in a truck that had a dead body in it?"

"It's not like the body was riding around in the cab with me."

Tully said, "You might want to think about replacing Jimmy's truck."

"My truck, and why?"

"Just seems a little strange," put in Uncle Ziggy, opening the fridge for another beer.

I grinned at them. "Kinda gives me a dangerous edge don't you think?"

Tully said, "Don't know about dangerous, but if you go driving that truck again you'll be officially over the edge."

CHAPTER 33

Marley and I set off with a list of must-haves from town while Tully and Zig wired up the chandelier. Clearing off while the two screw-ups had at it was a little cowardly, but self-preservation won out. I was giving odds that they'd have the house burnt down before we got back but Marley wouldn't take the bet, seemed she thought it was likely too.

"Let's see the list," I said as I pulled the safety belt around me.

Marley dug it out of the pocket of her jeans and handed it over.

"Polish — one, two, three different kinds, silver, furniture, granite — who knew there were so many? There's a lot I have to learn, isn't there? This party is…" I didn't get any further with my worries because we were at the end of the lane and a car from the sheriff's department blocked our path. Marley, always impatient and focused, laid on the horn even though the deputy was already getting out of his car and coming back to talk to us.

It was Deputy Quinn. He broke into a smile when he saw Marley.

He leaned on the open window and said, "Hello again."

Marley responded, "Hello to you too — now get out of my way."

"Just want to check your car, miss. We're looking for a real bad fella and we want to make sure he isn't trying to sneak away in anyone's car. Would you mind opening your trunk?"

"Yes I would. We are still living in the United States of America, aren't we?"

"Yes, ma'am."

"Then you have no right to search anyone's vehicle just willy-nilly."

"Willy-nilly?" I asked. "Where the hell did he come from?"

"I need to look in your trunk, miss, it's my job."

"Seems he isn't looking for Willy, Marley. Just pop the trunk and let's get on with it."

She frowned, her sense of injustice battling with her desire to get back to her primary goal of house beautiful, but she pulled the trunk lever and Deputy Quinn went to search it while we turned in our seats to watch. We waited for something exciting to happen but Deputy Quinn slammed the trunk and came back to the window. "Have a nice day, ma'am." His smile was big and warm, as if he'd like to help make her day.

"Nice butt and he likes you," I told Marley as we watched him stroll back to his cruiser.

"Don't be silly," Marley snapped.

"Why are you so sure you'll never meet another man, that David was all there will ever be for you?"

"Why do you want Jimmy's truck back?"

She always wins.

As we pulled onto the highway watching the cruiser in the side mirror, I told Marley, "He's following us."

"Why?" Marley wondered. "What in hell is going on?"

"I think he's following you. He likes them mean and nasty. I think he still hasn't gotten over his last little up close and personal with you."

She wasn't laughing. Her eyes searched the rearview. "What's going on, Sherri? This is starting to freak me out."

"Me too. Why don't you go back to Jacaranda?"

"Are you coming?"

"Think we can get Tully and Ziggy to come with us?" I said.

"No."

"That's what I thought too."

Marley asked, "You're staying because they're staying, right?"

"Guess so."

"Then I'm staying too." She checked the rearview again. "He's still following us."

"He's in love."

"And you're crazy."

Actually I was happy to have him following us. If I met up with Boomer, having a sheriff's deputy on the scene might make that crazy bastard think twice about acting out, that's if the whole sheriff's department hadn't been told to stay out of Boomer's face. How deep did the corruption go? How big a hold did Breslau have on Sheriff Hozen? Seemed the Breslaus might get to do whatever they wanted around Independence.

With all kinds of bad men I didn't want to meet at the back of Riverwood and being watched and searched at the front of the property, I was feeling caught in a net that was slowly closing. And I didn't even know why.

The deputy left us at the town limits, near a small Mexican cantina/grocery store with a tilting sign that said Tiena Mexicana. The cantina was cuddled up against a discount store selling everything from cowboy boots to dish towels.

This general store was Marley's first stop. They literally had it all; some of it rested in huge cardboard boxes in the middle of the floor until someone wanted what the box contained enough to dig for it. It looked like Western wear and leather gloves were only beaten out by cheap foodstuffs and housewares as the hot items. I picked up a half-dozen sets of small glass salt-and-pepper shakers to put out on the buffet but Marley had a cartload of stuff for which I paid.

The good news was that when we got back to Riverwood Tully and Ziggy had finished hanging the chandelier. They had it lit up and the house was still standing — no smell of smoke, no crackling noises. They were so excited I figured they were as surprised as we were by this.

Marley didn't leave any time for congratulations. She had us right back to work unpacking the last boxes. I sorted out the crystal drops for the chandelier, washing and polishing them.

I was drying baubles when someone called, "Hello," from the front door.

Marley and I looked at each other. She shrugged and dove back into a box. Nothing was as interesting as what was hiding among the paper and she was ripping off newspaper and set-ting the contents of the box on the floor around her before the next hello came.

I peeked around the entrance to the dining room.

April Donaldson stood in the front doorway. "I brought the dog," she said, looking around and taking in the chaos.

"Come in." I set the crystals down on the table.

April had actually combed her hair but her eyes were still hollow and red-rimmed.

"Why? Why did you bring the dog?"

"My sister called, didn't expect it but she'd heard about Lucan and thought I might want to come up and spend some time with them. Can't really show up with a dog, can I? And I'm not really a dog person; don't know what to do with him."

I was going back to Jacaranda. I wanted the dog like I wanted chiggers but you can't say no to someone in April's sit-uation, at least not if you're Ruth Ann Jenkins' daughter. "All right," I agreed, my voice full of reluctance.

I followed her down the steps to her beat-up old Honda. The back seat was filled with suitcases and boxes. It didn't look like she was planning on coming back anytime soon.

"Did you tell the sheriff you're leaving?" I asked.

"No." She opened the door of the car. "Why should I?"

"He might want to know." But then, if the old guys at the service station already knew she was going, and knew where she was going, the sheriff probably did as well.

I looked into the front seat where the dog was pretending I couldn't see him, hunkered down like he was expecting blows. "Well, are you coming out or not?" I asked.

He was beside me in one bound, shaking and trembling and leaning up against me like he just couldn't get close enough. I stroked his head, telling him he was in for a helluva life if he chose to stay with me. He didn't seem to dislike the idea, just stuck onto me like he was glued right to my leg.

"Will you be back for the funeral?" I asked April, figuring I might get a second chance to ditch the animal.

She frowned. "I called the sheriff's office to see when they were going to release Lucan's body. They didn't know."

"Want me to call you if I hear anything?"

She nodded, "I'll give you my sister's number up in Gainesville." She opened her purse and wrote down a number, handing it over to me. "How much does it cost to bury someone? I don't have much money put away."

"Maybe the Breslaus will help out. After all, Lucan worked for them."

"He only worked when the gates were closed."

"What?" It sounded like her mind was doing backflips but she was looking away from me and worrying her lip.

Her eyes came back to mine. "Always told me if I saw those gates closed to go right on home and stay put. Never knew why but I think you better do the same. Stay away from them people, especially when the gates are closed."

"Have you heard something in town? Heard about Boomer and me having a little trouble?"

"Oh, God no, you didn't? Get away from here. Lucan said Boomer was real crazy, not just normal disturbed but real dangerous crazy. Lucan hated him and was afraid for Kelly, said what he was going to do if Boomer Breslau came near his daughter again. That's why, well, why I was surprised that it was Lucan who died. Should have been Boomer. I really thought Luc would kill him to keep Kelly safe. The way Boomer has been acting that's what it will take to keep him off that girl. Luc was real scared for her. He even talked to Lovey about sending Kelly away to a private girl's school to finish high school. It was going to cost a lot of money but Lucan figured it was the only way he could protect her. Well, that or Lucan was going to have to kill Boomer."

"You think Boomer killed Lucan?"

"Maybe, but if it was Boomer who killed Luc, no one is ever going to charge him. Luc said the sheriff was as dirty as the Breslaus were. Whatever bad things are happening, the sheriff is involved. You stay well out of their way and stay away from Boomer." She was getting agitated, trying to convince me. "Just stay away from them all, you hear?"

"Don't worry about me. I know how to look out for myself, although this place is turning out to be worse than most of the bars I've hung out in — but with a lot less to drink."

She almost smiled. "Still, you watch out."

I nodded and said, "I'll keep your dog for now but if you decide you want him back you just swing on by."

"Okay," she said brightly, nodding her head in agreement as she got into the car.

"What's his name?" I asked as her car coughed to life.

"Whose?"

"The dog's."

"I don't know, just Dog. Luc just called him the dog, never heard nothing else."

I raised my hand to wave as she backed the car around and headed off.

"Okay, Dog, looks like it's you and me." I stroked his head. He seemed to like it. At least well enough not to bite my hand off.

"Sure you don't want to run after her?" I asked Dog, who was still leaning on my leg. He looked up at me and yawned with an open mouth that showed off all his teeth. "Bored with my jokes already?" I asked him. He seemed disinterested but I went on petting him anyway.

Tully was making his way back from the bunkhouse where he'd gone for a quiet nap, daily naps being only one of the things that were worrying me about Tully.

"Look what I got, a genuine dog."

"And an ugly one at that," he replied.

"Now don't you go disparaging my animal. I don't let nobody bad mouth you, although heaven knows there are plenty of reasons to do that, so nobody's going to dis my dog."

"Has it got a name?"

"Yup, didn't I just say it?"

"What?"

"Dog."

"But what's his name?"

"His name is Dog."

"You have got to be kidding. First he's an ugly brown dog with a tail too long, to say nothing of his legs that look like they belong to one of those things we're feeding in the barn. Every bone in his body shows through his skin and now you give him a name like that." He shook his head and headed for the house.

"Be careful," I warned Tully, "Marley is looking for someone to polish more silver. I'd like to see that, like to see you
polishing stuff."

"Tell her to get Dog to do it," he said and kept on going.

CHAPTER 34

"Are we ever going to get this done?" I asked. Boxes were everywhere and although the furniture was sitting where Marley thought it belonged it was looking bedraggled and haphazard. Marley had declared it all needed vacuuming and polishing. The kitchen counters were still covered with silver to polish.

"Of course we will," Marley said. "You just get on your dancing shoes and move."

"I'll get some real good music for you, that's what we need, some good music for dancing. It'll help us work too," Ziggy said and hurried away.

Marley watched him hustle out the door and asked, "Does he take everything literally?"

"Pretty much. Just don't say 'Break a move,' or he'll be looking for something to destroy."

"I love that man," Marley said, diving into a box. On her knees, she stopped digging through paper and looked back at me. "And I love this place, love Independence."

"Girl, you are crazier than I ever knew. This is one weird

place, people getting murdered, psychopaths on the doorstep and now mutant dogs."

"Do you think Boomer Breslau is a psychopath?"

"Oh yeah, the poster boy."

Ziggy's music turned out to be the greatest hits of the sixties, his old-fashioned boombox blasting out *Creedence Clearwater Revival.*

"Now that's what I call music," Tully said, grinning with delight.

"'Proud Mary' was an old girlfriend of yours, was she?" I asked.

"Tad hard to remember them all but I'm sure there was one named Mary."

"I'm sure there was too," I agreed.

Tully took the empty box I handed him. "The great thing about a misspent youth is it gives you something to think about when that's all that's left for you to do. Man, I'd sure hate it if those years were boring."

The work may not have gone faster with the music but it was a lot more fun. Things just got better when Zig started to do a solo performance to "Lookin' Out My Back Door." It was a bit like a hippo ballet but I sure got to say it really did lighten the mood. As he jerked his head and tiptoed around the room, in what looked a lot like the beginning of a convulsion, Marley went into spasms of laughter.

An hour later, when Marvin Gaye was growling out "I Heard It Through the Grapevine," I was standing on the table hanging the last of the crystal drops on the chandelier.

"Hello," a thin voice called from the front door. That was followed by, "Excuse me."

"April," I said. "Thank God, she's come back for the dog." I sat down on the table and slid to the floor.

"Just don't use it as an excuse to be gone all day," Marley said, stuffing newspaper back into the last cardboard box.

"You know, with a little more effort you could become a real pain in the butt," I told her as I went by.

"Saturday is four days away, remember? It's your party. I'm only doing this for you." She went to take the box out to the back porch where Ziggy was breaking the empty boxes down.

I went to see who was visiting us, with Dog clicking along beside me.

Laura Kemp stood beyond the screen door on the front porch. At the end of her right arm hung catalogues of material and in her left hand was a black portfolio case.

Struck speechless, a great rarity for me, I stared at her in stunned silence.

"I thought, for Clay's sake, I'd come out and go over a new design with you. He seems to feel you should have some input." Words seemed to stick in her throat and she swallowed before she got out, "For Clay's sake, I think we should put our own personal feelings behind us."

"How lovely," I said, with a smile every bit as sincere as her words. I opened the screen door. Dog, still hugging my side, stretched out his neck and sniffed her crotch. Not a dog lover, she yelped and jerked backwards, swinging her heavy portfolio around in front of her for protection.

"Please come in," I said and stood aside, waving her into the front hall.

With her samples behind her and the portfolio in front of her — to guard against all canine possibilities — Laura Kemp came reluctantly forward.

The hall seemed to startle her. She stopped, turned to me with her mouth still open, started to say something and then closed it; she looked back to the stripes Marley had us paint in the hall, at the round mahogany table in the center of the foyer with a big vase of lilies on it, and then into the dining room on the left.

"I brought in a few family pieces," I told her, which was not a lie. They were pieces that had once belonged to a family — just not my family. In the single wide trailer on the edge of a swamp where I'd grown up it had been Super Discount sales items all the way, and if it wasn't plastic and faux-grained we didn't own it.

I stepped around the stunned Laura and led the way into the dining room. We'd put the two extra leaves into the mahogany table, opening it up to its full length to fill the huge space. Uncle Ziggy had rubbed every inch of the rich wood down with beeswax. It glowed. The chandelier sparkled and gleamed. It had taken me an hour to wash and polish those little devils before I hung them. A silver champagne bucket on the table was filled with Peruvian lilies.

On the matching mahogany sideboard sat the silver tea set and two silver chargers, polished and waiting for food to be laid out. The red velvet drapes we bought at the secondhand store hung at the edge of the windows and pooled on the floor. The air smelled of beeswax and lilies.

In the carved rosewood mirror over the buffet I met Laura Kemp's eyes. They were filled with shock and defeat. I turned away and led the way to the sitting room across the hall, the most formal room in the house.

The sun coming in the bow window made Marley's shiny cream stripes the center of attention, but the rosewood settee covered in blue and silver satin looked pretty good too. A group of bronze greyhounds sat on a rosewood table in front of the settee while over the settee was a huge painting of horses in front of a grand house. The bay window was hung with more red velvet drapes. Two Victorian chairs on small casters sat on either side of a mahogany table with a glass oil lamp, a pot of orchids and a small silver box. The only other pieces of furniture in the room were a massive rosewood secretary with ivory inlay and two upholstered wingback chairs. The room was anchored by a Persian rug that covered most of the floor. The effect was that of quiet elegance and understated wealth.

"Would you like to see the rest of the house?"

"No," she shook her head. "No, not really," she said.

"How about the powder room? It's fabo."

"No," she said, stalking to the front door, no longer worrying about protecting herself from Dog, more intent on getting out of the house than she was on being sniffed. Laura was through the door and down the front steps before I could even offer her tea.

"But you haven't met my family," I protested as she pitched her samples into the back seat of her Audi. "You must stay and meet them."

"No," she said, without stopping or even looking back. But then she'd already met Tully and Ziggy. Understandable if she couldn't take the excitement of that twice.

"Well, you all come back real soon now, you hear?" I said, all biscuits and grits.

When she didn't reply I was thinking that a return visit wasn't going to happen in my lifetime. She slammed the door on her materials, hopped into her Audi and was gone. Dog leaned up against me and sighed.

Marley came up behind me, chewing on an apple and asked, "Who's that?"

"Laura Kemp."

"What? No shit! And I missed it. Damn."

"Seems she didn't want to meet you. I tried, but there was just no way she was going to hang around if you were here." I leaned over and kissed Marley on the cheek.

She took a big bite of her apple and said around her mouthful, "What's that for?" Bits of apple sprayed me but I didn't object. She held out the apple.

"That, Marley my friend, was for messing with Laura Kemp's mind and for saving my bacon. It's the first time I ever felt on equal footing with one of Jacaranda's gentry. Who knew it only took a shitload of heavily polished old wood." I took a bite out of the apple and gave it back. "You're ace."

"You're welcome," she said. "But I still wish I'd been here."

"She's worth seeing, the queen of bitches with the crown and sash to prove it."

We laughed. The great thing about our friendship is we can be as nasty as we like, behave as badly as we please, without the other one thinking less of us.

She looked out at the yard. "Crazy weather."

The air was heavy and hot, threatening rain. Barely a breeze stirred the leaves. Ominous and breathless, the darkening day seemed to be braced for what was to come.

I considered the sky and said, "We never get rain this time of year. Hope it stops before the weekend."

I always worry about the wrong things. It was silly to be worrying about the weather with what was about to hit us.

CHAPTER 35

I took my cell out to a rocker on the porch and called Clay. There was a little sweet talk and I was just getting down to telling him what was going on in Independence, when he said, "I've got something to tell you."

I waited, pretty certain I wasn't going to like what was coming.

"I'm in a little bit of trouble," Clay said.

I sat up straighter. "What kind of trouble?"

"Financial," he said and went quiet.

"I need a little more information than that."

"My contractor has gone bankrupt, leaving unpaid bills. The banks are calling in my loans, and my partners pulled out months ago. They read the writing on the wall. I didn't. I bought them out. Now, nothing's selling. This isn't the economy to sell vacation homes in the Florida Panhandle. Those retirees are all staying up North with their money."

"Yeah, I know. We've been seeing that at the restaurant;

business is down twenty percent over last year. The only thing that keeps it from being worse is having a restaurant right on the beach." I realized I'd taken over the conversation. "Sorry," I apologized, "you were telling me about your worries and I jumped in with mine. How bad is it, Clay?"

"About as bad as it can get. I used my other properties as security for this one when everyone started pulling out. The resort is half done, eating money, and without finishing the marina and the units on the water, the condos aren't going to sell. I have to have the whole package. I'm trying to refinance and bring in a new partner. Unless that happens, and happens quickly, I'm dead."

I started to make a joke and tell him he could always bus tables at the Sunset but stopped myself in time.

He said, "It may get worse." He went silent and I waited for the really bad news I knew was coming. Clay had a large chunk of money in the Sunset. I'd used Jimmy's insurance money and Clay had made up the difference on the multimillion-dollar property. The restaurant and the rental properties barely carried the mortgage, taxes and overheads — don't even think of profit. If I lost one of the stores, a definite possibility given the economy, I wouldn't be making the mortgage payments any longer.

"I'm sorry, Clay."

He said, "I can't make it home this weekend. Brian is here, we're working through the refinancing."

"But, I'm having…" I took a deep breath. "The house looks perfect. I wanted you to see it. And it's your birthday."

"I'm sorry, Sherri. I have one more chance at making this

right. I've got a meeting with a guy that may partner up with me on this. Can't you come up here?"

I said, "Let's talk tomorrow."

I'd have to let more staff go. Where would they find jobs? Nobody would be hiring wait staff and bartenders. If things got worse I wouldn't have a job myself. The little bit of money I sent Ruth Ann every month, where would I find that? There was a question I hadn't asked. If Clay lost his development in Cedar Key, would he also lose his share of the Sunset?

One minute everything was fine and the next, well, my life was swirling around the bowl and about to go for the big flush.

Marley stuck her head out the door as I hung up. "This is going to be the best party ever. When is Clay getting here? I hope it isn't until after most of the guests have arrived, won't be much of a surprise otherwise."

After dinner I slunk off to my bedroom to decide what I'd do if I lost the Sunset. Nothing came to me and hours later Marley burst in and started to tell me about her really good idea.

"I was watching this program on PBS, all about Western dude ranches in Arizona, Utah and like that. That's what Clay should do with this place. It would be great. Hundreds of acres to ride through, creeks to canoe down and Independence even has a rodeo — every one of these little towns out here has a rodeo in the tourist season. And the beaches are only an hour away."

She was bouncing with excitement, planning the layout from turning the bunkhouse into a guesthouse to constructing more. "Of course, at first we could treat it like a B&B with horses and trails — there's enough bedrooms, might need more bathrooms. Do you think every bedroom would need to have its own bath or would people be willing to walk down the hall?"

I nearly bit her head off.

"All right," she said, "but I still think this is a great idea and I'm going to tell Clay about it no matter what you think. And if he goes for it, well, I'm going to be part of it." She slammed the door on her way out.

CHAPTER 36

In the morning, after we walked all the horses out to the paddock, my nearest and dearest piled into their vehicles and left the ranch. Marley didn't say what her plans were, barely spoke to me after I told her I was canceling the party, but Tully and Ziggy were going to look at Lovey for an hour. Ziggy just had to get his fix and the eagerness with which Tully tagged along convinced me Tully had been bitten by the same bug as Uncle Ziggy.

I stayed behind on the farm to talk to Clay. I wanted details, wanted to know if there was any hope.

"I have a meeting with some of my lenders on Friday," he told me. "If that doesn't work, I'll file a legal action, an assignment for the benefit of creditors, which is really pretty much like bankruptcy but it may force my lenders to take a proper look at things and negotiate with me. The problem is my property in Cedar Key has lost value so the banks want me to make up for this. If I don't come up with the money, they won't renew the loans on the land; if I can't renew, I'm in default and they can take all of my property here plus what I put up as security. The banks are telling me to come up with the additional money or they will force me into foreclosure."

"Sounds like you've really got your tail caught in the door. What about Riverwood, can't you use that to make up the difference?"

"It isn't enough. And besides, it might turn out to be throwing pennies after dollars that are already gone. Even if I were willing to put up Riverwood, it wouldn't be enough to keep the banks from moving in and the question is, do I protect what I've got or push everything onto the table and risk the whole pot?"

I asked the really big question, "What about the Sunset?"

"If I lose my securities, it means you'll have a new partner."

"The bank?"

"Yeah."

"Which will tear it down and put up condos." Clay had always said that the moment the Sunset stopped carrying itself he was going to replace it with condos on the beach and that's exactly what the banks would do.

"Not in this market," he assured me. "Nothing's going to be torn down and rebuilt in this economy and, besides, to do that they would have to buy you out."

"Yeah, but how much will they pay for it? I'm betting the value of the Sunset is less than we paid for it."

"Not according to what they lent me on my share. I don't think you'll lose money."

"So we still have something left?"

"We? There's still a we?"

"Hell, yeah," I said. "You haven't killed anyone, have you?"

His voice was so quiet I could barely hear his next words. "I thought you might leave me."

"Now how am I going to make your life a misery if I leave you?"

"I should have told you I was in trouble sooner but I didn't want you to worry."

"Okay, I can see that, but not worrying over a specific problem now means I worry all the time about what might be happening that I don't know about."

"I'm sorry."

"Don't keep secrets." It didn't escape my attention that I'd been keeping a few secrets of my own but that was different, wasn't it?

"I may be starting over, no more penthouse," Clay warned.

"Well, I know a great trailer park. Drunks, losers and even the odd saint passes through — they'll make you feel real welcome."

"Don't joke. I'm more than a little scared it'll turn out to be true."

I laughed. I'd always known that the penthouse wasn't permanent. One way or another it was bound to end, but it had been fun while it lasted. "Being poor isn't all that hard. I'm real good at it; I'll show you how."

After our tender goodbyes I settled in to cancel the party, a party being the very last thing Clay would want to deal with if he got back Saturday night. Come to that, a party was the last thing I wanted to deal with. While I was joking with Clay, I'd also been saying goodbye to the good life in the penthouse on the beach. It was sweet while it lasted.

When I finished with the e-mails and calls, I moved restlessly about the kitchen, trying to decide what came next. Marley had left a couple of oddities from the last of the unpacking in the hall. I took the box of leftovers upstairs to the junk room.

The binoculars where still where I'd left them. I picked them up and went to the back window to check out where I'd last seen Boomer. Two ATVs burst out of the woods, one ridden by Sheriff Hozen, with a rifle across the handlebars, and the other by Boomer, also carrying a weapon. They got to the opening to the lane, following something on the ground, and came on a hundred yards before they had a discussion. Red Hozen pointed behind them and turned back but Boomer didn't. He looked up at the house and then down at the ground and then back at the house, shouted something over his shoulder and came on towards the house.

I threw down the glasses without waiting to see where he was headed. I just ran.

CHAPTER 37

I was getting out of there. If Boomer was coming to visit I wasn't going to be sitting on the porch waiting for him.

I grabbed my purse off the back of the kitchen door and bolted for the drive shed, with Dog at my heels.

Reality brought me to a dead stop; there was neither truck nor car sheltering under the tin roof, no way of escaping. I was trapped out in this wilderness with a madman.

Dread and fear prickled along the hairs of my arms. My palms were damp. My heart was racing and I was whimpering with fear. Beside me Dog growled. Did he sense my mood or was danger closer than I knew?

What were my choices? Even if Tully and Ziggy had cell phones there was no time for them to get back to Riverwood before Boomer got me. Hide, I had to hide. That was my only choice, but where? "Think, think," I told myself. I looked behind me at the house. It was impossible to secure the house. Not enough time to close all the windows. He could punch out the old-fashioned screens and step into the house through any window. And upstairs there were no locks on the bedrooms.

I could hear the machine getting louder. Clearly, whatever I did, I had to make up my mind quickly. The deep threatening drone was coming closer. "Hurry, hurry," I whispered aloud.

"Come on," I said to Dog and headed back to the house. I opened the door to the kitchen and let him in, closing the door quickly behind him and trapping him inside. "Sorry," I told him.

The problem was I couldn't trust Dog to be quiet. He might growl and give me away and, while he'd do his best to protect me, a dog was no match for a gun. I had no doubt that Boomer would shoot Dog if he got in Boomer's way.

The angle of the lane, swinging away from the barn around a stand of trees and then back towards it, put the barn between the house and where Boomer was coming up the lane. For a few seconds more I was out of Boomer's sight. I raced for the barn but stopped at the door, not going inside, flattening myself against the wall.

The front and back doors of the barn were open to let the air blow through. Anyone coming up the lane could see right through the barn. If I stepped into the opening Boomer would see me silhouetted against the light. He could drive right into the barn on his machine and run me down.

The sound of the ATV was loud. He was at the barn. My time had run out.

On the side of the barn was a lean-to, a place to store old machinery and the ride-on lawn mower. It was the only cover. The creak of the rusted hinges on the door was barely covered by the sound of the machine.

Inside, dust motes danced in the light from the grime-filmed window. A green tractor, a bailer, an old wagon and various other pieces of equipment — I headed deep into a dusty tangle of forgotten machinery, crouching down between the wall and a wooden box of spare parts. Not the best. If he had any idea where to look for me, I was done.

My heart was pounding. I heard the sound of Boomer's machine make the turn around the barn to the house. The sound died. I held my breath, struggling to hear everything. What was Boomer doing? Was he heading for the barn? Senses working overtime, straining to hear, I tried to guess.

The tension was too much for me. I couldn't bear not knowing where he was and what he was doing. I took down a rusted pipe wrench hanging on the wall and crept out of my hiding place to the grimy window. Boomer had parked by the back door and was on the kitchen porch. He reached for the door. The fact that the inside door was open, that only the screen door was in place, well, Boomer must have been sure someone was there, but he didn't knock. He was going to open the door and walk in.

But he had to get past Dog, who was going crazy. Boomer thought better of stepping into the kitchen. He circled the house, heading for the front door.

Dog was going ballistic. He must have raced from the kitchen down the hall to meet Boomer at the front door.

I could hear the second machine, growing louder and getting closer with each second that passed.

Dust tickled my nose. I sucked in my breath and pinched my nostrils, trying to stop it, ending it in a cough of a sneeze.

The roar of the other engine filled the shed. I eased back to the window. Sheriff Hozen came into sight outside the grimy pane. Boomer walked around the side of the house to the edge of the porch and leaned on the railing.

Their first exchange was lost in the noise of the machine but Boomer's body language was saying he wasn't happy with what he was hearing.

When the engine died I heard the sheriff's words clearly. "Forget the girl, we'll get her later. Keep your mind on what's important."

Boomer cursed viciously.

"Look," the sheriff said, standing up on his machine, "This is your fucking disaster. Get your ass out there and solve it. The bitch can wait."

Boomer kicked the railing. I heard the spindle crack. He stomped down the stairs and marched to his ATV.

I stayed where I was until the sound of their machines faded. Would they come back? There was no way I was going back into the house to wait and see if they showed up again.

And no way I was hiding in the shed until Tully and Ziggy came home. What if Boomer returned and did something awful? Crackling fire, the smell of gas, and crawling from a burning trailer — those memories kept me from running for the house.

Slowly, I opened the creaking door, not quite believing they were gone, more than half-expecting them to be waiting for me. The yard was empty and quiet.

I slipped from the shed and hesitated. Should I get the dog? I didn't know if he would be an asset or a liability. Best not. I started down the lane towards the road, feeling vulnerable in the open. My steps faltered and stopped.

I could head for the road but there was a deputy waiting there. There were open fields to the right of the lane. Across them was Sweet Meadow Farm. Being on foot, I would be caught in no time. There had to be another way.

Joey was rubbing his neck along the boards of the gate as if waiting for me to come and get him, and for once he came along like a prince when I grabbed his halter and led him towards the barn to get the saddle. Don't ask me why I thought that piece of dog food would be any help. I just wanted to be able to move if I needed to, moving being preferable to hiding or being caught out in the open on foot. And to ride him, I needed a saddle and bridle. There was no other way.

I was tightening the girth when I heard the sound.

CHAPTER 38

It wasn't a big sound, more a dry rustle, like someone moving in the wood shavings in the stall off to my left.

I froze. My hand stopped in the act of lifting a stirrup down, every hair on my body at attention, taking in sensory information and not liking the results.

Humming softly to myself, moving around Joey, ducking under his jaw and away from the sound, I looked over the saddle in the direction of the noise. Nothing.

How did Boomer get back into the barn without me hearing or seeing him? The thought made my legs go weak.

A scream bubbled in my throat.

I gathered the reins. Would Joey let me mount him from the wrong side? Always twitchy at the best of times, he would probably dance away from me while I had one foot in a stirrup. Even if I was able to mount him, could I kick Joey into action and bolt outside before the unknown man leapt out of the shadows and grabbed his bridle? If that happened the stupid creature would probably go crazy, dumping me on the concrete floor in his own horse chestnuts, and then stomping me to death. Besides, Clay had drummed into me that I was never supposed to mount before I was out of the barn.

Maybe the noise I heard wasn't human. Maybe what I heard was a rat. Somehow this thought didn't give me comfort, rats being only one of the many things that scare the shit out of me.

Keeping Joey between me and whatever was hiding in the empty stall, I started to lead Joey to the door. We almost made it too. A man stepped out of the stall. He stood between me and the light at the opening.

He was a small dark man, with piercing black eyes. His clothes were in threads and I could smell his feral scent over the odor of horses and hay. Long hair grew wildly around his head and a scraggily beard covered the bottom half of his face but I knew it was the face I'd seen in the woods.

CHAPTER 39

Joey tried to rear back, lifting me off my feet. "What do you want?" I said.

"*Por favor*," he said and then went off in a long string of words I didn't understand.

Words from high school Spanish came back. "*No entiendo*," I don't understand.

He tried again, even faster this time, which did nothing for my comprehension. I didn't have to tell him my Spanish was bad but I did anyway. "*Mi Espanol es malo.*"

He nodded and gave me another string of words but I didn't get one of them.

And then I remembered another phrase that always came in handy: Can you speak slowly? I tried it in Spanish. "*Puedes hablar mas despacio*" or something close to that.

"*Si*," he said and nodded. "*Tengo hambre, tengo sed.*" He pointed at his mouth. Hungry — he was saying he wanted something to eat or drink. This I could handle.

"*Si*," I said. All I had to do was convince him to wait here for me and then I could run to the house and call for help while locking myself in one of the bedrooms. My mind was already calculating which door was strongest, which one would actually lock, which one I could shove something in front of while I waited for help.

I said, "*Regreso en un momentito.*" I just hoped I'd told him I'd be right back and not that I had bags of cash in the living room. We didn't get to find out.

Tully and Ziggy made the turn into the yard. My Spanish friend dove for cover in the empty stall.

"Get out of here," Tully told me when I'd explained the situation.

"And leave you here to do what?"

"Don't know, but I really can't see why this guy is our problem. You don't know what he's done."

"The sheriff and Boomer are out there looking for him with guns. That tells me the guy in the barn is in a lot of trouble."

"Still not our problem," Tully said.

"Why hasn't the sheriff told us why he wants him?"

"It doesn't matter to us why the sheriff wants him."

"True, but damn, do you want to leave him to the mercy of the Breslaus? If we turn him over to them, I don't think he'll ever make it to jail."

"Can't hurt to talk to him, Tully," Uncle Ziggy put in.

Tully rubbed the back of his neck.

"Please," I begged, "let's just give the guy a chance. I'm all for turning him over to the authorities, just not ones that have Boomer on their team."

Tully wasn't happy but said, "All right, I'll go out to the barn and figure out what we've got."

"I'm coming with you," Uncle Ziggy put in, and then said, "Wait a minute." He went to his truck and came back with a length of heavy pipe.

"You always have one of them handy?" I asked.

Zig nodded. "Pays to 'cause some guys just don't listen real good, so's you have talk to them in a language they understand."

"Not a bad idea, Zig." Tully headed for the bunkhouse, leaving us to watch the barn door, expecting the guy to come charging out to attack us. Joey hip-hopped about. I stroked his neck, trying to settle him down as Tully returned with a handgun hanging down by his side.

"Do either of you speak Spanish?" I asked. They shook their heads.

"Then I'm going with you."

We were still arguing about that when Marley pulled in. "I speak Spanish," she said when she heard the story.

"It's true, Marley was real smart in school," I assured Tully.

"Yeah," she said, with a nod in my direction, "While Sherri was studying anatomy in the back of a car, I was studying all the other subjects."

"What?" Tully asked, hung up on the anatomy lesson.

"Let's go see what he has to say," I said.

The guy was more frightened than we were, cowering deep in wood shavings in the farthest corner of the stall, waiting for the blows to start falling.

"Why didn't he run?" I wondered aloud.

"Too done in by the looks of him," Tully said.

It was true. The man, skeletally thin, was beaten; there was no running left in him. He was curled up in a fetal position with his bare feet, swollen and cut, poking towards us. On his left foot a sore had festered and was draining white pus. Insect bites and scratches covered his bare arms, which protected his head.

"And there's nowhere left to run," I added. "Boomer and Red Hozen are out back waiting for him. They probably chased him in here."

Marley bent down and started to talk to him. Her voice was soft and kind, almost as if she were talking to a hurt child. He uncurled and looked up at her with hope in his face.

We waited. This talking went on for rather a long time until finally Marley said, "Oh, shit."

"What?" Tully asked.

She looked up at Tully and said, "He's been held as a slave."

Tully made a sound of disgust. "He's lying. Why would he think we'd believe that?"

"Because it's true," Marley said. "I've heard about it happening."

"I haven't," Tully said.

"Yes you have," Marley said. "Think of women from foreign countries held as prostitutes. We've all heard of it happening."

"But in Florida…here?"

Ziggy patted my arm. "Go get him some water and something to eat, Sherri."

I stuck Joey in a stall and went for food. When I came back with the plastic grocery bag of sandwiches, bottled water and fruit, Marley was sitting in the shavings with the ragged man.

When I handed over the food, he tore into it with both hands. Marley told him to go slowly but, although he nodded in agreement, it didn't stop him from shoveling in the food.

"What's the story, Marley?" I asked as we watched him eat.

"The Breslaus are into human trafficking," she replied. We all jumped in with questions, our words tripping over each other and making no sense, sure she was making a mistake, wanting her to be wrong.

"It's true," Marley said. Her quiet words were sad and spoke of defeat.

She had accepted the truth but Tully shook his head in denial. "It doesn't happen here. The guy is just trying to get your sympathy."

"I know it's true," Marley said. "Florida is the third largest state for trade in humans, right behind California and New York." She pushed her hair back from her face. "David told me this is happening all over the state. There's a bill before the Florida legislature right now to stop human trafficking. David went up to Tallahassee to represent a coalition of churches. The churches have been working hard to change the law." Her eyes were full of tears. "Victims, those who get away, are usually too afraid to go to the police because they get deported. David's church sponsored one man who escaped, I've met him, and I know it's true." Tears washed over the brim of her eyes and ran down her cheeks.

Uncle Ziggy went to Marley. "It's okay, honey," he said, patting her shoulder. "It's okay."

Nothing was okay. He was just trying to wipe away the hurt and grief from her face.

CHAPTER 40

"Tell us what happened," Tully said. "How did he get away?"

"As near as I can tell he was brought to the Breslau place late on Thursday night along with five others. They were chained to the walls in a transport truck. Three men were left in the truck to be moved on somewhere else while Ramiro and the other two were taken off the truck. They were taken upstairs in the house and each of them was chained to a wall in a different room. The next night they were taken out and put back into a truck." She wiped a knuckle under her nose. "They were being moved to a new farm. He doesn't know where. He got away Friday night."

I could've wept a river of tears at the sheer awfulness of it. "Who did this?" I asked.

"He doesn't know the names of his captors but I think from the description one of them was Boomer." She ran her hand up her arm. "Does he have tattoos up and down his arms?"

"Yeah, that's him," I agreed.

"Ramiro," she looked at the man. "That's his name."

"*Si, si*," the man agreed. He pounded his chest with the flat of his hand. "Ramiro Aguila."

"Yes," Marley agreed. "He wants us to remember his name. He's afraid he'll be taken and never heard of again. He wants us to remember him. He's Ramiro Aguila from Jalapa, Guatemala."

"*Si, si*," the man said again. "Ramiro Aguila, Jalapa." The rest of what followed was beyond me.

Marley translated. "He says please tell everyone who he is and that he was here."

We all nodded and agreed that was who he was and that we would remember his name.

He went off on a long excited speech which was too fast for me to follow but from Marley's horrified look it was pretty dramatic. "His family doesn't know where he is or what's become of him." She consulted him for a minute and then she said, "It's been over a year."

I reached out my hand for Tully's arm, needing to hold onto him, needing to feel safe. Dying in a strange place, where no one knew your name or who would remember you, and with no one ever to tell the people you left behind what had happened to you — well, the thought made us edge closer together.

Tully squatted down in the straw with knees that cracked and held out his hand to Ramiro. "I'm Tully Jenkins, son." The man shook Tully's hand.

"I'm not going to let anything bad happen to you if I can help it and we'll remember your name." Tully looked to Marley. "You tell him what I said and tell him I'm not a man that goes back on a promise."

Marley did as Tully asked. "*Gracias,*" Ramiro said, nodding his head and smiling. "*Gracias.*"

Marley asked a question and Ramiro nodded his head and began to explain something. Twice Marley asked him to slow down; that I could understand but none of the rest. He just seemed to want to get it all out there while he could, before he was swept away again. Maybe he really didn't feel he'd been rescued; perhaps he saw us as only a reprieve not a safe harbor. And maybe he was right. Could we save him, no matter what Tully vowed?

At last Ramiro ran out of words and Marley turned to us. "After dark, Ramiro was the next to the last one taken out of the house to be loaded into the truck by two of the men. The old man and another man were upstairs bringing down the last captive — Ramiro uses the word *slave.*" She lifted a shoulder and wiped her face across it. "That's what they were you know, slaves, part of a crew that was moved from place to place to work. They were beaten and worked nearly to death. At night they were locked in the back of an old transport truck with nothing for a toilet but a bucket."

It was hard to hear. None of us could look at Ramiro anymore.

"They'd been held on a farm." With a bark of a laugh she wiped her palms across her face. "The American dream turned into the American nightmare for cheap tomatoes. The crop was finished there so they were being moved again to a new farm."

Marley pushed back her hair and took a deep breath. "He has no idea what today's date is. When I told him, we worked it out. He's been held for fifteen months." She looked up at us and wailed, "How could anyone do that?"

Sitting in the shavings beside her, Ziggy hugged her to him.

"The two men were quarreling. When they put Ramiro in the truck, before they chained him to the wall, they started yelling and shoving each other, this young man and the older man. They'd been arguing all night. The older man started pushing the younger man away from him towards the back door of the truck. He was screaming at him. They started fighting. Overhead the hatch was open for ventilation. Ramiro went out the hatch and down the side of the truck while they were still fighting. He was in the woods before they knew he was gone but they came after him pretty quick. He's been out in the woods since then. While they searched for him, he's been living out in the palmettos, trying to stay alive. He ate grubs and ants and drank from pools of water. One morning he saw a panther. He was afraid to go into the jungle, that's what he thought it was, thought he'd get lost and never be able to find his way out. He wanted to stay close, near other people. By Sunday, after he'd spent a day hiding in the palmettos and drinking groundwater, he was really ill, he thought he was dying. He couldn't travel then.

"He saw them, saw you and I out riding, and he saw the airplane searching for him too. They nearly caught him twice. He's really exhausted. Even though he's terrified, he can't hide from them anymore. He wasn't sure when he came here if he wasn't running back to the place he escaped from. He never saw the house in the daylight. But he thought it was different because the place he ran from seemed to have more trees and underbrush closer to it. But he was totally disoriented and lost in the woods. He just hoped he was doing the right thing, hoped we weren't going to put him back in a truck."

We were stunned into silence. Tully was the first to recover. "What are we going to do with him?"

"We have to be careful who we tell," I warned. "Red Hozen is a part of this. He was out there with Boomer today. We can't turn him over to the sheriff. Ramiro would never make it to jail."

"All right," Tully said. "Are we all agreed whatever we do we don't turn him over to the sheriff?"

We were all agreed. Uncle Ziggy had some rather heated things to say about the sheriff and his relatives, present and past and future, before Tully cut in with, "But what are we going to do with him? They've been watching Riverwood pretty close. They must know he's somewhere on Clay's property."

There was something bothering me. "We only have Ramiro's word for all this. He could be a common criminal. He may have heard of trafficking in humans and be using it to get our sympathy. We don't know if what he's saying is true."

"The sheriff was real short on the details of the guy he was searching for," Tully said. "You pointed that out yourself. And you saw the sheriff out there with a gun, hunting with Boomer. Something bad is going down, for sure. Do we want to get in the middle of this?"

Marley's answer to the question came from out of left field. "Remember Anne Frank?"

"Who?" I said.

"Anne Frank, we read her diary in grade nine."

"What about her?"

"I always wondered if I saw my neighbor being dragged out in the middle of the night, what would I do? Well, this is sorta like the Gestapo coming for our neighbor. If the bad guys want him, we shouldn't let them have him. I'm not brave, never have been, you know that, but I'll be damned if the one time in my life I'm called on to do something I'll fold without trying…not for him, you understand, but for me, for my own self-respect."

"Marley's right," Uncle Ziggy said, jutting out his chin, determined and ready to fight.

Tully said, "We don't know if he's lying to us, although I don't think he is, but even if he's telling us the truth he could still be dangerous. Desperate people can do desperate things. That's still no reason we should turn him over to that gang with guns. I said I'd make sure he got somewhere safe and I will. We need to get him away from here and turn him over to people who can sort it out."

"Okay," I said, "Let's put him in Uncle Ziggy's rig, cover him with blankets and run him into Jacaranda. The police there will take care of it. We need to turn him over to someone else quick."

Tully shook his head at this idea. "We can't take him out. Since last Monday we've been stopped by a deputy every time we went off the property."

"Don't break cover," Uncle Ziggy warned. "That's always the first rule, isn't it Tully? That's what we learned in 'Nam."

"Ziggy's right. We have to bring help here rather than try and run to it."

"I'm calling Styles," I said. It was a comfort reflex. I trusted him to tell me how to solve this problem.

Detective Styles and I had developed a mutual respect. If I

were honest, it was even more than that. The physical attraction was something I mostly chose to ignore, but the fact that it was there meant that when I called I was sure he'd come…except this time. This time he was still up in Tallahassee at the conference and out of touch until Thursday, one day away. I left a message, giving an outline of the situation and asking him to come out when he was finished in Tallahassee.

Twenty-four hours wasn't much, was it? We had it all under control. If Ramiro was still on Riverwood tomorrow, Styles would take care of him. We could hold out twenty-four hours. Just sit tight and wait until tomorrow and it would all be over.

CHAPTER 41

Tully and Zig took Ramiro up into the small loft. I was more than willing to leave them to take care of things but first I had to unsaddle Joey and put him in the paddock. I did think of offering the stupid animal to Ramiro and let him make a break for it, figuring it would take care of two problems.

Marley followed me to the paddock. "He's exhausted," she told me as if I hadn't been able to see that for myself.

"Why don't we take him in the house where he can sleep in a proper bed?" Now that Marley had taken on the work of savior she was going to do it up right.

Silly idea, but I wasn't about to use those words to Marley. "Like Tully said, we still don't know if he is dangerous, don't know if he's lying."

"We know that those men are after him with guns. Doesn't that prove his story?"

"He could still be a criminal. Even if his story is true, there may be more to him than that."

"The sheriff isn't trying to arrest him for shoplifting."

"There may be a reason he left Guatemala. Both things could be true. He could be escaping from slave labor and he could be a criminal as well. The point is, you don't invite strangers into your home…well, not unless you're my mother, and you know how often that went sour."

But for Marley, Ramiro had gone from a raving maniac to the second coming. Secretly I'm sure she wanted to hide him in the attic and pretend we were under occupation, which was just about what it was feeling like, surrounded by armed men and vehicle checks. True, we could still pick up the phone and dial 911, but who was going to come?

Back in the barn Marley tried to convince Tully of the rightness of her view.

"He stays in the barn," Tully said, no room for argument. And then he added, "And you girls stay out of the barn. Me and Zig will take care of him."

Uncle Zig came out of the stall with the empty water bottle and plastic wrap, tidying up and hiding all evidence of our visitor. Ziggy pointed out reasonably, "Like Tully said, the man could be lying to us."

"We better have a weapon close at hand, Zig, when we're in the house," Tully added, herding us out of the barn.

"Not in the barn," Zig agreed, "case he tricks us and gets it away from us, got to be real careful."

"What if they come here looking for him?" Marley whispered. "What are we going to do?"

"We have to just act normal," I told her. "Although there isn't anything normal about this family."

Tully laughed and waved us towards the door. "That may be true but then I've never met these normal folk we all aim for."

"And we aren't family," Marley put in as if that somehow made a difference. Marley always has a great need for accuracy and truth. Strange, even with my good example, I've never been able to dissuade her from this silliness.

"Family has nothing to do with DNA," Tully told us. "Family is people who love you and who guard your back."

Tully only went as far as the back porch while Zig went to the bunkhouse and returned with a big old double-barreled shotgun that had belonged to my grandpa. It tended to have the bad habit of firing both barrels and sitting you on your ass so it was a good thing Zig was the size he was.

Marley and I stood at the kitchen window watching the barn. Marley asked, "Do you really think Ramiro is a danger to us?"

"There's no easy answer to that. Whether directly or indirectly, whether he does the deed himself or brings violent men here, we are caught in the middle, and innocent bystanders take as much flak as soldiers. I just want to turn him over to someone we can trust. That's why I called Styles."

"Oh," she said in mock surprise, "that's why you called him."

"What are you talking about?"

"Oh, you know what I'm saying. I've seen the sparks that fly."

"As usual, you're wrong. I called him because we need someone in authority who we can trust to sort this out." I looked from the barn to Marley. "It's a bugger, isn't it? Who do you call when you can't rely on the police?"

Marley said, "Maybe we should call the FBI."

I looked at Marley in shock. "I never thought of that. Won't they call Sheriff Hozen and ask what's happening? The last thing we need is to tip the sheriff off. We need someone we can trust, someone who will believe us before anyone else."

Marley nodded. "People are always letting us down."

"Comes with being human." I picked up the thick writing tablet and a pen she'd been using to make lists and handed it to her. "Write everything down so we have a copy of what Ramiro told us. Later we'll get him to write his story down in Spanish. It will help when we get him somewhere safe." What I wasn't saying was that if the sheriff took him or he ran off we'd have some kind of record left behind.

"Right," Marley agreed, pulling out a chair and sitting down at the table. She began to write without thinking, earnest and determined to get it all down.

Tully came in and went to the den, returning with a rifle. He went out to the porch and laid the rifle beside him on the floor. Through the door I watched Dog sniff the gun. Then Dog went around to the other side of Tully and flopped down.

Should I mention Clay's handgun to Tully? I decided to keep that one for myself…as backup. Besides, they had quite enough firepower to scare me.

I left Marley to her writing and stepped outside. "Did you hide him well?"

"Pulled down some bales and made a safe little hidey-hole," Tully told me. "Don't worry, it'll take a real serious search to find him."

"I'm betting a real serious search might not be too far off."

An afternoon thunderstorm was building up out towards the gulf. The trees swayed and the wind picked things up and tossed them about the yard. The air was charged with a current of violence that was almost palpable, as if the weather could feel the human tension and wanted to get in on the act. "Crazy weather, I just don't understand it," I said.

We were on the porch finishing our lunch when the sheriff's car careened into the yard. He was followed by pickups towing trailers.

I put my glass down on the floor. "Showtime," I said. "Better hide those weapons or the sheriff is going to think he's come to the right place."

Right off the bat I noticed Boomer's big-assed truck. It was hard to miss, lording it over the other vehicles. The door opened and he jumped to the ground. His eyes found me. The doors of the pickups opened and men and dogs poured out, making an ungodly racket.

Boomer reached into the truck and pulled out a rifle.

Beside me Tully said, "Easy girl, stay cool."

Boomer slammed the truck door shut and started towards the house, the rifle in his left hand. Tully's hand went to my arm.

Sheriff Red Hozen jumped in front of Boomer, blocking Boomer's progress with his body. Bits of their conversation, mainly Boomer's curses, reached us. It took some time, but finally Boomer swung away and went back to stand by his truck.

Red Hozen marched to the porch. Tully and Zig and I stood on the porch steps waiting.

"We're going to search this property for a wanted criminal," Red Hozen said. Marley came out from the kitchen, letting the screen slam behind her. The sheriff's eyes flicked to Marley and then back to me. I guess because I slept with Clay he thought that put me in charge.

"We're searching for a dangerous criminal, a murder suspect." The sheriff's attitude said he expected a fight and was ready for it.

"Not looking for Howie Sweet then?"

"If Howie Sweet is out there, we'll find him." Sheriff Hozen turned to Tully. "Fact is, it would be better if you and your family went back to town until this criminal is caught. It's too dangerous here with this fella on the loose."

The sheriff looked back to me. "This is no place to be with a fugitive on the loose, Mrs. Travis. I suggest you leave."

Tully raised a hand. "My daughter is leaving, Sheriff."

"Good. Things are a little different out here than they are in the city."

"Yes, I've noticed that," Tully said.

Sheriff Hozen's eyes narrowed, looking for the insult and then he said, "These men are going to go out back and chase this fugitive out. Best you be gone in case he heads this way."

I asked, "Have you asked for Clay's permission to search his property?"

"I don't need anyone's…" the sheriff swallowed a curse, and said, "…permission." The word was distasteful to him. "I'm only telling you this as a courtesy," he said. "If you won't leave, just stay out of the way. Best you all stay indoors with everything locked up nice and tight. Remember, one man has already died."

Involuntarily my eyes looked out to the black pickup where

Boomer Breslau stood. Around Boomer men were backing the three-wheeled vehicles off the flatbeds and loading up the dogs. Boomer ignored them. There was only one living thing Boomer was interested in and that was me. He held his bandaged hand up as if he wanted me to see it, as if giving me the finger. It was both a promise and a threat, saying he'd be coming for his revenge.

Tully sounded bored when he said, "Knock yourselves out, Sheriff. You boys just go out there and have all the fun you can."

The sheriff swung away and jogged to join his men.

A man, built like a fire hydrant, came up and started talking to Boomer who looked away from me and nodded. His eyes swung back to me and stayed for a moment longer and then Boomer watched the man unload his mechanical mount for him.

The chaos and racket of the dogs were beginning to blend into some kind of order. Men mounted their machines, called up their dogs behind them and started off. Every man was armed.

The searchers roared off around the barn and down the narrow lane between the fenced fields, setting startled horses running from the noise.

Sitting down on the porch railing to watch, I said, "Maybe this is the time to run for Jacaranda. Put Ramiro in the back of Uncle Zig's truck and get the hell out of here."

CHAPTER 42

"We stay put," Tully said. "Let them run around out there all day, what good is it going to do them?"

"The dogs are a worry," Ziggy said. "They pick up his scent, they could track him back here."

Tully frowned. "I been thinking on that. How likely is it that those dogs have been used to track men? More likely they're just coon dogs. My guess is the Breslau clan is getting desperate, trying to flush him out, trying anything to find Ramiro. We stay put and let the fools wear themselves out."

"One day is all we need," I added. "Tomorrow Styles can take over."

"For now, I'll just go to the barn and make sure Ramiro understands what's happening and stays out of sight." Tully picked the rifle up from under the papers and handed it to Ziggy, but Ziggy had already toed the newspapers off the shotgun and picked it up so Tully handed the rifle to me.

"I'm coming with you," Marley told Tully. "He can't understand you."

They headed for the barn while I took the rifle inside and put it on the kitchen table. Then I went to the window and leaned on the sink to watch Marley and Tully going to the barn, wanting to call them back, wanting them to be safe. Who knew how frantic the guy in the barn might be and what he might do. Everyone I was closest to was put at risk by this rescuing business and I didn't like it. I only hoped Ramiro was worth it.

When Marley and Tully disappeared into the barn, I went back out to the porch and picked up the empty plates. Back in the kitchen I watched Uncle Ziggy pace up and down the porch, never taking his eyes off the barn, the open shotgun hanging loosely in the crook of his arm but ready to be slammed closed for action. His restlessness mirrored my own anxiety, the wanting to do something when all there was to do was wait.

The rain began to fall, big round drops that drilled holes in the dust and pattered on the tin roof of the porch.

I turned on the tap, rinsing dishes before putting them in the dishwasher, forcing my mind to practical matters I could do something about. My head buzzed around the problem of who you call when you can't trust the police. Who do you trust? It all came down to that. Who do you trust with your life?

Out here in nowhere land where no one knew me or cared about me, without a dozen guys leaning on my bar who I could turn to for help and no Miguel in the kitchen with a cleaver, I was downright lonely. I missed them. Feeling cut off from other people was bad. If I was going to be in deep doo-doo I wanted company, lots of it.

When Tully and Marley came back to the house, the rain

239

was falling in earnest. Thunder crashed and lightning streaked across the sky. At least I wouldn't have to water the flowers. Better than that, the rain would destroy any hope of them tracking Ramiro back to the barn.

"Is he well hidden?" I asked Marley.

"As well as we could hide him. I still think we should bring him into the house, it would be safer for Ramiro."

But would it be safer for us?

I said, "The sheriff and his men won't be out there long, they can't do any good riding around in the jungle, throwing up mud."

We waited. And we worried. And we watched some more. Tully sat on the back porch, a rifle at the ready. Zig went upstairs to the junk room with the binoculars and the shotgun while Marley and I hovered around the window with mugs of coffee growing cold in our hands.

"What's going to happen?" Marley asked.

"I don't have a crystal ball."

Marley upended her mug into the sink. "I'm going upstairs with Uncle Ziggy." I could hear her feet pounding up the bare stairs, adrenaline driving her in a frenzied rush. Anxiety, adrenaline and caffeine — we'd all be bouncing off the walls in no time.

I went outside to sit with Tully and watch the rain that fell straight down like water on a fountain wall.

He reached down and scratched Dog's head. Dog's allegiance seemed to be wavering between Tully and me. When we went in opposite directions, he'd look from one to the other, trying to decide which one of us to choose. Even dogs can't have it all.

"Sure as hell, sooner or later, they're gonna search the barn and house for him," Tully said. "You know that, don't you?"

"Why?" I asked.

"'Cause they figure he's here."

"I don't see how they can know that he's here. How do they know he isn't miles away?"

"Could have spotted him. And maybe Boomer found something out there. I was figuring the guy must have at least been wearing sandals when he got away. Wonder where he lost them and when."

"Can they just search the house?" I asked. "Don't they need a warrant or court order or something?"

Tully just snorted. "How you gonna stop them? Around Independence the law is pretty much what the sheriff says it is. You might take him to court weeks or months from now but it wouldn't do us any good today."

"I want to be away from here," I said. "Back where I know the rules and how things work. Let's make a run for it. While they check one car, the other takes off."

"Not going to happen. They always block the lane with a car until they have a good look in the truck. Are you ready to use force against a deputy? Ready to use a gun for someone you don't even know? 'Sides Ziggy's right, the first rule is never break cover, that's when you expose yourself."

"I'm ready to jump out of my skin."

"The waiting is always the hardest, knowing it's coming and not knowing when or where. Stay down and stay put, that's the way to survive in the jungle."

I looked quickly at him, worried this was bringing 'Nam back a little too vividly, but he was just sitting there, rifle across his lap, feet up on the railing and squinting at the faraway woods. And waiting.

CHAPTER 43

I rubbed my arms, suddenly cold. "Are you sure he's well hidden?"

"Oh, yeah. We can only hope he has enough good sense to stay there until Styles comes for him, but this boy knows better than us what's waiting for him if they take him."

"I'm worried about the dogs."

"We closed up the end doors downstairs; going to be hot as hell in there for Ramiro but at least they can't drive right in there with the dogs. Long as we keep the dogs out of the barn, we're doing fine."

"There were a lot of men with the sheriff. Are you sure anyone is still waiting at the end of the lane?"

"No, but just because the sheriff called in all these men it doesn't mean he hasn't got someone waiting for us to make a run for it. I bet he has more men coming onto Clay's property the way Boomer came, trying to panic Ramiro into running. They're hoping to scare him, or us, into running, flushing him out. That's what all this is designed for. The sheriff may not be as dumb as he looks."

"Well, it would have worked with me. I would've run. Who are those other guys with him?"

"My bet is he called all the men who have been using this illegal labor. They've all got a stake in seeing Ramiro doesn't stay free."

"What about the deputies who are with them, think they're part of this?"

He gave it some thought. "Not necessarily. He might just send them elsewhere if they find Ramiro. There won't be any witnesses to what happens. But those other guys?" his shoulders went up in a shrug. "Hard-looking old boys."

"Do you think they'd kill Ramiro? Surely not."

"Kill him or put him back in chains on some farm while saying he'd escaped custody, either way Ramiro wouldn't likely get another chance. This is it for that boy in the barn. We're the only ones standing between him and real bad news."

"I still can't believe they're prepared to kill."

"What's your freedom worth? They're going to prison if Ramiro lives to tell his story. 'Sides, maybe there are other dead men."

"Shit. I hadn't thought of that. They belong in prison. We can't let them get Ramiro."

"No telling how it will end for him if they catch him. These guys have a lot to lose." Dog raised his head and yawned, looking up to Tully with eyes that asked, "Why did you stop scratching?" Tully's hand went back to Dog's head.

I said, "I've been thinking about what Ramiro told us.

There were four men in that house. I think it was the three Breslau men plus Lucan. One of those three men — Harland, Orlin or Boomer — killed Lucan because of what happened that night."

"My money is on that mean little bastard."

"Yeah, that would be my first guess. Killing wouldn't be a stretch for Boomer, except—" I started to tell him something else, "well, I'll tell you about that later. That night with Ramiro, the two men who were fighting, that was Boomer and Lucan, wasn't it?"

"Sounds right to me," Tully agreed.

"When Lucan came into the Gator Hole, he had already been drinking, maybe started before Ramiro got away. April said he wasn't afraid of anything when he was drinking. I figure when they took those guys out to lock them in the truck he was telling Boomer to stay away from his daughter, Kelly Sweet. April said Boomer had been bothering her, and you and I know that Boomer doesn't take real kindly to the word *no*. I figure after Ramiro escaped, the Breslaus looked for Ramiro but Lucan didn't. It was too dark to have any hope of finding Ramiro. Howie said Lucan came into the Gator Hole first, later Harland and Boomer, and later still Orlin came in. I figure Orlin delivered the captives in the truck while the other two came looking for Lucan. Maybe Lucan was willing to tell everything he knew to save his daughter by sending Boomer to jail. If Lucan threatened to tell the authorities, they'd want to shut Lucan up. It explains why he died that night."

"You've given this some thought, haven't you?"

"Yeah, a little." I had thought it all through while waiting in the kitchen. "Strange that Lucan did such awful things but also such noble things. He loved Lovey and his daughter right to the end."

"Have you figured out where Red Hozen comes into it?"

"Nope, but he's involved somewhere. He's just as eager to find Ramiro as the rest are."

"Well, just pray Ramiro doesn't get put in the back of Red Hozen's car or that's the last anyone will see of him. He'll be dead or back at work in a field."

There was something bugging me. "Yesterday, Harland Breslau was with Boomer searching out back. Where do you suppose he is now?"

"If it was me," Tully said, "I'd have armed men I could trust cruising up and down the next concession making sure the guy I'm hunting doesn't get out of the net. Those guys waiting for Ramiro to break cover would have to be prepared to shoot. Bet that's where Harland and Orlin Breslau are."

"So there may be more guys than we can see. All of them can't be dirty."

"A fair number of those guys may have been using slave labor."

"Yes, but would they go any further than that?"

"I wouldn't want to go to jail for that crime, especially not here in Florida."

"They can't all be prepared to kill."

"Which ones you going to trust?"

His words echoed my own thoughts.

Tully added, "Sheriff Hozen has told the deputies they are looking for a wanted man. Seems to me if they caught Ramiro the sheriff would take over. Even if the guy that caught him wasn't in on it he's never going to know what happens to the prisoner. The sheriff would see to that."

I got to my feet. Dog raised his head to see if I might want him to come along. "I'm going in and send an e-mail to everyone I know telling them what's going on here. People have to know what's happening out here, what's happening in Florida. However this ends, too many people will know about it to shut it down."

Tully looked up at me. "You think that's wise?"

"It's the only thing I can think of. I want his story to be out there so they can't deny it."

"You're afraid something's going to happen to all of us, aren't you?"

"I don't know. That's the problem."

"Why don't you and Marley go? There's nothing you can do here. If you go into Jacaranda, you can tell the police. Bring help."

"Or maybe they'll just call Hozen and tell him about the crazy woman standing in their office accusing him of crimes. Tell Hozen about the fugitive in the barn. That would work well, wouldn't it?"

"Even so, there's no reason for all of us to stay."

"Well, I'd go, you know I'm all about looking after number one, but Marley has decided to be a martyr and she'd never let me live it down if I left without her." I picked up the papers. "I'd hate to let her have that to hold over me."

"Yeah," Tully said, "I can see that would be a problem." He reached down and stroked Dog's head. Dog settled down again. "We got to find a name for this animal. Why don't you think on that for a while?"

I opened the screen door but before I stepped inside I turned back and said, "Styles will come. He'll come tomorrow. We have to hold off until tomorrow."

Inside, the land line was ringing. I picked it up without thinking.

"I'm going to get you, bitch," Boomer hissed down the line. "I'm going to kill this guy and then I'm coming for you."

I hit End and then I unplugged the telephone. My cell phone was on the counter. I switched that off as well but then I put it in my pocket just in case.

Looking out the kitchen window I tried to see Boomer. He was out there with a cell in his hand, able to reach out for me as he searched for a man he was going to kill. It was time to run. Maybe we'd already stayed too long.

CHAPTER 44

The rain stopped and the sun came out and cranked up the heat and humidity, just to hold our attention.

After I sent an e-mail to everyone in my address book, I paced the kitchen waiting. Waiting was the worst. I had to do something useful or I was going to freak out. I pulled out some apples and began peeling them for a crumble. Crazy thing to be doing, but I couldn't sit and wait.

I heard Marley's feet on the front stairs, heard Uncle Ziggy's heavier tread following her. I already knew what it meant before she flew into the kitchen and said, "Here they come."

From the kitchen window I saw the last of the machines break out of the woods. I dropped the apple and knife into the sink and followed Uncle Ziggy and Marley out to the porch.

"What do you think?" Zig asked Tully.

"I think that boy better keep his head down," Tully replied.

"Get rid of the gun, Tully," I said. "It will just complicate the issue."

He looked up at me set to argue but changed his mind, getting to his feet and going into the house.

"Where's the shotgun?"

"In the junk room with the binoculars," Uncle Ziggy said. "But I'd feel better if I had it with me."

"Look how many there are of them, all armed, let's just take it easy, make sure nothing stupid happens." Tully and Ziggy were not men that took to being pushed around and weren't always given to thinking before acting. Having to turn away to get their weapons might just slow them down a bit.

Tully came out of the house and said, "The rifle is in the cupboard under the stairs if we need it."

"Maybe they'll just load up their machines and leave." I opened the kitchen door and put Dog inside. No telling how he'd react to all this.

The world was soaked and dripping, the heat cranked up by the humidity, and the men riding the machines looked grim, sodden and unhappy. Some encircled the barn while others headed for the bunkhouse. None of them headed for trailers to load their ATVs.

The dogs jumped off the machines where they'd been riding, sniffing the ground and setting up a racket. Everyone had a gun somewhere in sight.

"Apes with badges," Ziggy said softly. "Psychotic rednecks, just trash that don't know no better. Stay close to the house and the girls, Tully. I'm going to the barn just to make sure they don't get any unfortunate ideas, don't decide to take those dogs inside." He limped down the steps, favoring the leg crushed when a trailer came off its hitch, and step-hopped towards the barn.

Sheriff Hozen spoke quietly to the two deputies beside him. They nodded and stayed back as the sheriff peeled off towards the house. Behind him some men were getting off their machines while others stayed put, their weapons ready.

Boomer followed the sheriff. The sheriff heard Boomer behind him. Sheriff Hozen stopped and started to argue with Boomer. Their raised voices carried over the engines to the house. "I'm in charge here and you'll do exactly what I tell you," the sheriff yelled. "Now get back."

This Red Hozen, sitting astride his machine, was a different man than the one who first came to Riverwood. In less then a week he'd aged years, like he'd been pushed beyond the breaking point, not a good place to be when making life and death decisions. I waited to see if Boomer was going to explode, hoping they'd get to fighting each other and forget about us. Boomer spun his ATV and headed for his truck.

"Wait here just a minute," Uncle Ziggy yelled, seeing two guys headed for the small door into the barn, dogs at their side. For a big man with the aches and pains of aging he still moved pretty fast, like the high school halfback he'd been. He blocked the small door set in the large barn door. "You ain't taking them dogs in the barn, we got a pregnant mare in there, no way you gonna upset her."

The men started to argue with him.

"Hold it," Sheriff Hozen yelled at the men facing Uncle Ziggy. He turned to us. "We're going to search the house and barn."

"Now wait here," Tully said. "You ain't got no call to do that. Like Zig says, we've got a mare ready to foal in there. Clay's going to be suing your ass off if she drops early."

Sheriff Hozen stood up on his machine. "Don't spout

rights at me. We're going to search the premises and you're going to stay out of it." He peeled off his yellow slicker and tossed it onto the back of his machine. What had once been a neatly pressed shirt now clung to him like a wet rag. "Stay out of it," he roared. His hand went to the revolver at his waist. He stared at us, daring us to defy him.

The confrontation at the barn was turning nasty. Ziggy had a shovel in his hand. Beside me, Tully moved restlessly forward but hesitated.

"And if we say no?" I asked. "What are you going to do, arrest us?"

"You don't really want to go there, do you?"

"There's no one here but us," I told him. "I don't know exactly who you're looking for or why, but whoever you're looking for it's a waste of time."

"It's for your own safety."

"We're doing fine," Tully answered.

"Two elderly men and two women?" The sheriff's disgust was barely contained.

I said, "I think you better come back when you've got some paper to show us."

"We're in hot pursuit of a felon, we don't need any paper. We can enter any property we need to."

"Hot pursuit? Well, it's true you look pretty warm. What did this guy do?"

"It's not necessary for you to have the details, you already know there has been a murder and you know that we are in hot pursuit, that's all we need to tell you."

A shout went up from Ziggy. He had his arm out pushing

off the guy trying to go into the barn. A second man peeled around Ziggy and was just about through the door when Uncle Ziggy hit him with the shovel.

It was a footrace for the barn.

A deputy I hadn't seen before was lying on the ground and another man had pulled his gun and was pointing it at Uncle Ziggy. Uncle Ziggy was red in the face and puffing, glistening with sweat, a heart attack about to happen. Even so, Ziggy stood spread-legged at the door holding off the others with the shovel.

Sheriff Hozen pulled out his gun and yelled, "Drop it."

Marley shoved through the men and ran past the deputy with a gun straight to Ziggy and planted herself in front of him.

The sheriff yelled again, "Drop that shovel."

Zig ignored him. Marley took the shovel out of Uncle Ziggy's hands. "It's okay. It will be fine," she soothed. The shovel dropped to the ground.

It was a no-win situation. "Okay, Sheriff Hozen," I said. "Just keep the dogs out of the barn, that's all we're asking. No point in hurting the mare."

"You men get these dogs out of here," the sheriff roared.

The men started moving away with the dogs. I punched Brian Spears' number. My lawyer and friend, one of the guys that hung out at the Sunset every night, Brian was always my first resort in times of trouble. And he knew Ziggy, had acted for him when Ziggy had been forced out of his junkyard. Assaulting a deputy was serious. Zig would need a lawyer.

"Come on," I said to the phone as Sheriff Hozen used plastic bindings to cuff Uncle Ziggy.

Uncle Ziggy didn't look like the only one who might have a coronary before this was over. Sheriff Hozen was a man close to melting down.

Brian answered and I explained the situation. The men were in the barn, spreading out and searching the empty stalls. One man picked up a pitchfork and began spearing a pile of wood shavings used for bedding. Anyone hiding in there would have been riddled with holes.

Only the one stall was occupied. The pregnant mare had been restless for the last day so we'd decided to keep her close so we could watch her. All of the other horses were still outside in fields, standing under the shade of a tin-roof shelter or resting in the shade of oaks that dotted the paddocks. It didn't take long to search the main floor.

"Let me talk to the sheriff," Brian said as men started to climb the stairs.

"It's for you," I said and handed the sheriff the phone. I ran for the stairs.

"Stay here," the sheriff ordered. He had a gun in one hand and a phone in the other. No way to stop me unless he was prepared to shoot me.

Marley and Tully were already on the stairs, following the deputies.

"I'm ordering you to stay down here," the sheriff shouted after us.

"Not likely," Uncle Zig answered, his hands tied behind him, and charging at the stairs. I leaned aside and let Uncle Ziggy push past me, reasoning that even Sheriff Hozen wouldn't shoot with an innocent bystander in-between him and his target. Head down and puffing, Uncle Ziggy barreled straight ahead.

Whatever happened in the loft there was going to be witnesses. No one was going to lie about this and get away with it unless they killed us all. Not a good thought.

CHAPTER 45

At the top of the stairs Tully swung back and raised his hand to stop me. "You and Marley get out of here," he ordered. "Head for Jacaranda and tell the cops in Jac what went down here."

"It's too late for that," I said. "We're staying."

Tully said "Listen to me…" but I was blocking the stairs. Sheriff Hozen pushed me aside and then Boomer, coming behind him, elbowed me in the side and jammed me against the rickety railing.

"Hey," Tully yelled. He grabbed me and kept me from pitching over the rail to the concrete below. Neither the sheriff nor Boomer looked back to see if I fell.

"Are you all right?" Tully didn't wait for my answer but started after Boomer, saying, "I'll throw the little shit out of the mow."

I grabbed the back of his shirt and held him back. "Let's just get through this and get them out of here."

That's when Marley started singing. The men in the loft stopped stomping about, and fell silent, more shocked than if gunfire had broken out. Don't ask me why Marley started singing — she just started singing some Spanish lullaby. Maybe it was to comfort the guy hiding in the straw or it could be she'd finally lost it. Standing at the top of the stairs she started singing in a pure sweet voice, her hands folded in front of her, and her face looking to heaven.

Sheriff Hozen wasn't impressed. "Get on with it," he yelled. The men turned away from Marley and started shifting bales. Some men climbed to the top of the mow and tried to shift bales there while others were doing the same below. The air was filled with dust and bits of chaff.

It was chaos and unbearably hot. Someone opened the doors at each end of the mow to give us some relief but even with them open it was well over a hundred in the hayloft.

And there were way too many people in the loft for the searchers to be efficient. An open aisle, not more than four feet wide, ran down the center of the mow between the bales. In the roof was an open trap door and below it was a larger trap door, closed now, for throwing down bales into the center aisle between the stalls.

The center aisle of the loft soon filled with bales. We climbed up on them to keep from being swamped. Some searchers where throwing bales out the open door to the mow. Tully protested but it didn't stop.

The pitchfork was passed up from the bottom of the stairs and a man started stabbing in and around bales, waiting after each thrust to see if there were any cries of pain.

Marley sat down on a bale of hay, hands folded in her lap, feet flat on the floor and sang, looking up to the heavens like some saint waiting to be sacrificed. I wanted to scream at her to shut up.

Uncle Ziggy went over and sat down beside her. "There, there, honey, don't you carry on so, these fools will be gone soon enough and it'll be all over, no one's goin' to hurt you long as old Ziggy is here, no harm goin' to come to you, we just goin' ta sit here and let these fools get on with their dirty business, you going to be fine, but I don't know what this country is comin' to when goons can just walk onto a man's property and scare the daylights out of the womenfolk, that isn't what we fought for." Ziggy's babble and Marley's continued singing formed a chorus as men stooped and lifted, shifting bales from one place to another and then back again. They were getting in each other's way. On the stairs the searchers who couldn't fit into the loft, watched or climbed on down to wait for it to be over.

A line of sweat slipped down my spine and hysteria bubbled up in my throat. Between Ziggy's monologue and Marley's singing, and the hundred degree temperature in the loft, I was about to lose it.

And the singing and the heat was getting to the men. The violent energy that had shot them into the barn was dissipating. Men were mumbling and giving up, heading for the stairs to wait as the watchers on the stairs drifted back down out of the heat.

Tully whispered to me, "Go." There was panic in his voice. He shoved me towards the stairs. "Hey, Sheriff," Tully hollered.

The sheriff turned to look at Tully and everyone else stopped to listen. "You don't need these women here do you, Sheriff?"

"Nope, get them out of here."

"Come on, Marley," Tully said. "You and Sherri go to the house; it's too hot up here for you."

But Marley sang on, her eyes firmly locked on heaven.

Tully bent over, his hands on his knees and gently coaxed, "C'mon, Marley." But Marley wasn't going anywhere.

Tully looked around at me and asked, "She all right?"

"Damned if I know," I replied

"Take Sherri to the house, Marley." It was a nice try on Tully's part, this subtle change in tactics, but Marley wasn't moving. She had found her Baptist duty and she was doing it. Hallelujah, sister. Me, I was ready to run, all finished with being brave and defiant. I edged to the top of the stairs.

That's when a shout went up.

A gun went off. There was cursing and an incredible crash as a body rolled from the top of the mow to the bottom.

CHAPTER 46

The noise echoed in my head. Everyone swung to face the shooter. Boomer Breslau held a handgun in his left hand. A hole in the tin roof sent a shaft of light down to the floor. At his feet lay one of the deputies.

"Oh shit," I said.

"Jesus H. Christ," said Sheriff Hozen.

The deputy groaned and rolled over.

"He isn't dead," I said stupidly.

The deputy, red-faced and sweating like he'd climbed into a shower with his clothes on, got to his feet, swearing non-stop at Boomer.

"Boomer, you crazy bastard, what have you done?" the sheriff yelled. "What in hell happened?"

"Gun just went off," Boomer said. "Not used to having it in my left hand."

The deputy pointed at Boomer. "The bale I was on rolled over. This idiot panicked and damned near shot me."

"Never did," protested Boomer, "wasn't even pointed at

you." Boomer reached out with his damaged right hand and shoved the deputy. His grimace of pain said this was a mistake. The deputy shoved back. Boomer was driven backwards onto the hay bales.

The sheriff, yelling at the top of his lungs, got between them. "You two get your sorry asses downstairs and out of my sight."

I stepped back behind Tully as Boomer slouched by.

Sheriff Hozen took off his hat and wiped his forehead and the sweat band of the hat. "All right then, what have we got left to search here?"

"Think we've done it all, Sheriff," a beefy guy said.

Sheriff Hozen didn't look happy. He looked from one end of the loft to the other and then his eyes fell on Marley. She'd stopped singing when the gun discharged, which told me she hadn't completely gone on a no-return visit to Gagaland. "Mike, you and Joe get her off that bale. She likes it so well it must be protecting something."

Marley started singing again. Deputy Mike Quinn and the beefy guy lifted Marley off the bale and redeposited her on the opposite side of the aisle. Marley kept singing but I heard the deputy whisper, "I'm real sorry about this, miss."

The officers tossed the bales aside where she'd been sitting. There was nowhere to put them. The aisle was already filled with bales. They threw more on top, forcing me and some of the searchers to the stairs. Uneasy at being separated from Tully, I scanned the bottom of the stairs for any sign of Boomer.

Finally Sheriff Hozen swore and said, "All right let's get started on the house."

That's when Marley snapped out of her singing trance. She jumped to her feet and said, "Oh no, you don't." She bolted for the stairs like a madwoman, pushing and burrowing though the people on the stairs and yelling for them to move it.

Did she think Ramiro was hiding in the attic of the house? Was that why they hadn't found him? Did she know something I didn't? I took off down the stairs in her wake.

Outside, Boomer lounged against his pickup. He shot to his feet when he saw me. I ran faster.

At the door to the kitchen Marley nearly locked me out. "Take off your shoes and lock the door behind you," she said and then she ran through the house to the front door. I did as I was told on both counts and followed her to the front hall.

"What's happening? Why are you trying to keep them out? If we couldn't keep them out of the barn, how do you think you're going to keep them out of the house?"

"I'm not trying to keep them out," she said. "Don't be stupid. They just aren't going through my clean house with their boots on. No one gets in this house unless he takes off his shoes."

Through the latched screen door she informed the sheriff of her terms for entry. Beside her, Dog growled low in his throat, threatening.

"Open this damn door or I'll pull it off the hinges," the sheriff yelled. Dog started barking in earnest while the sheriff's men sat on the railing to pull off their boots. A madwoman protecting polished floors was something they all understood and after dropping their boots onto the porch, they entered the house with their hats in their hands. I held Dog by the collar as they shuffled shamefacedly past Marley saying, "Sorry, ma'am."

"And I don't want your dirty pawprints over everything."

"No, ma'am," replied the men respectfully.

Wet and miserable, they shuffled into the hall. My mother, Ruth Ann, the demented Southern belle from the trailer park, would be sympathizing with them and asking if they wanted a cold drink…course, she'd have asked the devil himself to sit down and get comfortable if he was a guest in her house. I'd long ago figured out that wanting to be kind was what led to all her troubles and her bad choices in men. She'd let more than one sorry-assed loser move in because she felt sorry for him. Marley was made of sterner stuff. "Just see that you put everything back the way you found it," she ordered.

"Yes, ma'am," was the soft reply.

The sheriff scowled at her and said, "You, Mike, take half the men and start upstairs." Deputy Quinn tapped men on the shoulder and pointed upstairs. The men silently climbed the stairs as Mike Quinn followed. They'd lost their taste for the job.

The others stood shuffling their feet and waiting for orders. They were embarrassed and uncomfortable rather than threatening. That could change in an instant. The lives and freedom of some of these men were at stake. They still could turn dangerous again without warning.

Holding Dog by the collar, I shoved Ziggy ahead of me down the hall. I opened the powder-room door and pushed Dog inside.

In the kitchen, I sat Uncle Ziggy down onto a kitchen chair, ran a damp cloth over his face to cool him, and then started hacking away at the plastic tie binding his wrist. I tried to hurry.

Any moment the sheriff was going to remember he had a prisoner and lock Ziggy in a cruiser. I didn't want that to happen.

"Go outside," I told Ziggy when the band finally gave way. "Get in your truck and go for a drive until they leave."

Sheriff Red Hozen was desperate. There was a frantic edge to the guy that was getting worse the longer this went on. Spinning out of control, he was becoming more intense, more frantic, and my concern now was to make sure that he didn't take Uncle Ziggy away.

It wouldn't be a calm, routine arrest. He'd take his frustration out on Ziggy, might even decide that Ziggy could tell him what he wanted to know and not mind how he got his information. Uncle Ziggy could have a terrible accident while in his custody.

On top of this, Uncle Ziggy would not behave well if he were arrested, wouldn't wait calmly until we got a lawyer. He would shout his indignation and disgust to the rooftops.

Uncle Ziggy rubbed the red welts on his wrists. "Nope, staying right here, they want me they can take me but I ain't going anywhere, not leavin' you and Tully, no way no how, never ran in my life and I'm too old to develop new habits." He went on grumbling and rubbing his wrists on his way to the fridge. Taking out a beer, he said "Sons of bitches acting like they're above the law, it ain't right." He handed me the beer and got one out for himself.

"The sheriff may forget about you if he doesn't see you."

"I'm staying," he said and shuffled off to watch the search with his beer in his hand.

I pulled out a chair and sat down. Where in hell was

Ramiro? Why hadn't they found him? I sat there letting the cold liquid slide down my throat and waiting for the next piece of bad news.

My cell rang. It was Clay. I'd forgotten that Brian was up in Cedar Key with Clay. Brian was working out the refinancing deal with him. I hadn't thought of that when I'd called Brian. Brian had been waiting for Clay when he came out of a meeting and told him about the search of the barn. I tried to explain the situation to Clay. It did not go well. I hung up, promising to call him back and explain everything as soon as the sheriff left. I shut off my phone.

Marley stuck her head in the door. "That nice young officer, Mike Quinn, just asked me out. What do think?"

"Think you better get your shots against peckerwood before you say yes."

"You've become truly negative when it comes to men." She came the rest of the way through the door, letting it swing shut behind her, and reached for my beer.

I leaned close to Marley. "Why didn't they find him?" I whispered.

She shrugged. "Don't know." She tilted the beer up and emptied it down her throat. "I don't think I mind peckerwood."

"Let's get through this before you make any rash judgments."

"Fine." She set the empty back on the table. "Come help me watch these guys so they don't pocket anything."

Her keen delight in possessions was even stronger than fear, or maybe now the searchers had left the barn she thought the worst was over, relaxing back into the comfort of things known, like keeping the floors clean.

But we weren't out of the woods yet, weren't even close to the edge of our woods. "After your imitation of a Christian martyr waiting for the lions they wouldn't dare touch anything."

"One can only hope," she said and went off to make sure.

An ATV roared to life. I went to the screen door. Boomer peeled around the other vehicles and charged towards the house. Torn between running for help and wanting to know what he was up to, I braced myself on the door frame and waited for him. At the edge of the porch steps he stopped. He looked up at the screen door. "I'm coming for you, bitch," he yelled.

He peeled away, heading for his pickup. Hardly slowing, he drove his ATV up onto the flatbed trailer he was towing. I watched as he jumped from the gate and lifted the ramp, struggling with the locking mechanism.

"What are you planning, Boomer?" Fear made me wrap my arms around myself and hug my anxiety to me.

Something moved on the roof of the barn, catching my eye. "Oh, God, no."

Boomer was focused on the house, planning his revenge, and didn't see what I saw.

"Please," I prayed. "Please don't let Boomer turn. Don't let him look up."

Boomer stamped to the open door of his truck, climbed in and slammed the door behind him.

CHAPTER 47

I bolted upstairs, wanting to block the one window that would reveal the north part of the barn roof.

Upstairs, the guys making up the search party were just going through the motions, obeying orders hurriedly and doing their best not to offend. They looked in closets, under beds and pretty much moved quickly on through the rooms, no longer committed to the program, and not believing they were going to find their runaway on Riverwood. They just wanted out with whatever dignity they had left.

The men trailed down the stairs and bunched up in the hall. Some slid past the sheriff, saying polite goodbyes to Marley and went out onto the veranda in their sock feet, distancing themselves from the sheriff and wanting to be gone.

Red Hozen knew he'd lost the men. He let out a defeated sigh. "All right," he said. He looked around the hall. "I'll leave one of my men here."

"Isn't necessary, Sheriff," Tully said. "We can take care of it."

"No," the sheriff said and looked around for support, looking for someone to volunteer to stay behind. No one would meet his eye as they slipped past him. None of the men were putting themselves forward as the guy to be left behind. They quickly went out onto the veranda and retrieved their boots. Some carried them around to the back of the house, wanting to be away from the sheriff.

The sheriff wasn't happy. He was either going to call one of them back or stay himself. "Shit," he said and stomped out the door, the only man who hadn't removed his boots. He seemed to have forgotten that Ziggy had attacked one of his men with a shovel or maybe he didn't want the whole story to be told to a judge. Now we just had to hope he didn't order one more search of the barn. We stood on the porch and watched them load up their machines.

"Is it over?" Marley whispered. "Is he safe?"

I stopped her. "Are they all gone? Have they left anyone behind?" We looked back into the house. When Jimmy was murdered, my apartment had been broken into. It never felt the same after that, felt alien and foreign, like the guys who broke in still lingered. I felt that now.

"Seems like they're all gone," Tully said, but still we were all uneasy.

"Just like those sons of bitches to leave someone behind, those buggers don't care about rules or laws," Ziggy said. "I tell you I'd like to have had the shotgun, I'd of taught them some manners."

We watched the last of the vehicles pull away. "We have to check on the mare and straighten some of those bales," Tully said. "Is everything all right in the house?"

"Yeah," Marley told him. "They were really quite nice about it."

"You stay with the girls, Ziggy. I'm going to make sure everything is okay in the barn. I'll need to patch the hole in the roof."

"Clay will be home come the weekend," I told him. "He can worry about it."

Tully frowned at my slowness. "Oh," I said, realizing Tully wasn't really concerned about the hole, just speaking for anyone who might be listening. And we all thought someone was listening. We still felt the presence of our unwanted visitors. It's hard to feel comfortable in your home when strangers have tramped through it.

"We'll check real good and see they didn't leave anything behind," Uncle Ziggy said.

"Let Dog out of the bathroom and keep him with you," Tully told us. "He'll tell you pretty quick if anyone stayed behind." Tully headed for the barn while Zig followed Marley, saying, "I'm going upstairs with Marley and make sure everything is all right." We wouldn't trust it was over until we'd checked every corner. I headed for the powder room to let Dog out.

Marley and I were on the back porch waiting when Tully came out of the barn. He climbed the steps slowly, deep lines of tiredness etched on his face. All of this was too much for him. If I chased him out to the bunkhouse for a nap he'd get stubborn and refuse, but he was looking like he was about to drop.

"Well?" Marley said impatiently. "Is he all right?"

Tully nodded. "He did exactly what he did to get away from the Breslaus the first time. He didn't stay in his hiding place but went up. He was up on the roof, hanging onto the edge of the hatch opening while the posse was searching."

"I saw him go back inside," I said. "It's a miracle no one else saw him."

Tully sank down onto a chair. "His hands are sliced and bleeding from the edge of the metal roof. We need to take out some bandages and ointment and clean those cuts."

"Okay," Marley said. "I'll take care of it." The screen door slammed behind her.

"Why didn't he let go when he heard that shot?" I wondered. "I would have."

I sat on the railing thinking what it would be like to hang from a hot tin roof, twenty or thirty feet about hard-pack ground, with the metal cutting into your hands and waiting to be discovered. And then a gun goes off.

A vehicle entered the yard. I jerked around to see who it was and then I got to my feet.

CHAPTER 48

"Jesus, what now?" Tully asked. "Maybe they've sent someone back."

"Wait," I put out a hand to stop him from rising. "I know that van." Beat up and crapped out, it had been used more than once to pick up supplies for the Sunset. "It's Miguel."

"Who?"

"Miguel, the luncheon chef from the Sunset." Miguel and I'd worked together for about five years and over those years we'd become friends. One night, when Jimmy and I were at the height of our marital wars, Miguel had come to my rescue. And when Hurricane Myrna hit Jacaranda, Miguel and his family moved into my apartment. Miguel was the kind of guy you wanted to see when trouble was about. I went to meet him.

"What are you doing here?" I asked. Not the most gracious of welcomes but it was a surprise to see him — and a worry. The night might bring more grief than I wanted to think about.

Miguel hitched his jeans and said, "Rosie was doing homework and she read your e-mail."

"Shit. I'm sorry, Miguel, sorry if I upset her."

"No importa," he said. "What's happening here? I've been trying to call but your phone is off. It says your voicemail is full."

"Damn. I'm sorry, Miguel, I turned off my phone when the sheriff gave my cell back to me. I must have scared the life out of everyone." When I sent that e-mail, I was just doing what I always do in times of trouble, gathering friends around me like a blanket. "I better send a new message. The sheriff just left. He searched the house and barn."

"What did he find?" Miguel asked.

"No one he was looking for. But why did you come? It isn't safe for you here."

"You're here," he responded, indignantly. "Is it safe for you to be here?"

"Well, it's sort of my place, at least until Clay gets back."

"So, the fact that you live with Clay, that makes this your problem?"

"Yes, but it isn't your problem."

"*Por que?*"

"Look, there are some real bad guys out here. Ones you don't want to mess with. You have a family, Miguel, go back to Jacaranda."

"How do you think my parents got here?" He shoved his hands in his back pockets. "The man they are looking for, well it could have been one of my family."

"Okay, but what happens to your family if you get hurt or in trouble?"

He considered my question for a moment. "I have a family but I have a country too, this is my country now. No way I'm going to let some bastards destroy it without trying to stop them. This can't happen here. Not anymore."

"That's hard to get your head around, isn't it? That this can happen here? We hear of it happening other places and we say, 'Oh, well, what do you expect in a place like that?' But not here."

"So I will stay." His flat statement left no room for argument.

"Was there a police car at the end of the lane when you came in?"

"*Si*, he wasn't happy to let me in."

"They don't want people here. You can't get away with as much when you have witnesses, harder to cover up."

A smile lit his face. "And that's why I'm staying...to be a witness, *si, el testigo*."

I started to argue with him but another car was pulling in.

"Maybe this is the man the sheriff is sending to watch us. Why don't you go up on the porch," I suggested. "The sheriff and his men were looking for a Hispanic man; they might not discriminate between them. Jesus, Miguel, this so isn't where you should be. Go in the house."

"You want me to hide?"

"God, no." And then I recognized the driver. "Holy shit."

Miguel looked from me to the car. "*Quien?*" Miguel asked.

I didn't tell him who it was. Instead I said, "I don't believe this."

Anil Pereira, my wine merchant, and his wife, Sheryl, pulled up beside us. But before their doors opened, another car swung into the yard.

"What have I done?"

It was only the beginning. Over the next hour the area in front of the house and around the barn filled with cars.

When people couldn't get me on the phone and the e-mails they sent weren't answered, some of my friends got in their cars and headed for Independence to find out for themselves what was happening. A few people saw the deputy blocking the lane and kept on going, going home to send messages that began, "I hope you are all right." But an amazing number, like Anil and Sheryl, demanded to be let in.

When most of them got out of their cars they were truly frightened at what they were letting themselves in for. But like Miguel they were all there to be witnesses.

I really don't know how many people finally came to Riverwood. In ones and twos they got out of their cars, talking to each other, getting angry or being quietly proud but most of all they were determined to see justice done.

Tully snaked his way through the crowd towards me, leaned over and whispered, "Remind me never to share a secret with you," then shook his head in disgust and disappeared out to the barn to sit with Ramiro.

Miguel and I followed him to the barn. Tully was sitting on the bottom step to the loft, ready to stop anyone from climbing the stairs. He and Miguel went upstairs and brought Ramiro down. Ramiro was crying when he came down with Miguel, frightened and traumatized.

I held out my cell phone. "Tell him to call home," I told Miguel. The call took some time and brought on another wave of emotion. Then we took Ramiro to sit on the front porch while our guests sat on the hoods of cars, leaned against them or stood on the grass to watch while Marley finished bathing his hands and poured peroxide over them. After she wrapped bandages around them, Ramiro cupped a mug of soup gingerly in his hands.

And then, with fresh water in the pan, Marley washed Ramiro's damaged feet. People watched silently, caught up in a modern rendition of the sacred rite.

All through this, Miguel talked quietly to Ramiro. When Marley finished drying Ramiro's feet and rubbing salve on them, Miguel leaned against the pillar at the top of the steps and interpreted while Ramiro told his story once more. Ramiro's voice was almost inaudible in the beginning, but after a few minutes Ramiro got up from the creaking wicker chair and limped to the railing, leaning out to look people in the eye. Impassioned and intense, speaking faster than Miguel could translate, he told his story.

Tears began to flow down faces. Listeners were breaking down all over the place, and not just the women. Maybe it was a loss of innocence and having to live with this new reality, the realization that even in the greatest nation on earth this could happen. No one is safe from evil and we aren't protected from the worst depravities of humanity by an accident of birth.

When Ramiro was finished, everyone started grumbling and speaking at once. The noise was deafening.

They all had a different idea about how to make Ramiro safe and how to end the horror he'd been through. None of their suggestions were pretty and some were downright vicious.

"How can this happen?" Anil Pereira asked. "I just can't believe it."

"Greed, that's what this is about," Jack Harris answered. There was a nodding of heads. "Greed and corruption are ruining this country." More nodding of heads, more anger. "Hang the bastards," Jack roared.

A cheer went up. Confidence, pride and anger were growing in the crowd. They were taking something back they'd lost. Anil, always calm, started, "Elected officials represent us," but was interrupted by Jack shouting, "They don't represent me."

There's always one politician in every crowd and Jack was turning into ours. As he started into a long diatribe about dishonest politicians, people were talking back, shouting out their encouragement or their objections.

If the sheriff turned up now, if they tried to take Ramiro away, there would be blood, a riot of it. And it wouldn't all be Ramiro's. They were also close to turning into a mob.

Exhaustion, lack of food and fear took their toll. Ramiro slumped down onto the porch, unable to stay on his feet. Marley moved down beside him and put her arm around him. "Look at him. We have to get him to a doctor."

After loud discussions it was decided that we would take him out of Independence in one long line, the first cars stopping to be checked and when the deputy moved aside the whole line would follow without stopping, head back to Jacaranda in a long convoy heading straight to the hospital.

It sounded like a good plan to me but some felt that the whole line of cars would be checked before the deputy moved aside. Others feared that the car holding Ramiro might get separated from the rest while some argued that we'd lose control once Ramiro was in the hospital and we couldn't protect him.

"Whatever we do, he needs a doctor," Marley said.

Tully put in. "And a shower and clean clothes won't hurt either. After that we can decide what we need to do."

They didn't need any help from me. I turned away and headed for the kitchen with Miguel following me.

"This isn't the party I'd planned," I said as I turned on the tap and washed my hands. "But it looks like it might be turning into a good one."

He laughed. "I never went to a better one, Sherri." He looked in the fridge and started pulling out stuff. "What's in the freezer?"

"Everything. I can't help myself. Talk about greed, I just keep on buying." I pulled three-quarters of a French stick out of plastic wrap. "I'll slice this really thin, toast it with garlic butter and chop some nice fresh tomatoes to put on top." I stopped in shock and looked at Miguel. "Tomatoes, who the hell picked these tomatoes? Do you think they were picked by slave labor?"

"It's a question we'll be asking ourselves for a long time, but we can't just throw out all the tomatoes just in case. We still have to live."

And there was the quandary of our lives. Even if we want to do the right thing, how can we identify what the right thing is?

"Is there any basil?" Miguel asked, putting aside unsolvable problems.

"Nope, but there's a bunch of parsley. I'm going to use parsley, black olives and onions instead of basil on the tomatoes." The one thing Miguel and I knew how to do was to serve the customers.

"Okay," he agreed and we started our dance to the kitchen gods, moving smoothly around each other, handing things off like America's best dance team. People wandered into the kitchen and were given things to pass, chop or fetch. We couldn't seem to help ourselves. From depression and disgust came a feeling of bonding and togetherness, of wanting to stay in this tribe we belonged to, wanting to say that we would stop bad things from happening to each other and celebrate the good.

Sheryl Pereira, a writer for *Floridian Life* magazine and a beauty with ice green eyes, came into the kitchen and asked if she could help. I handed her napkins and a plate of veggies to pass around. Out on the lawn, tramping the weeds into dust, people argued about what needed to be done, took the food she offered and went right on arguing.

The fairy lights came on, waved and twinkled in the breeze, and went unnoticed. The barbeque was lit, chicken, hotdogs, burgers and all the goodies meant for Clay's birthday party were pulled out. Miguel created amazing salads out of the cans in the store room, like black beans and corn along with parsley, tomatoes and celery. With every vegetable I chopped, I wondered. But as Miguel pointed out, people have to eat.

Mary Lou Churchill, an emergency nurse at Jacaranda Hospital, came back into the kitchen from checking on Ramiro and told me, "Sleep is the best thing for him right now. Tully is keeping watch on a chair by his door."

I picked up the celery out of the colander and said, "Tully should tell Ramiro to move over and just stretch out with him. It's been a long day and Tully is dead on his feet."

Lou and I had been friends since high school. We know the

gritty bits of each other's lives and don't have to fill in a lot of back story. I stopped chopping and looked up at her. "Have you any idea how sick Tully is?"

"Nope," she answered. "Have you?"

"I'm only his daughter. The doctor won't talk to me. That's why I'm asking you."

"Why would I know?" She pulled a stick of celery from the colander.

"'Cause I know he was at the hospital for tests. Couldn't you just look up those tests and see what's going on?"

"No. Why don't you ask Tully?"

"He claims he's in perfect health."

"Well, don't ask me, I can't help you."

I picked up a tray of cheese and crackers. "Then if you haven't any information for me, at least make yourself useful by passing around this tray."

"Yes, ma'am."

Uncle Ziggy took a couple of buckets to get the beer and wine from the fridge in the bunkhouse. Along with the beer, he returned with his old boombox and the greatest hits from the sixties. Sheer craziness broke out…dancing in the face of the unbelievable.

And so began our first party at Riverwood.

CHAPTER 49

Lou came back into the kitchen. "There's a man out there asking for you. Better hurry, people are getting pretty worked up. You could see he was someone official the moment he got out of the car. They won't let him near the house."

I dried my hands as I went.

On the steps to the porch, Jack stopped me and said, "How do we know he isn't with the sheriff's department?"

I looked at the man in a suit. He looked quite calm despite the fact that he was surrounded by people who were clearly angry. "Are you with the sheriff's department?" I asked.

"No. I'm Ian Welbee from the Department of Immigration. Detective Styles sent me."

"Thank God," I said. "The cavalry has arrived."

A cheer went up.

"Come on up," I told him.

"Wait," Jack said. "Don't you think we should know what's going to happen to Ramiro first?"

I wanted to kick him. I just wanted someone else to be

responsible. But all around us people started to worry out loud that Ramiro would be sent back to Guatemala. There were offers to sponsor him, to give him a job and all sorts of things in between.

I was betting, on sober reflection in the morning that they'd all have second thoughts, enthusiasm giving away to caution. Tomorrow they'd be worrying about this stranger they were taking into their lives. Or maybe I was just being cynical but I've seen too many morning-after recaps not to know how these things happen, although Ramiro's rescue was bound to have a better outcome than most bursts of enthusiasm fueled by food and booze. Hopefully together we could make it happen without any one of us risking all.

"Let's just tell Agent Welbee what went on and take it from there," I said.

While Ramiro slept overhead with Tully standing guard, Marley and Miguel sat down with agent Welbee in the dining room and told him the story from start to finish.

I added what I'd learned from April. "I think when the gates are closed they have their captives on the property. She said Lucan only worked when the gates were closed. April said she didn't know what was happening but I think she knows more than she told me."

I turned over April's telephone number. "The Breslau place is surrounded by eight-foot chain-link and guarded by dogs. You'll need company when you go in."

"Oh, don't you worry about that, we'll go prepared."

"And they're armed. Everyone on those ATVs had a rifle. I

don't know how many men will be at Oxbow but there will be at least three, Harland Breslau, Orlin Breslau and Boomer. He's the one you really have to watch. There won't be any reasoning with him."

He nodded. "I'll keep that in mind." He didn't seem too impressed with the idea of Boomer.

"Are you going to tell the sheriff you have Ramiro?"

"No," Agent Welbee said. "I think your plan of leaving in a group is a good one."

"What about the sheriff's deputy when you take Ramiro out? He's been stopping us every time we go out. If you tell him you're an immigration officer he'll repeat it to the sheriff and the Breslaus will be warned."

He grinned at me. "Hey, we're just a couple of guys leaving a party."

"Okay, and Ramiro?"

"Just one of the guys. They haven't been flashing around a picture of him, have they?"

"No. I doubt they have one."

"Then they won't recognize him with clean clothes. He can pretend to nap like he's had a little too much to drink."

"You better make sure you explain all this to Ramiro so he doesn't panic."

He gave me a look that said he wasn't really interested in advice from me. Funny, I get that look a lot.

Ramiro didn't get much rest. Welbee woke him and he got to tell his story all over again and then Agent Welbee took Ramiro away, probably to be held in another jail. His freedom had been an illusion but at least he would be better treated and he would be safe. Lots of people from the party would be checking in on him and offering their support. It was the best we could do. The convoy idea everyone supported earlier was put into effect. A line of vehicles went out the drive with Welbee and Ramiro in the fourth car.

Those of us remaining at the house were pretty subdued, talking in soft tones and whispers, waiting and expecting a bomb to go off or shots to ring out.

A comfort level had been removed with the people who'd left. The few people remaining grew restless, uneasy in the night that seemed darker outside the circle of Japanese lanterns and fairy lights. We'd all come too close to evil to feel safe anymore.

My cell rang and everyone went silent.

"It was a non-event," Agent Welbee told me. "We told the deputy the party was over and he just moved out of the way and let us all out."

"Do you think he had any idea what was going on?"

"No way of knowing, but he knew a no-win situation when he saw it."

The half-dozen people remaining were in a hurry to be gone now and they drove out the lane together, calling when they had cleared Independence to tell us they were all right, wanting to reassure not only us but also themselves that they were out of the danger zone.

But we weren't. That small fact was becoming clearer and clearer with each car that left.

CHAPTER 50

As the last of the taillights disappeared, I said to Tully, "Maybe we should go into Jacaranda for a few days."

"Who will look after the horses?" he asked.

I heaved a sigh. "Let's discuss it in the morning," I said. "Truthfully, I'm too whacked to even think about driving anywhere tonight."

"Me too," Tully agreed. "Just don't have the energy I once had." His eyes were dark and sunken.

"Go to bed. No need to roam the corridors tonight, we know now there's no one out there in the dark, creeping up on us."

"We know that, do we?"

I shivered. "Go to bed anyway. Tomorrow we'll decide what to do."

He tipped up a long neck and drained it. He set the empty bottle on the porch railing saying, "That's the best idea I've heard all day."

"Sleep in the bunkhouse so no one disturbs you."

"Nope, I'll stick to the house. The Breslaus don't know their problem has moved on."

"I'm trying not to think about that, just telling myself it's over."

"They have to know from the sheriff that there was a load of people here tonight, that might keep them away. Then again—" he hesitated, staring off into the darkness as if he might be able to see what dangers hid there.

Overhead the Japanese lanterns swayed and shone brightly. Their gaiety didn't stop the fear Tully's words delivered.

"It isn't over, is it?" I asked.

"Not by a long shot. This has gotten real personal. I don't think there's much reasoning left with Boomer. He's just plain crazy. It's about more than Ramiro now and even Jacaranda might not be safe. He's going to come after you and when he does I'm going to be here."

Tears stung my eyes. I put a hand up to wipe them as the lights of a car swept across the clearing of the yard, too late for someone coming to our aid. Was it the final unknown danger we'd been dreading? Tully and I looked at each other. I reached out a hand for Tully, wanting the comfort of touching him.

"I'll get the rifle," Tully said.

"Wait." I knew the car. I flew down the steps to grab the edge of the car door as it opened.

Clay rose from inside the car and took me in his arms. "You all right?" he asked, into my hair.

"I am now you're here."

I bent back in his arms and took stock. Clay's obsidian eyes were tired, but they crinkled into a smile. It was those eyes that first attracted me to him. Hard and unyielding and giving away nothing, those eyes watched me pulling pints and delivering drinks a long time before Clay acted. Lean and darkly handsome, he was wearing a dress shirt with the tie undone and no suit jacket. He looked perfect to me.

"Man, you scared us," he said softly.

Brian rose out of the passenger seat of the car and looked over its roof at me. "What in hell is going on?" he demanded.

It took a while to explain.

It was one in the morning. Brian was asleep in the den off the kitchen, Zig had gone to the bunkhouse and Marley had dragged herself upstairs.

Tully announced, "I'm off to bed," and made for the hall. At the door he turned back to look at Clay. "When you gonna make me a grandpa, boy?"

"I'm working on it, sir."

"Well, work a little harder," Tully ordered. "C'mon Dog, you better sleep with me tonight." Dog clicked down the hall behind Tully and followed him up the stairs.

With a lift of his shoulder and a smile Clay said, "Well, you heard the man."

I laughed. "It's going to take more than an order from Tully Jenkins to make that happen."

Later, Dog sounded the alarm, telling us the situation was even worse than we knew.

CHAPTER 51

Fighting to come awake, I asked, "What?"

Out in the dark, Dog's bark was a crazed and vicious sound. A gun exploded. Someone yelled.

I jerked upright, my heart pounding while Clay bolted out of bed.

A second gunshot, louder and heavier, answered the first. "What's happening?" I asked.

I reached for the light.

"Don't," Clay said. "Don't turn on the light."

I lowered my hand, looking to the window. We hadn't pulled the drapes. The light would make us targets, backlit and vulnerable. "Oh." I pulled the tangled sheet across my chest, crippled with panic and fear while Clay's shadowy image pulled on clothes.

"Tully?" I asked. "Was that Tully yelling?"

Clay was at the closet, taking down the wooden box that contained his handgun.

Outside, Uncle Ziggy or Brian, I couldn't tell which, shouted, "Tully, Tully. Where the hell are you, Tully?"

"He must be outside," I said. "Oh, Clay, what's happened to him?" It was a stupid question. How could he know any more than I did?

He searched the back of a drawer for the box that contained the shells. "Stay here." There was the click of the safety being released and Clay was gone.

"It's my dad," I told the empty room. "Someone shot my dad."

I picked up the phone and dialed 911. It was Sheriff Hozen's men who would come with the ambulance, might even be his men out there in the dark, but dialing the emergency number was all I could do.

A calm woman's voice asked me questions, while I searched the floor for my jeans. The night had not ended tidily. Clothes had been discarded in frantic haste. My foot hit rough denim. I pulled on the jeans, phone cradled in my shoulder, and searched for my tee-shirt. In the moonlight I could see Clay's white shirt puddled on the floor. I picked it up.

"I have to go," I told the woman and dropped the phone.

In the hall the red transom over the front door blocked the light of the moon. Carefully, feeling for each step in the dark, I slid along the banister and down the stairs. Scrambled voices came from the back of the house.

The shotgun, where was the shotgun? Hadn't Ziggy left it upstairs in the junk room? I hesitated, about to go back up the stairs to get it. But it wouldn't be there now. Uncle Ziggy would have it with him.

"What's wrong? What's going on?" Marley asked from the top of the stairs. Her white nightshirt hovered there like a ghost in the dark.

"I don't know what's happening. Don't turn on the lights. It will…" I couldn't tell her that it would make us targets. "I'll come back and tell you what's happening as soon as I know."

"No," she said. Her night shirt bobbed down the stairs. Beside me at the newel post she said, "They don't know Ramiro's gone, do they?"

"No."

She turned slightly away from me and then moved in close. "The front door's open," she whispered. "I can feel the air."

"It's okay. Clay must have gone out that way."

But had he? The two of us stood there, barely daring to breathe, straining to hear, to pick up wisps of data from the very air around us. There was only silence, no smell, no sound and no awareness of anyone else. Night settled down. No voices called, no dog howled. The old house creaked and groaned, easing its warped bones back down.

The two of us were alone in the dark house, unarmed and with someone laying siege to Riverwood. Had I done the right thing in calling more of them in?

Marley's breath was warm on the side of my face when she whispered, "I'm going to close that door."

"Why?"

She didn't answer, just tiptoed softly towards the front door.

I took a deep breath, exhaled and started boldly for the kitchen.

As I passed the powder room under the stairs an arm snaked out and captured me. "I told you I was coming for you, bitch."

CHAPTER 52

My toes fought to touch the hardwood floor. The forearm across my throat cut off my air. I couldn't scream. I could barely breathe.

"I'm going to kill you, kill every living thing on this farm."

A sound gurgled from my lips, nothing loud enough or strong enough to be heard by anyone, anyone except Marley creeping back in. Behind us I heard the slap of bare feet running. The front door squeaked. Boomer swung me, a rag doll hanging from his arm, around to face the door.

My nails dug into his forearm.

"Who was that?" His bristled face scratched across mine. The smell of stale beer wafted from his mouth. "Was that your little friend? Don't matter, my friends out there will get her."

Boomer's arm tightened around my neck. The muzzle of a handgun bored into my side. He pushed and lifted me forward into the kitchen. "I'm going to kill you first, bitch, and then her." He shoved me into the kitchen and dragged me in front of him to the door.

Only the screen separated us from the night. Headlights swept into the yard, red lights pulsing on the roof like blood, the light throbbing in the kitchen.

Motion detectors turned on the barn lights. The car hesitated at the barn and then came on towards the house. It halted at the edge of the lawn. The door of the car swung open and a tall figure stepped out.

"In the house," Marley screamed from somewhere on the porch. "He's got Sherri."

A beam of light from a flashlight led the figure towards the back door. Boomer's arm rose from his side. "Come on, sucker." His voice was a low growl in his throat.

The porch light flicked on, freezing the deputy in its glare. "No," I screamed.

The sound of the gun was deafening. The flashlight fell. Then the figure holding it crumbled slowly. When the man reached the ground, Boomer shot again. The form on the lawn jumped in response.

Boomer pressed me up against the ragged screen door, the gun raised beside my face. The smell of the gunshot, and Boomer's body odor, filled my nose. Crazy, I stared at the hole in the screen and thought of insects I wouldn't be around to worry about.

Intent on the fallen figure, Boomer's arm seemed to tremble, on the edge of shooting one more time, and then he said, "Best save some bullets for you." His arm relaxed. The light went out.

There was a snarl, a blur of something flying towards us, and then the screen imploded.

Boomer's gun blasted in my ear as we tumbled backwards. A shower of plaster fell. Dog yowled and fell in a lump on the floor.

Flat on my back on top of Boomer, my hands were trapped between us. Boomer's arm crossed my chest to shoot at Dog again. I dug my fingers deep into Boomer's crotch and squeezed.

Boomer screamed. His body bucked. I didn't let go until he threw me away.

My body landed on Boomer's arm, the arm with the gun. I twisted on my side and held onto his arm. I dug my nails deep into his wrist and then sank my teeth into his flesh. Another shot blasted into the kitchen wall.

Dog was on Boomer. Boomer was screaming in pain.

I had both hands wrapped around the gun now, not trying to get it away from Boomer as much as I was trying to stop Boomer from using it on Dog.

Boomer let go of the gun and picked up Dog with both hands and threw him out through the screen.

Dog cried out.

Boomer crawled to his knees and got to his feet. He came towards me, saw his gun pointing at him and stopped. He turned back to the door.

With his hand still raised to push the door open, a shot rang out.

Boomer jerked backwards. The screen door bounced open and then shut again as Boomer caught the door frame and pulled himself forward. He stood there as if he couldn't decide what to do next. Another shot. Gradually, slowly, very slowly, Boomer pitched forward. The broken screen held him for a second and then, with a great cry, it released him.

Falling through the frame of the screen, the bottom of the door caught Boomer at the knees and swept him off his feet. He pitched face forward onto the porch with his legs sticking up into the kitchen.

I heard Tully cry, "Don't shoot, my daughter's in there."

Down the hall, at the foot of the stairs, the heavy front door creaked opened. I rolled on my belly to face the door, holding the gun out in front of me.

CHAPTER 53

"It's okay," Marley said.

I laughed. How many times have I heard those words?

Marley crept forward and took the gun from my hand. "It's okay."

She went to the edge of the door and flicked on the porch light. "It's okay," she yelled, staying well back from the opening. "Sherri and I are fine."

I got off the floor and went to huddle beside her with Boomer at our feet. Out in the yard the officer knelt on his right knee, his left leg stretched out to the side with his left arm hanging useless.

"It's Mike Quinn," I said. "I called him peckerwood."

The lights came on at the barn. Tully called, "Don't shoot." Tully walked from the barn with his arms above his head. But Officer Quinn wasn't going to shoot anyone. He didn't even turn to look at Tully, just sorta collapsed back to the ground.

Tully ran to Quinn's side and then looked up at us. "Get towels, lots of them."

But for me everything had shut down.

"I will," Marley said and wrapped her arm around my shoulder. She led me to the front hall, away from Boomer, and out onto the veranda. "Wait here," she said. "I'll be right back."

I barely took in what happened after that. It was just noise and confusion. My body and my mind were frozen, unable to process what I was hearing and seeing. Time stopped.

Clay came from the barn. I recognized the men he pushed along in front of him. I'd seen them in the woods with Boomer. Behind them came Brian.

"Ambulances are coming," Brian said. "How many people are hurt?"

"Just the cop," Tully told him. "Boomer is dead and Dog is shot."

Marley was kneeling in the dirt beside Quinn, pressing towels over his wounds to stop the flow of blood while Tully tended to Dog.

"Why?" Brian was asking, the question we all wanted an answer to.

"He was going to kill me." They were my first words. "He said he was going to kill every living thing on this ranch."

Their eyes, incredulous in pale faces, turned to me.

"He was going to kill us all," I added, wanting them to understand. Clay wrapped me in his arms.

Uncle Ziggy came out of the barn and said, "We have to move the horses." He held up a small plastic pail.

"What is it?" Clay asked.

"Rat poison, I think. Maybe they were trying to kill the

horses, poisoning the water bowls, or maybe they were putting these pellets in their hay bags; either way we have to get those horses out of the stalls before they drink any water or eat any hay." Uncle Ziggy set down the pail and headed back into the barn at a trot.

"Will you be okay?" Clay asked.

I pushed him away from me. "Go."

"Tully, keep these guys covered," Clay said and held out his gun.

Tully rose from beside Dog. "Sherri, come look after Dog."

Dog raised his head and made an attempt to stand up. His hindquarters wouldn't cooperate.

My own legs barely obeyed. I stumbled to Dog's side, fell to my knees, and pushed gently at his shoulder, "Stay down."

A long smear of blood oozed along his hip where the bullet had torn the length of his flank before taking off most of his tail. His tail slapped the ground and blood sprayed from the nub that remained. The warmth of his blood splattered across my face and left a dotted line of red across the front of Clay's white shirt.

"No, no." I said, holding down both his neck and his hindquarters.

A long keening noise came from him. "Shush, you crazy animal." I leaned over and kissed him. "You didn't need that long tail anyway."

But he kept trying to wag his tail, only to send more blood pumping out in an arc. I felt clots of blood hitting my hair. "I need a towel to wrap around the stump." I started to get up. Dog tried getting up as well. "Stay still," I told him.

Tully offered me his shirt. I wrapped it gently around Dog's tail, squeezing tightly. Blood seeped out under my fingers.

"It's okay, Champ," I crooned. "You're gonna be fine." Those same words, the same promises, yet again. What else do we have?

Tully asked, "Champ?"

"We're going to call him Champ because he's a champion, aren't you?" I leaned forward and stroked along the dog's face with my left hand. Champ lifted his head and tried to lick my hand.

"Champ it is," Tully said.

My mind was starting to work again. I asked, "What in hell happened?"

"I've got an old man's prostate, had to get up to take a leak and couldn't go back to sleep. I was going out on the back porch to have a smoke, left the rifle on the kitchen table. Champ was with me. He started to growl, started to go crazy. He went for the barn and I went for my gun. I heard the first shot before I got to the barn. I went for the back of the barn, because the motion light had come on out front when Champ went in those front doors, figured whoever Champ was after would want to avoid the light. There was no car so I figured the guy in the barn had gone in from the back of the barn, come from the woods."

I stroked Champ's leg as I listened to Tully.

"I met this guy coming out back." He waved the gun at the guy on his right. "Bastard tried to kill me. He was quick but I grazed him, drove him back in. Then Zig and Clay came and had the front covered. We had them cornered. That's when the cop showed up. We didn't know Boomer was in the house."

"I'm glad he's dead," I said. "We never would have had a safe night again with him alive. He would have come after us until someone died."

"Yup," Tully said. "And we're lucky that young deputy was sitting in a car at the end of the lane. Keep that tight around Champ's tail until it clots. And try and keep the silly fool from wagging it." He patted me on the head. "Soon as Clay gets back to watch these guys I'll go in the house and get something to bandage it with."

I sat there with Champ, thinking that it was over. But the evil hadn't died with Boomer.

CHAPTER 54

Cars from the sheriff's department filled the yard before the last of the horses had been moved to new stalls. Red Hozen wasn't with them.

Two ambulances came. They loaded up the guy Tully had wounded.

Marley held Mike Quinn's hand as they wheeled him to the ambulance. "Please," he said softly to Marley as they started to put him inside.

"May I go with him?" Marley asked and climbed up inside the ambulance without waiting for them to agree.

Champ wasn't trying to stand anymore. He seemed sleepy and lethargic, perhaps from shock or perhaps from blood loss. Tully and Ziggy wanted to take him to a vet. A bit of a noisy argument broke out when the deputies wouldn't allow Tully and Ziggy to leave the property. Tully and Ziggy put Champ on a blanket and carried him into the bunkhouse between them, away from the noise and confusion to keep him warm and quiet until they could get him help.

We weren't allowed back into the house because it was a crime scene so I sat on the front step with Clay, who rocked me in his arms until I stopped shivering.

As the night slipped away, each one of us gave a statement. The body of Boomer Breslau was photographed and moved to a stretcher from a mortuary van. The body was being wheeled to the van when a gray sedan pulled up beside it. Agent Welbee got out of the back seat. He was wearing an armored vest.

We rose and went to meet him.

"Hold up a minute," Agent Welbee called to the mortuary guys. He went to the trunk and took out a wheelchair.

The driver of the sedan opened the back door for Harland Breslau. He held Harland's arm as they came around to the front of the car. Harland's hands were locked and folded in front of him, and he looked around in confusion while the agent opened the passenger door, reaching in to help Amanda to her feet. When she was on her feet, Amanda held onto the top of the door and looked to Clay and me, never looking at the stretcher draped in white. Agent Welbee rolled her chair into place. She positioned herself over the chair. With Agent Welbee and the driver supporting Amanda, together they lowered her onto the seat.

Harland shuffled closer to the wheelchair. His eyes were downcast, fixed on the top of Amanda's head, and his fingers picked at the rubber handle of the wheelchair. Amanda sat there regally, composed and elegant.

Clay whispered. "Who are they?"

"Harland and Amanda Breslau."

"No shit?"

Agent Welbee moved Harland aside and pushed Amanda's chair to the stretcher. We followed.

The agent lifted the sheet. A moan of shock escaped Harland. Amanda reached out for the stretcher, clasped the edge of it and pulled to lift herself. Agent Welbee helped her rise. "Is this your son, Justin Breslau?"

Amanda stared down in silence for some time before she nodded. "Yes, that's Justin." She twisted her body and looked over her shoulder towards Clay and me. Her face twisted and for a moment I saw Boomer again.

"Sit down, Mrs. Breslau," Agent Welbee said, clasping her arm and easing her down. He turned her chair to face us.

"He was shot by a deputy," I told her. It was like I was trying to remove myself from any responsibility.

"Why?" Harland wailed. "I don't understand — why was he here?"

"Boomer came here to kill me." I pushed hair back from my face. "He was going to kill us all."

"We knew nothing of this," Amanda put in. "It has nothing to do with us." Her voice was harsh and angry.

"Are they under arrest?" I asked Agent Welbee.

"Yes."

"What for?" Clay asked.

"For illegal confinement."

"What?" Harland wailed. It was as if he was unaware of the handcuffs, had been in a coma when they were put on and suddenly came alive outside our barn. "What are you talking about?"

Agent Welbee replied, "I already told you the charge when

I Mirandized you." He started to explain again but Harland cut him off. "Both of us? But you can't arrest Amanda. Why would you arrest Amanda?

"Harland, it's okay." Amanda raised a hand to comfort him. "It's a mistake; it will be cleared up."

But Harland wasn't having it. "You can't take my wife into custody." He clasped her hand in both of his. "Can't you see she's not well?"

"Harland, shush," Amanda said. "They might as well take me if they're taking you. I can't go home without you."

The truth and the tragedy of this statement were only too evident.

Behind me Clay wrapped his arms around my shoulders and pulled me to him. I leaned back into the warmth of his body.

Harland was begging now, "Please, let me take my wife home."

"I'm afraid not," agent Welbee responded. "I already told you, you both have to answer questions involving trafficking in humans."

"What do you mean trafficking in humans?" Harland protested, outraged at the thought. For a moment I almost believed he'd had no part in it, he was so totally amazed.

Welbee began to explain with a voice that might just as well have been telling Harland how to plant potatoes. "Human trafficking is defined as forced labor obtained not only through the use of force but also the threat of physical force, and restraining or confining another human being unlawfully. Transportation, soliciting, harboring or obtaining another human for transport is defined as human trafficking. We have a witness who says you were involved in these activities and we have agents at twenty-nine River Road, searching your property for evidence as we speak. If they find any evidence that you, or the rest of your family, were in any way involved in this activity, that you were holding aliens unlawfully, it will go very hard on you. We are taking you to our office so you can tell your side of the story now. Mr. Breslau senior and Sheriff Hozen are already under arrest." Agent Welbee turned to look at me, "When your 911 call came in, we already had Sheriff Hozen in custody. The sheriff's office called Sheriff Hozen and we intercepted the call. We brought Mr. and Mrs. Breslau here to identify their son."

"But," Harland said, shaking his head in denial. "None of this is our fault." Tears ran down his face. "We didn't do it."

"Hush now, my darling. Don't say anything." Amanda put his hand to her lips. Tears slid over her cheeks.

Harland wasn't listening. He croaked out, "Can I take my wife home now?" He didn't seem to be able to grasp the concept that he wouldn't be able to walk away as if nothing had happened. He just didn't understand anything beyond Amanda.

"No sir," Agent Welbee's voice was flat and patient. "I have a warrant for your arrest. I've explained that."

"But what will happen to my wife?" Harland wailed. "You can see she couldn't ever hurt anyone. She wasn't part of this. And she needs me." Not even what happened to Boomer and his father penetrated Harland's concern for his wife.

"Harland won't harm anyone ever again if you just let him go," Amanda promised.

"What about Lucan Percell, doesn't his life mean anything?" I asked.

"What are you talking about?" Amanda leaned on her forearms, raising herself in her outrage. "Harland didn't have anything to do with that."

"Didn't he?" I jerked away from Clay, every bit as angry as Amanda. "It was the night Ramiro went missing, the night they were moving workers and Ramiro escaped. Harland never went to the Gator Hole but he did that night, the night Lucan died."

"That isn't a crime," Amanda said, "Going into a bar."

"No, but murder is. If Boomer had killed Lucan, well, he would have just killed Lucan and left him lying there, and Orlin's arthritis would never have let him lift Lucan into the truck." I looked from Amanda up to Harland. "But you're strong, Harland. You lift Amanda all the time. She told me last Saturday how strong and fit you are. And you promised me the murderer hadn't damaged my truck. Such a careful man."

Amanda looked up at him, uncertain. "Harland?"

His wail of distress was full of self-pity. "I had to," he assured her. "Lucan was going to tell. He wanted to put Justin in jail so he would stay away from Lucan's daughter. Lucan didn't even care if it meant he was going to jail too, didn't care if I went to jail."

"Why didn't you just make Boomer stay away from Kelly Sweet?" I asked.

He shook his head. "Couldn't, never could control him. His grandpa raised Justin. We had no say." Tears washed Harland's face. "Neither my son nor my father cared about us. I asked my father to sell enough land so that Amanda and I could have a little place on our own, away from them and start a new life. He wouldn't do it. Said we weren't in the business of selling land. Said we were going to keep the land together, going to keep all of us together. He wouldn't let us go."

"Can't you see?" Amanda said, "We were trapped there just as much as any of those men. We couldn't leave, had nowhere to go, no money of our own and no health care for me. My father-in-law controlled it all."

It seemed the damage they'd done to other people's lives had never entered her head.

Agent Welbee's phone rang.

CHAPTER 55

Everyone froze while Welbee listened silently. As he hit End and slapped closed his phone he said, "A body was found buried behind the house. The dogs had dug it up. The driver's license in the wallet they found says the body was that of a Howard Sweet."

Harland gave a whimper of distress and slumped forward. Welbee quickly moved to support him but Harland rallied and pushed the agent away. "I didn't know," he said. And then he added, "Why? Why would they kill Howie?"

"We don't know, sir," Welbee replied. "Those are questions yet to be answered."

Zig and Tully took Champ to town to find a vet while Clay and I sat in the sun on the porch steps long after Agent Welbee and the other men had left. I didn't think I'd ever be truly warm again and neither of us seemed inclined to move.

Elbows on his knees enclosing me, I leaned back and looked up at Clay, saying, "Grandma Jenkins used to say, 'Greed is the root of all evil.' The Breslaus sure proved that, didn't they? Anything was better than losing what they had. Didn't matter who else had to suffer. Other than that, it's real quiet here in the country."

"Yeah, no wonder you prefer the beach." His hands rubbed my shoulders.

"Shouldn't you be getting back to saving your empire?" I asked.

His hands stopped. "Things will change big time for us."

"I'm real good at being poor."

His hands went back to massaging my shoulders. "I'm not sure I am."

I laughed. "It's one of the few things you don't need to practice."

He leaned forward and kissed the top of my head. "I'm sorry."

"It will hurt if we lose the Sunset, no denying, but it's better to lose possessions than your humanity."

"There's a lot more than the Sunset at stake," Clay said. "We may lose everything."

"Well, if that's the worst thing that happens to us, we're golden. Boomer just showed me something a whole lot worse. But I sure as hell will miss my bar."

"I suspect you'll always find another one, and we haven't lost it yet."

I leaned back and looked up at him. "Why don't you get out of here and do your damnedest to hold on to it."

"I will," Clay said, getting to his feet and pulling me up, "But first I have something else to do, something for your daddy."

THE END

AUTHOR'S NOTE

On Monday, March 27, 2006, an article appeared in the Englewood *Herald Tribune* on human trafficking. It told the story of migrants coming to Florida from Mexico and Guatemala to find a better life, only to be sold into slavery. The article stated that Florida was the third state behind California and New York for human trafficking and that it was currently proposing a new anti-trafficking bill that would affect tens of thousands of people a year. The true extent of the problem is unknown because victims seldom go to the police for fear of being deported.

I had earlier read about migrants being held in container trucks, beaten and forced to work in Florida fields. The scheme was revealed when one of the workers was able to get away. I haven't looked at produce in a major supermarket the same since reading this article, wondering who picked that tomato or bagged the head of lettuce I'm holding. From this grew *Champagne for Buzzards*.

PHYLLIS SMALLMAN
ENGLEWOOD, FLORIDA

ACKNOWLEDGMENTS

Thank you to the Pereira family, Anil, Sheryl, Lucie, Bennett, Henry, Jaipur and Elysse for their generous support of Artsping on Salt Spring Island.

And thank you to Betti and Carl for the loan of the Pink Palace so I could finish this.